STELLA MANHATTAN

STELLA MANHATTAN

. . . . . .

by Silviano Santiago

Translated by George Yúdice

●

SANTI

DUKE UNIVERSITY PRESS ● *Durham & London 1994*

© 1994 Duke University Press   All rights reserved
Printed in the United States of America on acid-free paper ∞
Typeset in Galliard by Tseng Information Systems.
Library of Congress Cataloging-in-Publication Data
appear on the last page of this book.
Lyric excerpt from "Oh, What A Beautiful Mornin'" by
Richard Rodgers and Oscar Hammerstein II copyright © 1943
by Williamson Music. Copyright renewed.
International copyright secured.
Used by permission. All rights reserved. Lyric excerpt from
"Like a Rolling Stone" by Bob Dylan copyright © 1965 by
Warner Bros. Music. Copyright renewed 1993 by Special
Rider Music. All rights reserved. International copyright
secured. Reprinted by permission.
The translator received the generous support of
the New York State Council on the Arts.

For Auggie and Minnie

God doesn't want me to write,
but I know that I must write.
—Kafka

STELLA MANHATTAN

PART ONE

. . . .

It's not about painting life.
It's about giving life to painting.
—*Bonnard*

1

· · · ·

Manhattan Island, New York
October 18, 1969

I

Gardening woman, why are you so sad?
What's happened to you?

Stella Manhattan hums as she opens the small living room window of her apartment. She takes in the cold and polluted air of an October morning in New York, filling and emptying her lungs, her warm body pushing a compact cloud of smoke through the mouth, like the large billboard ad for cigarettes on Times Square. *"Oh what a beautiful morning! I've got a beautiful feeling!"* she sings quietly. As she exhales, Stella opens her arms and shuts her small almond-shaped eyes that long for the tropical sun and the carioca heat of Rio. The smoke issues lazily in a rounded cloud from her lips as she languorously releases the word "heeeaaallthhhh," indolently embroidering the vowel and spitting out the final *th* with a sputtering thud. Before inhaling again, her naughty little south-of-the-border odalisque eyes open wide, and Stella continues: "Here's to your health, your sex life, and many years to enjoy them." Her eyes open, she inhales; they close and she exhales: "heeeaaallthhhhh."

Stella can see—how could she not see?—the old neighbor across the way observing her through her window with a mixture of curiosity and fright. From the orchestra seat of her sill, she comments on Stella's morning show, making all kinds of gestures and directing her words to her husband who is lying immobile in bed. She concludes:

"He's nuts."

"Who's nuts?"

"The Puerto Rican who lives in the building across the street."

Stella breathes in and blows out the polluted morning air: "heeeaaallthhhhh." Gradually she's overcome by a frisson of nostalgia for summer, for the beach, for a glass of thirst-quenching mate, for the sun and the sea breaking over the burning sand, for spearmint and peppermint drops, for coconut desserts from Bahia, for ardent, sweating bodies. *Ricky my boy, my boy Ricky, we'll fly down to Rio.* (She remembers saying those words an hour earlier while lying in bed.) She goes on thinking of the muscles and thighs glistening on sensual bodies smeared with tanning lotion, stretched in studied abandon on Copacabana mats, lovely place Brazil. "Why don't you and I fly down to Rio."

She exhales and stretches out her arms like a vedette in final apotheosis in a burlesque review at Tiradentes Theater. If she stood before a staircase, she might sashay up the steps regaled in plumes, rhinestones, and sequins, luxuriously making her way to the top where in a long and tuneful trill she would bless her delirious admirers with a star-shower of kisses as they screamed: "She's the greatest! She's the greatest!" Amid frenetic clapping her voice would reverberate against the vaults of Manhattan's skyline. Stella Manhattan, the Star of Manhattan.

"Here I come, divinely. Hold on tight, 'cause here I come divinely," she cries as if mounted on a broom, flying Mary Poppins–like across the sky. Suddenly a gust of wind from the Hudson knocks something over in her apartment and wipes the rapture from her face. She turns and sees a picture frame. She shuts the window angrily.

"Merda!"

Through the window she sees the old gringa making faces at her from behind her own window. She returns the favor. "Don't mess with me, don't mess with Stella, you old bitch. You don't know what she's capable of. One of these days she'll wring your neck." The old woman disappears behind her dirty curtains. Yes, she sure knows what Stella is capable of, ever since she crossed her path on the street and she blurted out snakes and lizards at her. Stella told her to stop sticking her nose in other people's business, to tend to her own dirty windows and curtains. "They're as filthy as your mouth, look at them!"

"I hate New York," Stella cries without conviction from behind her window as she looks at the gray autumn sky and at the empty street with its gray strip of asphalt, bordered by two unending multicolored rows of cars. *No little wind,* she thinks, *is going to drag me down from this glo-reee-ous autumn morning.* And imitating an old-time photographer in front of a pouting boy, Stella says to herself: "Smile, Stella, come on, let's have a smile. Don't drop the birdy. Come on, climb the horsey. Look up at the stars. Life is beautiful. Maravilhosa! New York is beautiful! You're beautiful. Here comes the sun. It's all right."

Stella woke up crazy, joyously crazy, this Saturday morning. The need for stage, footlights, and audience made it hard to stay indoors. Already she had gotten up twice, the second time around ten thirty. Ricky's mint-scented body was no longer at her side.

Several hours earlier, at six, Stella was relishing dreams of a South Sea island paradise when she felt a nudge. Stella rolled from side to side. At the next prodding she opened her eyes, and—wow!—was astonished at the unshaven face of her dream hero standing before her in the flesh. She rubbed her eyes and stretched to a lazy yawn as she asked what was up.

"Time to go," she heard Ricky's voice with eyes closed again.

"Oh no! Not now."

As Ricky got dressed in the dark, Stella noticed that his automatic movements were those of a professional heel who gets up in the dark and is out the door before his lover has even gotten his slippers on. Stella ran to the door after him to say goodbye: "Call me later. You have my number, I gave it to you last night at the bar."

Stella got up for the second time a little while ago. Her eyes glittered euphorically as she had breakfast. She ate in silence, though, in a repressed euphoria, waiting for the right moment to burst out. And how she burst! She went into song again

> *The camellia fell off the branch,*
> *gave two sighs*
> *and died.*

Stella is about to make the morning's momentous decision, but first she ponders out loud: ". . . and it died," and languorously sings:

"it died of love." She sighs: ". . . oh, oh, que pena." *It's Saturday and I really have to get this apartment cleaned up. What a mess! Dear, dear Stella, you have to do something. One of these days you'll get up to find a mouse running back to its hole. Good morning, Mr. Mouse,* she imagines herself saying as she shakes her finger, the same index finger with which she draws paths across the dusty furniture.

She rolls the drum *ratatá, ratatá,* blares the trumpet *ta-ta-ta-tum-ta-tum* and *ready or not here I come* she stands erect to meet the challenge, and then at ease again. With a feigned gesture she winds an imaginary red bandana from Azuma's around her head to protect her from the dust; in her imagination she rapidly slips into a sleeveless calico shift. No need for a sash, the flesh is still firm. She pinches both buttocks as proof without registering the love handles that winter put on her hips. She dons imaginary Havana sandals, arms herself with an imaginary broom and vacuum cleaner and "tweedle-dum, tweedle-dee" tackles her weekly fatigue duty, bending backwards at the waist and thrusting her legs forward in counterpoint.

What a cute little thing, she looks in the mirror, *coochie, coochie coo, Mama's little boy,* she pinches her morning wind-reddened cheeks. *I am deee-vine, aren't I?* She imitates Snow White without her seven dwarfs. *What Charming Prince, Ricky, wouldn't give his eye teeth for this tropical wench! And you have the nerve to ask me for twenty dollars for a taxi as you leave!* "What lack of imagination!" she pouts out loud in disappointment, but she gets hold of herself and turns on the vacuum cleaner to drown out Ricky's voice asking for taxi money at six in the morning. She turns on the vacuum cleaner and no sooner turns it off, *where's my head today, how can I vacuum if I haven't done my fatigue duty yet?*

"It's not on account of the money," she tries to convince herself in front of the mirror. "No, it's not that. Twenty dollars? If I had spent the rest of the night in the bar it would have cost much more. It's the lack of love, I can't get it out of my mind, Ricky. There was no love between us. Do you understand? No love!"

She hums ironically in order to ward off the tears and the bad mood that begins to envelop her:

> *No love, just fucking.*
> *No love, just money.*

No fucking, just love.
No money, just love.

But the word love continues to reverberate in her foolish little head, bubbling glub glub like a gold fish in a restaurant aquarium. The more it bubbles glub glub, the more Stella's fried fish eyes pore over the four corners of the room, glub glub, in search of something that might restore the memory of the previous evening. But Ricky had touched nothing; they went directly to the bedroom and from there to the door, but not before Stella said, "You'll call me so I'll know it wasn't only on account of the . . ." She censors the last words to create a suspense effect.

2

Badly dressed, afraid of his own shadow, and depressed; that's how Stella Manhattan, alias Eduardo da Costa e Silva, arrived in New York. One and a half years later he goes to work at Rockefeller Center decked out in a Bloomingdale suit, button-down shirt, and Brooks Brothers vertical-striped tie. Although he's not a career man, he was placed in the passport section of the consulate, where he attends the public.

In the beginning he begged everyone's forgiveness, even God's, for anything and everything; what he'd done, hadn't done, done wrong, even done right. As time went by he no longer felt like a cornered beast with yellow streak against the wall, begging for the coup de grace. Yellow gave way to lighter, happier, more spontaneous colorings. Reticent but smiling, he now let loose when he succeeded in tossing a saucy word into a conversation.

Eventually he cut a good working relationship with his office mates: three thirty-ish women who had outgrown their college jeans but hadn't yet settled into auntie-hood, although their colors had begun to turn autumnal. After a while they hit it off, engaging in all the indiscreet and confidential whisperings—watch out, the walls have ears—that friendship entitles.

By the end of the second or third month, however, there was a metamorphosis in the twelve-by-nine area circumscribed by the counter on one side and by the door that led to the back offices of the consulate on the other. The three women gradually came to treat Eduardo with a one-way intimacy, the kind engendered by jealousy. Since they worked sitting down and Eduardo standing, jealousy was translated into deference, which stratified the reception area into higher and lower levels. His and theirs. It even affected the way in which they called him for the four o'clock coffee break, when the office was closed to the public. It's not difficult to read self-interest into those invitations for they had found out—and did they ever wag their tongues about it—that Eduardo had lunch with the military attaché on Wednesdays, the only day he came to the consulate. They could not and would not permit such a low and dirty blow from one of their own. Eduardo always went alone. He never invited any of them, not even one.

Maria da Graça, without lifting her eyes from her typewriter, would say to the other two:

"There's something fishy here," and Terezinha, looking over at da Gloria, would add:

"If there is, only those who don't want to can't smell it." Da Gloria never said anything, she just smiled tight-lipped as if only she and her mouthwash knew the real reason why Eduardo and the military attaché lunched together every Wednesday.

Da Gloria's was not the smile of someone who listens and keeps quiet; it was a tic, poor dear!, a tic that came upon her as she day-dreamed her way through the empty day, her mind swept clean by the palm-swaying breezes of Pajuçara. This pseudo-smile was enough, however, to capture the imagination of the other two in a plot against her.

Standing behind the counter, Terezinha said:

"Friends grow on trees when you hit the jackpot. If you're drown-ing, they pay no mind and rush ahead, saying you're just crying wolf."

"People like that will get theirs, they'll get it good. If not in the here and now, then up there," Maria da Graça would add, rolling her eyes from floor to ceiling like a Sunday school teacher.

Da Gloria didn't say a word.

"There's so much injustice in the world," Terezinha was mono-loguing as a young man came into the reception area. He asked to see Eduardo.

". . . that, that disgra . . . ," she almost finished the word but re-gained enough presence of mind to cut short her loathsome rant.

She turned and spoke to da Gloria as if she were a life raft in the middle of a shipwreck: "This young man is looking for Eduardo. Do you know where he is?"

"Ladies, isn't he having lunch with the attaché?" Da Gloria responded somewhat confused, her empty little head filled with palm-swaying breezes.

Maria da Graça's and Terezinha's gossip-mongering was always hushed and never went beyond the reception counter or the door to the back offices of the consulate. Should anyone's words leave the slightest stain on a military uniform, there could be big trouble. These were risky times. And more so if you took into consideration that da Gloria's uncle was a four-star general whose untitled portrait hung from the ceiling like a guardian angel, providing her with anonymous and not exactly disinterested protection. She was, after all, the only one of the four who never did anything, absolutely nothing. She spent the whole day staring into space to the beat of the palm-swaying breezes.

No sooner were the three women left alone, especially on Wednesdays when Eduardo had to attend to other matters and Terezinha was temporarily put in charge of her former position at the reception counter, before Maria da Graça and Terezinha winked at each other and set their tongues—which had been itching like ticks on a hind—a-wagging:

"Nail and flesh couldn't be any closer than those two." To which Maria da Graça responded:

"Eduardo can look pretty strange . . ."

Terezinha, taking her turn again as she looked at da Gloria, added: "Ah, but the ambassador hasn't noticed. If it were one of us, we'd already have a pink slip in hand, even without receiving prior warnings. Don't you think so, da Gloria?"

Da Gloria was still wandering off in space, sitting silently at her desk under the pathetic gaze of her colleague. When Terezinha repeated the question, she perked up and said:

"No, I don't think so."

"Why not?" insisted Maria da Graça, winking at Terezinha complicitly. Now they had cornered the beast. Terezinha turned her head, Maria da Graça came forward.

"Ladies, the young man might be working for the attaché."

"Doing what?" asked Terezinha with overtones of jealousy and envy, conveying with her voice that she was the only one who had to make sacrifices while Eduardo clowned around on Wednesday afternoons.

"Working, what else? Or do you think that an officer has nothing to do, that he just twiddles his thumbs all day?"

Da Gloria wasn't very precise, she didn't need clever arguments or examples to convince her fellow workers who immediately felt the presence of her four-star guardian angel, sashed in the green and yellow colors of the flag and hanging from the ceiling. They didn't say another word. To go on could lead to an open expression of doubt about Colonel Vianna's dedication to his duties. And that they could not do. It would be worse than death.

Eduardo's luncheon appointments with the attaché also piqued the curiosity of others. More recently, the group of Brazilians with whom Eduardo associated and considered himself a part of, had begun to question and speculate on these lunch meetings.

It wasn't in Eduardo's nature to cultivate solitude or to court depression by staying home. He began to attend every cultural activity that had anything to do with Brazil. He had no idea that behind his back he was suspected of spying on the intellectual life of Brazilians residing in New York. Eduardo treasured love and camaraderie too much to think that certain details of his work in the consulate could be interpreted as forming part, like pieces in a jigsaw puzzle, of some diabolic scheme. But in the wake of the 1964 military coup, paranoia was the only logic by which Brazilians reasoned. The things they told him so that he might relay the (false) messages to the military attaché! Whatever they wanted the colonel to think, all they had to do was tell Eduardo.

The only cock that crowed politics in Eduardo's apartment was Stella Manhattan. And yet the substitution of President Costa e Silva by the military junta went in one ear and out the other. Stella wasn't very nationalistic. She wished for a new and libertarian politics that was personal and collective. She imagined it silently without arriving at any formulations; perhaps she wasn't capable of any. Hers was more a feeling deep inside, in her heart of hearts, a feeling that had no rational and verbalizable formulation. It was only by permitting Stella to leave the four walls of the room, exit the apartment, go down the elevator, walk along the streets swaying her limp hand and speaking to passers-by that Eduardo was able to take political distance from the Brazilians whom he sought out.

For not taking her to Woodstock that summer, Stella forbade Eduardo from going to the movies for a whole month and from eating plum ice cream. For not allowing her to go to bed with John Lennon and Yoko Ono, Stella threatened Eduardo with visiting the consulate and having a no-holds-barred discussion with the three Ivory Girls at the reception counter.

The more Eduardo worked his way into the group of Brazilians, the more they worked themselves up into a paranoid frenzy. Eduardo had the same last name as the ex-president of the Republic. That made him a close relative, a son, according to some, or at least a nephew or a grandson, according to others.

Eduardo wasn't a career man; he had been hired by direct orders from the SNI, the National Intelligence Service. They needed a trustworthy insider who could infiltrate the cultural milieu of the Brazilian exiles. His literature degree from the National University was a help, a real help. No one would suspect him. Why, he's one of us.

From his position in the passport section he would have a better opportunity to oversee applications and to approve documentation, duly alerting the Service to all suspicious cases.

The Wednesday luncheons with Colonel Vianna, a key figure in the organization and planning of the 1964 coup and the subsequent police repression, consolidated Eduardo's image as a spy and justified all other suspicions. Wednesday was the day all politicians from Minas Gerais held their backroom conversations and exchanged secret information. Likewise, the colonel and Eduardo exchanged information on Wednesdays; the colonel told him what was going on abroad and Eduardo reciprocated with local information. It was not for nothing that they went to a small and little-known restaurant on East 82nd Street. The tables, distant from each other, were not conducive to indiscretions.

The lowdown on the restaurant and the luncheons was provided by Carlinhos (an alias) who worked there as a busboy. His curiosity was aroused by the apparent complicity of the two as they spoke in hushed tones seated at a table off to the corner. One afternoon he even saw the colonel endorse a check and hand it to Eduardo.

All these conjectures, of course, were wrong.

"Eduardo a spy? You must be kidding." It wasn't until Marcelo arrived from Brazil that little by little the mystery that surrounded

Eduardo da Costa e Silva was dispelled. There was only one detail in this whole business that might have proved compromising for Eduardo. But no one knew about it, only the ambassador, and, of course, the two protagonists.

It was Vianna who, on the request of his childhood friend, Eduardo's father, got Eduardo his position at the consulate.

3

Stella Manhattan walks into the kitchen to get Ajax, ammonia, a sponge, and rubber gloves. She would begin her cleaning in the bathroom. She has made her decision but first she turns on the faucet to get a drink of water; she's got a pretty bad hangover. It burns her throat worse than the first shot of whisky. She lets the water run until it turns cold.

The squeaky faucet and the waiting send her back to Ricky's body shuddering with a violent, eye-popping pleasure that makes you lose your breath, huff and puff like an asthmatic in the midst of a fit. *Protestants are like that,* she thinks as she reviews in her mind Ricky's face with its eyes popping and his body bucking like a bronco. *They're little blond, blue-eyed saints, porcelain figurines made for glass showcases, but when they come they bellow like an entire church chorus. Hallelujah! Hallelujah!*

"Hallelujah! Hallelujah!" She repeats the phrase aloud imitating Handel's *Messiah*.

He remembers black protestant church services on Sunday morning TV programs. He pictures in his mind immense black women wearing hats and immaculate white collars, seated ladylike, good mothers that they are, surrounded by eight little urchins. Well-behaved like any faithful on a day of retreat and prayer, only their eyes betray a histrionics too lively for the setting, the mischief of a voyeur looking through a keyhole. Suddenly they begin clapping, swaying as if possessed, their bodies shaking and gyrating more wildly than *Bahianas* dancing the samba in Carnival procession. Then wailing like loons, eyes a-poppin', they run, almost fly, through the church waving their arms like windmills, their emotions totally out of control. *I don't even want to think what it must be like when they screw, their tongues hanging out and all that. Protestants are like that. Cold as ice on the outside and hot as all hell on the inside. So much the better.*

And again she imagines Ricky's body glued to hers when she began to sing those orgasmic hymns. Stella, zealot of noise-making that she is, doesn't back down but rises to the occasion, hooting in chorus, getting hotter and hotter, full throttle ahead and to the point of explosion. He thinks of his friend Bastiana, his parents' cook, black, strong, and fat like a zeppelin. One hot Rio summer morning, never having seen her with a man before, he caught sight of her in an alleyway kicking, moaning and screaming in near epileptic throes. Up to now, Catholics, he thought, fucked in silence, hidden from God's eyes *as if it were a curse and a punishment to fuck*. His mother and father were Catholic. He doesn't regret having left his parents' house for the States.

"Stella, shake a leg, girl," she says to herself, starting nervously and shaking her body as if to throw off the torpor that took hold of her as she reminisced. "What about your cleaning chores, Stella? You're not just going to stand there dreaming about Ricky with his eyes bugged out. You're not your Cuban girlfriend La Cucaracha." She fills her glass with water, drinks and smacks her tongue, which crackles like a dry leaf in flames.

In the bathroom, she puts on rubber gloves as if they were made of kid skin and holds them up for inspection. She wants to make sure that all her fingers fit correctly. She puts her right hand on her hip to signal that she's not sure where to begin: the sink? the bathtub? the toilet? No need to bother with the bidet. She hates cleaning the toilet bowl; she deee-spize-zes it. That's why when she has to clean the bathroom she holds her nose, mutters under her breath and calls her friend Bastiana for help, she can do anything. *Me? I'm not cut out for that*, Stella says to herself. *I rather like cooking but I'd never soil my angelic fairy hands on that mess. God help me!* She blesses herself all over as if that could keep the mess far away.

"Sebastiana, over there, that's right, hose down the sides first and then sprinkle some Ajax on it and scour it good with a sponge."

Bastiana goes about her house cleaning chores, docilely obeying Stella's instructions. Stella stands there wrinkling her nose. She'd close her little almond-shaped eyes too but she fears tripping up and making a real mess. The toilet bowl turns copper yellow under the acidic wash of New York's water; it has to be wiped up immediately to keep the porcelain from staining like a rotten tooth. The yellow swashes give way to Ajax whiteness with each stroke of the sponge, forcefully and expertly propelled by Sebastiana. When the torrent of water plunges the muck into the drain, leaving behind a translucent porcelain surface, Stella smiles and slaps Bastiana on the back, praising her to the skies for her expert handling of the job.

As she started on the tub, Stella gradually lost interest in cleaning and began to think about the real *carioca* Sebastiana who commuted daily from the outskirts. Taking bodily form, his thoughts wandered throughout his parents' apartment. It was the beginning of 1968, right after Carnival. He could see himself lying in bed, locked up in his room for two months, disowned by parents who could no longer accept him as a son after what had happened, after the near scandal that remained hushed thanks to the good offices of influential family friends.

Eduardo felt like an old potato sack abandoned by his parents in some corner of the house. He didn't understand their sudden distance; it all went against the theories regarding family ties and family unity that they had drilled into him from infancy. *They're absolutely intolerant and they want to punish me with their silence and their distance. They want to annihilate me,* Eduardo thought when he realized they wanted to get rid of him like an object that had outlasted its utility. "Go ahead, throw me in the garbage. You'll be doing me a favor." He puzzled over his father's religiosity, his praise for Christian charity and wondered how he could let their intimacy, which he so desperately needed, chill over. "Why don't they just pawn me off!" he cried in anguish as he got up from the table, already knowing how the whole mess would end up, and even dreaming up the ways his father would take to deal with the impasse.

The windows are shut tight. His perspiring body is stretched out on a sheet that begins to sop. The hot Copacabana sun shines outside and the scintillating sea and summer beach wink a seductive "come hither." Inside the room it's all silence and shadows, sadness and all kinds of fantasies filtering through his mind. Thoughts of vanishing from this earth without his parents' support or their understanding, as Bastiana opens the door—the only person to enter his room in those two months of confinement—and lays down a tray of food and starts to tidy up and put things in their place. *Would you just rather wallow in this pigsty?* she used to say.

"They argued throughout their breakfast like two fighting cocks. I don't know . . ." Sebastiana shook her head. That old black woman would enter his room smiling those sweet white eyes at him with a tenderness that dispelled the rage he felt against himself and the whole world. She would open the windows and the breeze and the sunshine, bursting in, would animate every object in the room. That old black woman touched on the subject one day, never to take it up again: "You know, I have a nephew who's also . . ." But her eyes didn't well up with tears, she didn't cry out of pity; instead she smiled a joyful smile of complicity, drawing close to the bed like a fairy godmother, stroking his head with a hand that felt like a magic wand: Shoo, shoo bad dreams, shoo, shoo, little baby don't you cry, shoo, shoo bad dreams.

Now Eduardo realizes it was Bastiana who prevented the worst from happening. That very afternoon he found himself all alone. He searched high and low through his parents' bedroom for the pistol his father claimed to have whenever he fretted over the danger of a burglary. He was looking for the pistol when he heard Bastiana's voice asking if he wouldn't like a cup of coffee, freshly brewed, hot off the stove. "Would you like one?" Thanks to her his confidence in the world began to return. He didn't hesitate for a second, "Right now, I'll go this very moment," when his father announced on a late April afternoon that he had arranged to send him to New York to work in the Brazilian consulate. Eduardo breathed a sigh of relief.

"If it wasn't for Vianna, I don't know . . . , I don't know . . . ," his father shook his head.

"Careful, Bastiana, that water's skin-peeling hot," Stella warns her as she herself feels the burn she got on her forearm when she inadvertently passed it beneath the bathtub faucet. It was so hot it even burned her through the rubber glove.

"What are you, on the moon, Sebastiana?" Stella asks her, reproaching her for her lack of attention.

"Me? On the moon? You're the one who stands there staring like a dummy remembering the waters of the past, and past waters won't turn the mill, you know," Sebastiana answers, making up to him as always.

"Oh, you're an ungrateful woman. I have my heart in my mouth worrying about you, and you, you tell me I'm a dummy."

Sebastiana keeps silent, feeling quite flattered by Stella's concern.

For a moment Stella is transfixed in thought with her gloved hands stretched out as if to receive a manicure. She comes out of her trance upon noticing the burn mark left by the hot water on her forearm. She's about to turn and give Sebastiana a scolding but she remembers that she meant to protest, look-a here now, where's the rest of your nephew's story?

"What for? It happened so long ago. Why go on forever chewing the same old cud; I'm no cow and he's no ox."

Stella listens to Sebastiana's advice and once again feels thankful for her kindness.

Stella would like to say something to Bastiana but she contents herself with the wish to say that it isn't easy to undo the past, at least not like she thinks. Stella wanted to, she wants to make an effort to erase what happened but the past returns like a thief to the scene of the crime. She would like to explain—but desists—that a crime was committed against her and that the phantoms who stalk her now are the same old criminals who, not satisfied with their crime, return to reexperience the pleasure of inflicting pain on a sensitive living being. They twist and turn the blade in his open wounds. And Eduardo ends up saying nothing to Sebastiana because he knows that she'll defend his parents and ask him to be more understanding like a good son, when they themselves weren't willing to be understanding with him.

"Oh, how I wanted to tell someone everything that happened," Eduardo pours out the feeling of oppression that he's been harboring, but only the white walls can hear him. Buried deep in his heart, it awakens him sometimes in the middle of the night, his body trembling with imaginary chills and tears running down his cheeks. Finally he allows the anguish to descend the length of his body and emanate like a thick, suffocating rain cloud. It hovers there threatening to unleash a storm.

He needs some kind of shelter now. He needed it yesterday. He searched for it but didn't find it. There was no place to turn to.

One day he stumbled on a sure fix for these nighttime anxiety attacks. He remembered a samba by Dircinha Batista and started to hum it, then a ballad by Edie Gormé, later a bolero by Daniel Santos, and finally a pop tune by Brook Benton and Dinah Washington: Hit the road, Jack, and don't you come back no more, no more, no more, no more . . . Little by little he began to feel better and even found the brighter side of the woes that weighed heavily on his heart. He smiled good-humoredly, seeing in himself the flirtatious, seductive tropical queen that hit New York, all by her lonesome, so all alone and unprotected, in need of the strong shoulder of a good man. Only that now he had found someone even more in need: Ricky. *A gente se mete emcada buraco. It's easy to get into a royal mess,* he thought. In any case it turned out alright, everything turns out for the better, he warbles mimicking the emotional falsetto of the one and only Angela Maria, alias Sapoti.

4

"Back to work, Sebastiana. There are many things left to do and there you are greasing your jaws." Stella, who had been sitting on the lowered toilet seat, stands up and remains entranced. *Entranced and daydreaming that in a little while the phone will ring and between the Ricky queridos and the Stella* dears *the day will slip by and the housecleaning won't get done.* All that's left to clean is the bathroom sink and then onto the kitchen floor. She'll grab the plastic pail and sponge mop, dip it in the ammonia solution and start to scrub the tiles. But just the memory of the smell of ammonia sets her cursing: "What a damn stench!" and making the faces that Sebastiana made whenever she killed chickens in the service area of the apartment. And to think that ammonia smelled like perfume to La Cucaracha's nostrils, accustomed to the public bathrooms of the subway. "That's where the action is, silly girl," he'd say, encouraging Stella to make a pilgrimage.

If it hadn't been for La Cucaracha who knows what would have become of Eduardo in his first months in New York. Sad, afraid of his own shadow, and complex-ridden, the first time he felt that his body still existed was at the end of the first month when he got his lion's mane cut at the Italian barber shop on Eighth Avenue. Maria da Graça had taken him aside and told him that it didn't become an official of the consulate to run around like a long-haired hippie. You know how people are, their first impressions lead them to hasty judgments. Actually, Maria da Graça went easy on him, she didn't tell him that people were gossiping about his Afro. That mountain of ringlets brought out his negroid features more clearly. "He looks like a Black Panther," they'd say. As he was getting his hair cut he could feel the barber's hand brush against the skin of his face. Since he had arrived in New York no one had gotten that close. He hadn't felt the warmth of human skin, of another person, of a stroking hand. The mechanical hand movements of opening and closing the scissors were like a caress he wished would go on forever.

La Cucaracha, a.k.a. Paco, baptized Francisco Ayala, was a Cuban refugee who had emigrated at the beginning of the sixties. He was a fanatic anti-Castro gusano who decided to make his new home in New York rather than Miami. To justify his choice he'd say: "For someone like me who had always lived in Havana, there were only two cities on the planet I'd live in: Paris and New York." And he'd add: "Paris is in the hands of communists and New York is in ours, we lovers of freedom."

He lived on the same floor as Eduardo and from time to time they'd meet face to face in the elevator. On their third or fourth encounter La Cucaracha greeted him in Spanish because I knew it all along (tapping his heart with his forefinger) that *you could only be a Latino*. "Brazilian! You don't say" he screamed almost hysterically in the ascending elevator, leaving Eduardo perplexed and speechless until they got off on the fifth floor. They chatted a little while longer in the hallway and Paco asked his new friend in for a drink, telling him make yourself at home, my house is yours. Eduardo accepted the invitation.

A few days later, after two or three visits to Paco's apartment, Eduardo discovered why Paco went hysterical when he found out he was Brazilian.

La Cucaracha had been, was and will always be, madly in love with a Brazilian journalist, the only love of his life, who not only moved in with him for three months, eating him out of house, home, and bar, never giving him a dime, leaving a trail of bills until one day he disappeared into thin air. Like a bat out of hell. He didn't leave a farewell note or say goodbye, not even I'm-getting-out-of-here-and-I'm-never-coming-back, ciao. He just up and left with everything. He even took, how shall I say it, he took certain things, Eduardo—which Paco didn't specify out of embarrassment but which Eduardo guessed had to do with his deep passion.

"You'd have to see it to believe it, chico, qué macho!" he said as he concluded his sad story of unrequited love. He sighed and rolled his little eyes to the ceiling as only he could do, taking on the angelic demeanor of a kneeling saint with upturned gaze. As if God would send back to him what he most desired on earth. And how he desired! Ardently. Woefully.

During that same encounter, he took Eduardo to his bedroom and showed him a bookcase filled with books and glass figurines. He told him to look on the middle shelf. There he kept a black bound

Bible opened to the middle, where Eduardo saw a dazzling color plate of an enormous pair of scissors, like those of a professional tailor. A Brazilian mãe-de-santo, a priestess he had met through some Cuban friends from New Jersey as she passed through New York, had told him how to get his fleeing lover back.

"Bull's-eye!" he intoned in a heavy Cuban accent. He spoke loudly and firmly as if to buttress confidence in his esoteric beliefs, like the faithful who reinforce their vows of humility and obedience by praying, thus camouflaging their real driving desires to have some favor granted.

Paco and Eduardo had sealed their friendship on that first exchange in the elevator. They became friends at first sight.

Eduardo accepted the invitation to have a drink in Paco's apartment. May was drawing to a close and it was already hot on the streets outside. But it was even hotter inside the apartment with that humid, sticky New York heat that makes people sweat until their shirts drip even if they keep still. Paco opened the living room windows but that didn't make things better; there were no breezes coming off the Hudson River. The only thing that came in through the open windows was the steady drone of the afternoon rush on Eighth Avenue.

"You can take off your jacket and tie if you like," said Paco as he pulled his own jacket off.

He asked Eduardo what he'd like to drink.

Eduardo asked what he had to offer.

Paco answered "almost everything, except cachaça" and he tittered discreetly, hinting at some kind of in-joke that Eduardo was at pains to figure out.

He asked for a whiskey on the rocks.

Paco had his usual: gin and tonic with a twist of lime and mucho mucho hielo, lots and lots of ice, switching into his best rendition of cocktail loungese. Only then did Eduardo notice that all along he had been speaking Portuguese and Paco a macaronic Spanish quite different from what he had learned at the National University. It was a bubbly and strangely pleasing mixture, like the syllabified Portuguese spoken by foreigners along the Avenida Nossa Senhora de Copacabana.

"Without music, no hay alegría," Paco said and wafted, glass in hand, over to a four-in-one TV-radio-record player-speaker combo console on the other side of the room. He didn't have to select a record, he had one ready and waiting on the record player. One of those sentimental boleros that abounded in the Mexican tearjerkers he had seen in Rio as a kid and to which people went to laugh at as much as to cry.

"Javier Solís, a Mexican singer. Do you like him? I think he's divine."

Eduardo didn't say yes or no; first he'd listen and then he'd give his opinion. To be congenial he asked what the name of the song was.

"Shadows," answered Paco, almost in tandem with Javier Solís, who was singing the word at the very moment, with a background of violins weeping the words "*échale, échale*," "oh yes, oh yes," as only Mexican musicians can make them sound.

> *Only shadows,*
> *Between our lives.*
> *Only shadows,*
> *darkening my love.*
> *I could find happiness*
> *But I am living death*
> *And suffering my tears*
> *In this undying drama.*

Paco asked Eduardo to speak about Rio. He remembered the numerous stories about Rio told him by a young Carioca he had met years back. They were so fantastic that Brazil, with all its picturesque place names, had become in his head a country of fairy tales or a gigantic postcard. He had never been there but he knew its streets and plazas as if he had walked them, as if he had stretched out on the sands of Copacabana and sunbathed on the reef at Arpoador or on a yacht off Ipanema's shore, as if he had taken the lift up to Sugar Loaf Mountain or Corcovado and surveyed the marvelous sprawling city. He saw himself as a child taking walks through Rio, wandering along the routes in the stories told by his nanny as she rocked him on her bosom on hot and starry Havana nights.

Paco remembered all this with dreamy nostalgic eyes. Something about his look neutralized the irony that threatened to break out on Eduardo's lips or the gleam in his eyes as always happened when he beheld the raising of the eyes, the half-opened mouth, the slow-motion walk, the dovelike waving of the arms, and the breathless rapt attention to the velvety crooning voice of Javier Solís, "the best Latin singer of all time."

La Cucaracha couldn't hold back anymore the urge to know about those beautiful, those lovely, gorgeous, cinnamon-skinned boys with luscious thighs and . . . God help me! And the more he spoke the more he raised his eyes, his carnal delight ascending to the rarefied heights of the angelical. With his third gin and tonic with mucho mucho hielo he grabbed Eduardo—who was also on his third whiskey—by the arm and told him he wanted to confess a secret.

"May I?"

"Of course! You can trust me, Paco."

What La Cucaracha liked about Carioca boys was the way they walked along the street, placing all their weight on their hips, like this! From the waist down they seem heavy and solid, like statues made of marble or, better yet, of steel or bronze. And from the waist up they're light, elegant, ethereal, as if their bodies, solidly rooted to the ground, were always about to take flight. And yelling shazam, he took a little Captain Marvel leap.

Gringos are also cute, he went on, but they're such clods. There's no life to them, no salsa, he summed up and got to his feet, smiling, pouting and waving his arms, mimicking Carmen Miranda clanging her bracelets and swinging her gold earrings, all hot and saucy like all women from Bahia. But he overdid it; no Bahiana would wave her arms like an octopus.

Eduardo began to laugh at Paco's antics with that mischievous and complicitous snicker characteristic of his future confidante, Stella Manhattan.

Paco asked Eduardo if he had already found the sitios de atraco in Manhattan.

Eduardo did not understand the Spanish phrase and remained expressionless throughout the rest of the conversation hoping he could somehow guess the meaning.

But the rest of the conversation came to a standstill because Paco stopped speaking, taking his cue from Eduardo's reticence. Maybe he had taken his queenly frolicking too far. *Hold your tongue, for Christ's sake,* he thought, *you talk to him as if he were your girlfriend from way back. Maybe he's only listening to be polite.* When he went back to change the record in that strange combo cabinet in front of the sofa he limited himself to clicking his waggish tongue. The singer he would hear now, he announced, was the Puerto Rican Daniel Santos, who sounded to Eduardo like a cross between Nelson Gonçalves and Miltinho with a pinch of Francisco Alves. Paco returned to the sofa minus La Cucaracha's mannered gestures, served himself a drink and, sheepishly looking askance at Eduardo, served himself still another drink without reference to the twist of lime and the mucho mucho hielo.

Eduardo caught on to the icy turn of the conversation and realized he hadn't yet answered Paco's question. This time he took the initiative, like the potential wallflower who, noticing after a few dances that her partner won't ask her again, works up her courage and asks him for the next one. He explained that he hadn't understood what Paco had said before he changed the record.

At first Paco made like he didn't hear, like the guy who is asked for the next dance: *Not with you, fool, not with you.* But he quickly changed his mind and got into the groove forgetting protocol and all niceties.

"Sitios de atraco, pickup spots, you didn't understand that?"

Eduardo nodded and Paco burst into laughter, feeling at ease again and summoning back La saucy Cucaracha.

Places where you meet people, Eduardo said to himself, mentally at first and then out loud, his gaze getting brighter as his interest waxed. This set La Cucaracha going on about how New York was Paradise on earth, you can't imagine, chico, anything you want you can get here and he went on enumerating all the possibilities, unaware that Eduardo had suddenly become serious, withdrawing behind an impassive demeanor. He sank—or was drawn back—against the arm of the sofa, thus retreating from his complicity, which he conveyed from the moment he entered the apartment.

"Mira chico, after walking through the streets, squares and bars of the Village, and the streets and docks of the harbor, looking over the truck drivers on a beautiful summer afternoon, you'll see. And wait till you get hold of the movie district, wow! Watch out, though, the people on 42nd Street can get pretty rough."

Eduardo's face was strained with the effort to exercise self-control. The more he tried to hide his agitation, the more his rigid muscles erupted in myriad tremors throughout his body, which no force of self-control could weld into the appearance of being at ease.

"¿Qué te pasa, chico?" Paco asked in alarm at this gratuitous display. "What's wrong, for Christ's sake?"

"Nothing, it's nothing really, I'll be okay," answered Eduardo halfheartedly. He felt he had to say something. "It's just a bad memory that came over me, that's all. It'll go away." He reached out for his whiskey but the glass was empty. He asked Paco for another.

Paco leapt from the sofa, grabbed the empty bucket and ran to the kitchen for more ice. When he returned he saw Eduardo bawling with no concern for what Paco might think.

Eduardo's body was doubled over and tears streamed over every nook and cranny, bathing it in an emotional weld quite different from the other one he tried to achieve by force of self-control. He was whole again now and had nothing to hide. And Paco, before this majestic image of release and total surrender to despair, calmed down, lost his fear, and sat silently on the sofa, his body turning toward Eduardo whose tears continued to gush like steam escaping from an overheated pressure cooker. The flow of tears eventually relaxed his muscles and his face regained that luminous aura that radiates from martyred saints in Renaissance paintings. At least that is how La Cucaracha saw the scene from his place next to Eduardo on the sofa.

He gazed at Eduardo and he suddenly saw a light so brilliant emanating from his face that he had to keep blinking in order to withstand it.

Fearful yet happy, like the magus who beholds the star that will lead him to the savior, Paco carefully drew near, placing his hands on Eduardo's shoulders and gently pulling the seated body toward him, which effortlessly let its head fall on his breast. La Cucaracha passed his fingers through Eduardo's hair like his mother used to on sunny and steamy Havana afternoons. He understood that he had just taken on a very heavy burden (months of rejection, suffering, and loneliness) and that his breast, like a soft down pillow, cushioned the impact of greater sorrows that might yet befall Eduardo in his traffic with the world.

Suddenly Eduardo's hunger pangs sounded the alarm, to which the two fell into each other's arms and, bursting into laughter, babbled in a jumble of Spanish and Portuguese that they just had to get out to eat.

Paco knew a good Chinese-Cuban restaurant where the ropa vieja era di-vi-na. It was on 22nd Street between Seventh and Eighth Avenues. Just around the corner.

"You can't imagine, chico, I'm so happy . . . like a clam at high tide."

2

. . . .

The telephone rings and Eduardo leaps, almost slipping on the wet tiles of the bathroom floor which he just mopped with ammonia. The phone rings again as Eduardo curses the goddamn fucking tiles. "Ricky, darling, I'm a-coming," he calls out as if he were in the next room. He takes off the rubber gloves and thinks to himself *wow! I never thought he'd call so soon.* He hums cheerfully to the tune of a well-known song, "Money Can't Buy Me Love," feeling like he just hit the jackpot. The phone continues to ring, making him apprehensive. *In a moment he'll hang up and never call back again,* he thinks as he flies across the living room and over to the night table by the bed. He answers huffing and puffing, barely able to make out the nervous, hurried voice.

"Eduardo, it's Vianna. I have to speak to you urgently. Wait for me at home and I'll be there in half an hour."

"What's wrong?" Eduardo asks apprehensively, feeling the weight of all his fears pitched above his head, ready to fall in one resounding blow.

"Hassles . . . but I'll tell you all about it personally in your apartment. It's too risky on the phone."

"Okay," Eduardo assents. "I'll wait for you, I had nothing to do anyway. Come whenever you want, whenever it's most convenient for you."

"I'll be there in half an hour at the latest," Vianna hangs up without saying good-bye.

The uninterrupted bustle of cars in the background, which Eduardo becomes aware of only after hanging up, indicates that Vianna spoke from a phone booth on a major thoroughfare. It also strikes him as odd that Vianna didn't even say "see you in a bit." Vianna was always very polite, to the point of obsequiousness in the attention he gave people, a remnant of his youth spent as a cog in the machinery of a very competitive career, never daring to raise his voice or even speak directly to anyone of higher rank. He never acquired that air of arrogance characteristic of those who never see themselves as subordinate because they come to the system with the privilege provided by good family or wealth. But now Vianna hadn't even asked if he had awakened him and if he had would Eduardo forgive him. Not even a good-bye. *It doesn't bode well,* Eduardo concludes.

He goes on forming hypotheses that leave him staring wide-eyed into space and waiting by the gray telephone. It sits there on the night table silently and enigmatically, taking on the appearance of a worm-eaten apple given to him as a gift and whose usefulness, since it's not for eating, he's at pains to discover.

He has a mind to call Maria da Graça and sound her out on whether or not there might be a squealer at the consulate. But it would be useless, with those three dimwits you've got to cross yourself and keep your distance.

But what on earth does Vianna want to talk about? And what's so urgent, on a Saturday yet?

Who knows, maybe he had dinner last night with the ambassador and got an earful of complaints. *Maybe all he wants is to help me, to warn me, Eduardo be careful, you understand, don't you? You can count on me, I'm warning you, am I not? I'm your friend, so don't worry, I'll be by your side, I'll get you off if anything goes wrong. You got me out of a bind the last time; I owe you one.* When they're alone together Vianna inspires trust, so it would be better, Eduardo thinks, to open up to him. But as soon as he considers that possibility he also figures that if there is any trust between them it's on account of their complicity rather than Vianna's good character. *Sweet words on the devil's tongue.*

Smooth and unctuous, he dons and removes his masks when it suits him. Charming with the ambassador and gracious with me, but in the end I'm the one who gets the shaft. He imagines Vianna all humble and obsequious with the ambassador, but then Eduardo changes the slide in his mind's eye and sees the ambassador, who's only a civilian, after all, walking a straight line in front of Vianna as if he were about to be chewed out by a drill sergeant for some triviality, shitting in his pants about the unforeseeable consequences on his career.

He lifts the telephone receiver and holds it in his hand for a second. He brings it to his ear and listens to the dial tone; it turns into a busy signal. He hangs up and realizes that the phone won't do away with the problems that will inundate the room as soon as he opens the door for Vianna. He dreads the moment, wondering what he's done for Vianna to come so urgently on a Saturday morning, banging on the door, just to talk. In person. It's too risky on the phone.

"I didn't do anything," Eduardo screams and shakes his body out of its torpor. "It has to be something Stella did, it couldn't be anyone else," he says as he starts laying into her:

"You're up to your old tricks, doing as you want up and down the street, and I'm the one who has to face the music."

"Calm down, Eddie, for Christ's sake, ree-lax," Stella answers him firmly. "It's not the end of the world, you know. And anyway, he's probably the one who's got his ass against the wall, that masochist friend of yours. It's obvious he didn't call you from his house. He called from the street, so he must have been at his apartment on Amsterdam Avenue and there's no phone there."

All of a sudden, Eduardo feels calm. He goes to the bathroom to give things a once-over before Vianna arrives. He decides to take a nice, relaxing hot bath like Stella recommended. That'll prepare him for what might happen, *whatever happens I always come out on top.* He puts the cleaning items and the vacuum cleaner in the kitchen cabinet. He didn't get a chance to use them. The dust on the floor and furniture will just have to wait another week. *I can't get it up to do housework after Vianna's call. What a drag,* he thinks, annoyed, and he gives the cabinet door a booming whack.

Your father, a letter arrived from your father, what else could it be? Something must have happened in Brazil: death, disaster, illness, anything and everything was possible because Eduardo had never written to his parents nor had he received a single line from them. At first, it didn't matter, he didn't know what to write or how, and if he had written, what he was thinking was not very nice, it would have brought on a quarrel for sure: you thankless, egotistic ingrate, and so on. Afterward he decided they didn't even deserve one word. They had treated him like a dog; worse, what they did to him they wouldn't have done to a mutt. Thank God they were pious people; imagine what it would have been like if they weren't. His first Christmas in New York, in 1968, Eduardo bought a card at the 42nd Street Library to send to his parents. He took it home and left it on his living room coffee table gathering dust until February when he finally threw it in the trash.

They tore me from their lives as if I were a peeling scab. Now it's my turn. I'm not going to cry or feel bad any longer. It's over, he felt his head clear up.

He got over the desire to write; it was gone, turned the corner, disappeared. And when Vianna asked him about his father, he'd lie and tell him that everything was fine, and so on.

Was his mother sick? Eduardo feels anxious and sad.

"Don't give in, Eddie," Stella, his companion for better or worse, recommends. "Don't get any ideas in your head that'll put you in a bind you can't get out of."

It was the first time he had thought of his parents since he had arrived in New York. He thinks about the both of them, not as the pretext for complaints, but because he misses them. It's as if he were looking at an empty vase insistently wishing a bouquet of roses into existence; they should be there but they're not. They had disappeared into thin air as in a magic trick. If there was someone to blame, it was the magician who artfully created the void, taking advantage of the spectators' momentary amazement. It all happened so quickly there was no time to feel the loss, the emptiness. But Eduardo does feel the loss.

2

Vianna was waiting for him at Kennedy Airport when he arrived in April of 1968. He was Stella Manhattan's first passion and he dove into it with all the foot-stomping tantrums of a spoiled brat: Mommy, Daddy's cock belongs to me. It was also his first unrequited, and fleeting, passion. "From now on we'll be the most intimate of girlfriends," one of them said, and the other added: "My very best girlfriend, despite the difference in age."

Vianna was a hunk; tall and handsome and not very Latin in his baby-face looks. Eduardo couldn't believe what he was seeing as Vianna came toward him with a photo in his hand and asked him if he was Sergio's son. No sooner had he said yes he was vigorously swept up into Vianna's arms, deriving much pleasure from the embrace of this fifty-year-old Rock Hudson who walked down the middle of the street without so much as blinking at the oncoming cars.

On their way into the city in a new Mercedes—Eduardo was impressed by the luxury but held back his awe—Vianna asked him how Sergio was getting on, it was so long since he'd seen him, and he began to remember their school years in Belo Horizonte in the forties, layering his remembrances amid long lapses of silence as if reconstructing the past were like stacking bricks on layers of time.

"You've been in Belo Horizonte?"

"Only once, I was born and raised in Rio."

"I was born in Espírito Santo but I moved to Belo Horizonte when I was twelve."

He went to the Colégio Mineiro and that's where he met Serginho, in his sophomore year, he specified after a brief pause.

He roomed with relatives in Renascença and in exchange for his room and board he slaved in his uncle's bar.

He had afternoons free to go to high school.

He worked the counter, went to the bank, made payments, worked the counter again at night and even washed the floor after the last drunk stumbled out of the bar.

"I would take the Renascença trolley and your father the Lourdes bus and we'd meet every day downtown at Praça Sete where we'd take another trolley to school."

Vianna left Eduardo at a hotel on 45th between Broadway and Avenue of the Americas. He said he'd come by to get him on Monday at ten in the morning to make the customary rounds of introduction at the consulate.

So little Vianinha and Serginho spent their days together. Hmm, I'll get to the bottom of this, Eduardo mused as he looked over a filthy 45th Street below, all quiet on a Saturday afternoon.

He remembered that on the eve of his trip his father said some things that seemed to justify the favor that Vianna was doing for him. Eduardo began to reconstruct their Belo Horizonte friendship and projected it in sepia tones in his mind's eye. First he focused on a photograph of his adolescent father in the family album. Then he moved on to his father's spiritual or was it religious crisis, who knows? Eduardo imagined him going to mass every morning. He could see him with a group of youths at the church doors. Finally, in another photograph, he saw him as a member of the Holy Mary Sodality with a blue ribbon around his neck. He imagined his repentant father on his knees beating his breast bless me father for I have sinned.

"Repenting for what?" Eduardo asked himself. His question wasn't answered but he heard his father's voice saying that he had a physical need, that was the word his father used, a physical need to do good. He spent his entire monthly allowance, which was quite substantial, giving to charity and he even secretly gave his spare change to the maid's son. It was through these do-good activities that he came upon little Vianinha, a poor hick from Espírito Santo who lived with his aunt and uncle in Renascença. He was a penniless nobody but his soul was belíssima, his father said.

"Belíssima," Stella sighed as she looked out the window.

To the rhythm of his pity and in a choreography of good deeds, Serginho provided Vianinha with his notebooks, textbooks, erasers, and pencils. After graduation each went his own way and they never saw each other again.

Not until they were in their forties and ran into each other at the 6th lifeguard post on Copacabana Beach. They were both living in Rio now, Sergio on Rua Francisco Sá and Vianna on Rua Júlio de Castilhos. 1964 had ushered in a new order: God, the Brigadeiro Eduardo Gomes, and Carlos Lacerda formed the Holy Trinity of national politics; they had everything sewed up among themselves, in spite of the threat of international communism. God was lord of the heavens; the brigadeiro lord of the nation, and Lacerda lord of the city. And the lord was with Sergio and Vianna. Still clinging to their conservative beliefs and piously beating their breast, their friendship bloomed anew. The sower cast his seed and it fell on fertile soil. They couldn't believe how much time had passed and they wondered how it was that their paths had never crossed before, at least at the meetings of the Clube da Lanterna, which backed Lacerda. They went over some of those meetings, referred to friends they had in common, and they were amazed by the coincidences, the great coincidences. They tried hard but they couldn't figure out why they hadn't run into each other before.

Asked by Vianna what he did on his first weekend in New York, Eduardo said he made a reconnaissance trip around downtown Manhattan. He went as far south as the Empire State Building and then back up north to Central Park. What he didn't tell the colonel is that he had gone into a sex shop on 42nd Street.

He also slept a lot, which allayed his anxiety, he thought, but said nothing to Vianna. He felt that his body was getting more and more relaxed as the anonymous rhythm of the big city penetrated him and attuned him to the pachydermal pace of the few white trash, Puerto Ricans, and blacks who wandered about an otherwise deserted Fifth Avenue. It reminded Eduardo of downtown Rio on a Sunday morning. It was the first Sunday of the season that really felt like spring and everyone had left the city so it was quite a surprise when Eduardo stepped out Monday morning and found the street in a congested chaos worthy of Rio.

He remarked on the difference of rhythm between yesterday and today and Vianna suggested that they walk up Fifth Avenue to the consulate in the International Building at Rockefeller Center. It was only five or six blocks away.

Is it possible that Vianna knows? They plodded silently through the New York hubbub like swimmers in adjoining lanes. *He must know, papai must have said something to justify asking for a job for me.* Vianna, of course, knew everything, to the last detail. As they walked he looked over at Eduardo from the corner of his eye and thanked the heavens that Sergio had sent him this angel of salvation. He looked him over thinking that, come the time, he would make the perfect accomplice to aid him in his escapades. He had been wanting to get rid of his private chauffeur, a gringo wiseass from Oklahoma. The fucker had started demanding more pay. Said he was going to get married and that he needed more money to furnish a new apartment and . . . Vianna smelled a rat and thought up a scheme to get rid of him.

He purposely left his engraved watch and ring in the car, leaving Jack no other choice but to take them with him. That very night

Vianna registered a complaint with the police, feigning that he hadn't the slightest idea who might have stolen the goods.

"The watch shouldn't be too hard to find; it has my name engraved on it. It was given to me by my fellow officers when I was promoted to colonel. The ring I bought at Tiffany's and it's the only one of its kind. You won't have any trouble recognizing them," Vianna told the cops at the precinct. "I only want to do the right thing and help you, you know."

The cops fine-combed the West Side in search of the thief and came upon Jack in a bar on 100th and Broadway that he went to most nights. With watch on wrist and ring on finger he tried in vain to explain the situation to the cops:

"I found them in the car just tonight." He said he was only waiting until the morning so he could return them to his boss.

The following day Vianna had no choice but to fire Jack. How could he tell his wife and the police that he wasn't going to fire him after all the fuss he made last night. It was no sweat off his back to keep him on but people might get the idea that they were in cahoots. The best he could do was tell the cops to forget the whole thing, drop the charges.

Jack thanked him. He was going to get married and make a new life for himself. He would look for a new job, promise.

Vianna said it would be better that way. And he could expect a generous wedding gift from him. He himself could even choose it.

Jack asked for a refrigerator.

Vianna was looking over at Eduardo the whole time, encouraging his delirious ecstasies of freedom in the big city. Eduardo could only thank the generous gentleman for his hospitality.

"Cut all this sir stuff out. You can call me by my first name," Vianna insisted three or four times until he broke Eduardo's habits of politesse. He wanted to gain Eduardo's trust before he asked a favor of him. He needed help in setting up a scheme without the drawbacks of a lover roaming throughout the house all day long. Never again!

Vianna and Eduardo made the rounds at the consulate, going through all the customary introductions. Standing next to Vianna, the ambassador looked like a hick politician from Minas Gerais. He was short and fat, stuffed into a ribboned suit that looked like it had been inadvertently shrunken at the dry cleaners. He spoke in a low voice, like people with halitosis do; he obviously lacked the social graces of those diplomats who are groomed for the post from the moment they start to crawl.

Just like his own papai, Eduardo thought, one of those people who take on a lifestyle in their adolescence and follow it through to the letter and when they grow up they become what they already were in their youth: old men.

Eduardo couldn't help admiring Vianna, who cut a favorable contrast with the ambassador standing next to him. He felt shivers ricocheting up and down his spine; he was so entranced that he began to dribble, so proud was he of being Vianna's friend. The colonel's athletic body stood erect, his trousers perfectly creased like a São Paulo executive in the month of July. Towering over others like a lighthouse, his head, with its clear, moist eyes and a mouth that made Eduardo's water with desire to kiss it, shone brightly, attracting the passing officials to his side. Vianna was speaking with the ambassador about confidential matters off to the side. Eduardo looked at him and thought *I'd like to get him into bed.*

He couldn't help it. The colonel's strategy was effective and Eduardo was quickly succumbing to his charm. And not only on account of his eyes; Eduardo sought refuge from the depression that threatened to flare up again, that depression he had felt in the last few months in Rio, the fear and the insecurity that all outcasts feel.

A few weeks later, on a Wednesday, Vianna invited him for lunch. Eduardo couldn't believe his good fortune, he never imagined he would get the chance to seduce the colonel. *From here on it's easy sailing, just push a little and he'll come over. It's in the bag.*

At work new apprehensions stalked him. Since he and Vianna were tight, he suspected that his three coworkers would try to trip him up out of jealousy. Out of spite they would say something to the ambassador.

"Leave it to me," Vianna said categorically, like a superman who took flight to the heavens and descended again to battle (victoriously, of course) the forces of evil. It's a bird, it's a plane, no, it's Vianna.

As the colonel conversed with the ambassador, Eduardo, that Lois Lane of the passport section, kept looking over at his three coworkers. *They'll never forgive me,* he thought to himself, making a display of his elation and winking, in his mind's eye, at his newest girlfriend, La Cucaracha. She would really get a kick out of seeing him acting out the anxious Lois Lane waiting breathlessly for an encouraging word from Clark Vianna. *He said yes! Yes! Yes!*

No sooner had they ordered their meal than Vianna launched his surprise attack.

"I know everything."

"Everything?" Eduardo repeated.

"Everything that happened to you in Rio."

"Papai told you?"

"He did."

"He gave you all the details?"

"You know your father better than I do. He asked me for a favor and felt he couldn't keep anything from me. He couldn't lie. He didn't have the right to."

"Even so, he must have lied."

"Be careful, young man," he said apprehensively in response to Eduardo's unexpected boldness. "Is that any way to speak about a father. A good and honest papai like Sergio?"

"It's that I'm still hurting, I'm . . ."

"That doesn't make it right . . ."

". . . very hurt."

"I understand."

"They were too hard on me. Too hard."

"You'd never know from his letters. He spoke very highly of you. He said he was interested in sending you abroad."

"You mean to get rid of me."

It was obvious that the young man's feelings of rejection were still festering and that it would be better if he showed compassion. He dropped his derisive attitude towards Eduardo's recalcitrance.

"Do you really think he wanted to throw you out into the gutter?"

"I don't *think* so, I'm sure."

"He always spoke well of you in his letters. I think he was right."

"Of course, he's pretty crafty. How else could he sell you this bill of goods?"

"And he sold it."

"But that wasn't really the problem . . ."

"What was it, then?"

"What was it!"

"Yeah, what was it?"

"Oh, nothing at all. He could have been a little understanding, loving, protective. But that was too much for him, too much."

Vianna figured he'd better change the course of the conversation. He didn't want to have his lunch drowned in sorrows. They already had wine for that.

"You know, the ambassador told me today that he's quite happy with your performance at the consulate. He even thanked me for recommending you."

"So much the better. If it were otherwise I don't know . . ."

"Can I tell you something? A friendly word of advice?"

"Go ahead."

"I think you're too defensive."

"And I have no reasons for being defensive?"

"I'm not so sure. It's as if you wanted to take the whole world on."

"Take on the world?"

"Yes, take on, fight, strike out, pummel the next person that walks by whether or not he has anything to do with your misfortunes."

"I should be meek, turn the other cheek, and be agreeable. Is that what you're recommending?"

"I didn't say meek or agreeable. More considerate."

"You mean take my medicine and keep my mouth shut. Well, you've got the wrong guy, buddy."

Eduardo was getting unsettled.

"See what I mean? You're getting defensive."

"I guess you're right," Eduardo lowered his head, justifying the colonel's feelings of power as he stood before the tamed beast.

"I just wanted to tell you one thing."

Eduardo seemed not to be listening, like a snail withdrawn into its conch shell.

"Wake up, Eduardo!"

Eduardo shook his head and, poof!, he was back in the restaurant, rubbing his eyes as if he had suddenly happened into some strange place.

"I want to say something to you."

"Go ahead."

"It shouldn't go beyond these four walls. You promise?"

"I promise."

"You've got to promise for real."

"Cross my heart and hope to die. Now go ahead."

"I also have my proclivities."

Eduardo laughed at the word.

"Only you, Vianna, only you could come up with something like that."

Vianna drew back, intimidated by Eduardo's unexpected laughter.

"You already knew?"

"It never crossed my mind. Although, who knows, there are many ways in which thoughts can cross one's mind and in some crazy way that I can't begin to explain to you, it did cross my mind. Well, I can try. It struck me that . . ."

"Why did you laugh?"

"Me? Laugh? When?"

"When I told you."

Eduardo tried hard to remember.

"When I told you that I also had my proclivities."

Eduardo laughed again, rousing Vianna's curiosity even more.

"It's that word: *pro-cliv-i-ties*."

"What's wrong with it?"

"Nothing."

"Nothing?"

"I don't know, it sounds funny. It's such a euphemism. When you're with another faggot you don't have to beat around the bush. You just come out and say it straight: I'm a faggot too. Or if you're a stud, then, I'm a stud."

As they left the restaurant, Vianna gave Eduardo a ten-dollar bill to pay the taxi. He was already twenty minutes late for his turn at the passport counter. He gave the money back.

"Don't worry, I'll call the ambassador right now from the phone on the corner and I'll tell him you'll be late on account of business."

"You know, I remember you from Rio," Vianna added.

"Where in Rio?"

"The 6th lifeguard post on Copacabana Beach."

"At da Gôndola's?"

"No."

"On the beach itself?"

"No. On the beachside promenade."

The taxi stopped in front of them.

"We'll continue our chat next week. It's been fun. Wednesday again, okay?"

"Okay, Wednesday's fine," Eduardo, perplexed, repeated as he jumped into the cab.

He lay back in the seat and Vianna's past came before him, projected like a movie on the glass partition separating the driver from the passenger. *It has to be him* he thought as he saw in his mind's eye a black Mercedes gliding along the lane nearest the sidewalk on Avenida Atlântica. *It can't be anyone else,* Eduardo smiled, happy to have made the discovery. *The Black Widow. I'll bet she's raising Cain in New York,* he thought as the taxi hurtled down Second Avenue. *Who would believe it. No other than the infamous Black Widow here in New York! Wow!* his imagination effervesced, blending the carioca night scene with more recent images: a sleek new Lincoln waiting for him at Kennedy Airport, its shiny black laquer finish, the colonel seated next to him as he sneaked glances at him, *I've seen him some place before,* shaking his head and thinking *I must be imagining it.* These images fuse with an unknown face at the wheel of a black Mercedes that leisurely follows three recruits who had just been drinking at the Forte de Copacabana.

"The Black Widow attacks its prey in the wee hours," Eduardo remembers his friend Zeca saying.

The Mercedes stops and the driver signals for one of the recruits to get in, the one who can't hide his admiration for the luxury car inching along behind them. The driver doesn't get out, he doesn't even open the door. He doesn't have to, he's an elegant gentleman. The recruit who turns laughs several times and then leaves his friends on the sidewalk waiting for him.

"I'll be back here," the recruit yells at his friends and goes around the car to enter it through the door on the passenger's side.

The eyes facing him are shooting darts. "Finally!" says Terezinha harshly, at the service counter. Maria da Graça intercedes, explaining that the secretary had already informed them that Eduardo would be late.

Terezinha swallows her rancor.

3

Same day of the week, same restaurant, same table. A new conversation. Eduardo gets more daring.

"Didn't you drive a Mercedes in Rio?"

"A Mercedes? Yes, I had one."

"A black one?"

"Yes."

Vianna fixed his gaze cautiously; Eduardo waited in suspense.

"It was the last car I had before I left. I bought it from a fellow officer who brought it back with him from Germany. When I came here I sold it to a real estate broker. I can't even remember his name. It's the best car I ever had, it never gave me any trouble. I was sad to get rid of it." He stopped speaking and looked at Eduardo, not knowing why he was running at the mouth. He wasn't able to hide his curiosity and asked why Eduardo had brought up the car.

"I saw you many times in Rio."

"In Rio?"

"Yeah, driving the Mercedes."

Vianna smiled admiringly at Eduardo's perspicacity.

"I wanted to ask you for a favor."

"I'm at your beck and call, you don't have to ask," Eduardo said, losing all inhibitions.

"Don't be so obsequious, you'll be sorry afterward and it'll be too late."

"If I have any regrets I'll just tell you that I can't do it. Isn't it better that way?"

"One extreme or the other. Ah, today's youth!"

"Loose screws. I just don't have any sense."

"That's what your father told you."

"That's right."

"Let's forget about that pious old crank."

"Hey, you're getting better, Vianna. Go ahead, tell me what you want?"

"It's not easy to explain. It's complicated, you know. The wife, the house, the kids, the colleagues. I've got people all around me."

Vianna enumerated all the obstacles to a good pickup in New York. It was even harder now that he acquired a taste for the rough trade, he even went in for blacks and Puerto Ricans. And in New York without the right clothes you couldn't get anywhere. Different strokes for different folks, you've got to have the right uniform. That's why he had his leather duds hidden away at home. Only now he couldn't continue to keep them there without raising his wife's suspicions. He considered keeping them in his office at the consulate but coming and going with an overnight bag was sure to raise suspicions that he had become a smuggler. And what if, Eduardo, the consulate catches fire. The firemen open the drawers and *presto* there's the leather and you're kicked out of the army. Of course, you can always change in the car, go to the farthest downtown parking garage dressed in suit and tie and come out in full leather regalia. Everything can be kept in the trunk. But then the car could be stolen, you know they don't fool around in New York, and imagine what the cops would say when they found all the paraphernalia: cowboy boots, steel studded jacket and belt, motorcycle cop cap. You're in deep shit then, better not even think about it.

Eduardo understood that it wasn't easy for the Black Widow to cruise. He nodded his agreement.

Before, everything was easy as pie. The chauffeur was pretty good, from Oklahoma, built like a football player and dumb as they come. But he made things easier. When Vianna was under pressure he changed at the chauffeur's house. He would lie and tell him he was going to a party. The guy knew what was going on but he kept his mouth shut. In the end he had no choice but to get rid of him. He was afraid the chauffeur would tip his wife off about his carrying on. It was too bad. Months had gone by and he still didn't know how to solve the problem. He poured his heart out:

"I've been going through a real dry spell."

Eduardo laughed at the expression and commented on it. Vianna continued.

"Do you have any idea what it's like to see spring and summer go by and there you are sucking on your thumb?"

Eduardo commiserated.

"I know what you mean."

"I knew you'd understand."

"Sure I understand but I don't know how I can be of help to you." Eduardo suspected the Black Widow wanted to turn his apartment into an S & M wardrobe so he tried to change the topic before he got caught up in his friend's predicament.

Vianna failed to register the cue and continued complaining. Just the other day a truck driver slipped out of his hands because he had nowhere to take him. The guy didn't want to go to a hotel. Vianna said he'd pay for the room but nothing doing, that wasn't the problem. He was afraid of a setup. No one wanted to turn down a good lay but after all he did have a wife and kid. "Aw, come off it, I'm in the same boat," Vianna said, but that didn't get him anywhere. The guy just stood there on the corner until Vianna invited him for a beer. Vianna suggested meeting the following day. But, no way, it's now or never. So it was never.

Eduardo could feel it coming. Vianna wanted to use his apartment for his comings and goings. *No way man,* he grumbled to himself, *don't even think about it.*

"Why don't you rent an apartment?" Eduardo hurried to ask. To make his suggestion more convincing he added that he himself had always wanted a garçonnière but couldn't afford one . . . Before he could finish his sentence Vianna interrupted him and thanked him effusively.

"How did you ever guess?"

"Guess what?"

"The favor I was going to ask of you."

"You don't have to ask. Just say what it is."

Vianna told him he'd seen a cheap, seedy apartment on Amsterdam Avenue between 75th and 76th Streets. It was only two hundred dollars a month. The neighborhood is full of black dope addicts and Puerto Rican drunks. No danger of running into a friend or acquaintance on the street. "Imagine me all decked out in black leather running into the ambassador!" The neighborhood's not that bad; nothing wrong with the people there. Everything's right about it.

The favor was as follows: "I want you to rent the apartment for me. It'll be in your name, if it's okay with you. You won't have to pay anything. I'll take care of everything."

So much the better, Eduardo said to himself. Now he'd be free of the leather-clad Black Widow and her roughneck friends, those freaks she picked up God knows where. He agreed.

"I don't know how to thank you enough."

"One hand washes the other," Eduardo said ironically. Vianna, however, interpreted those words as a sign of the effectiveness of his plan. He was a strategist like no other. He had great admiration for himself, and for Eduardo too; again and again he thanked Sergio, God, Our Lady of Perpetual Help, and all the guardian angels that had brought Eduardo into his life.

That afternoon Eduardo didn't go to work.

"I've already let the ambassador know," Vianna told him before he even had a chance to say anything. It bothered him but *what can you do but take it one step at a time.*

They both jumped into a taxi and went to a real estate agency on the West Side. It was on Broadway just north of Lincoln Center.

The secretary, a very Jewish Bette Midler look-alike, was startled when the two gentlemen in suits and ties entered the office. She had to make rapid calculations: were they detectives or thieves?

Vianna, noticing the secretary's suspicions, elbowed Eduardo in the ribs: "Keep quiet, I'll do the talking." He told her the apartment was for neither of them. He wanted to rent it for a friend, a young man without means from their country, a student at Columbia who was going through hard times. Mr. Silva, the young man here, would be responsible for everything. He had a very good job and could provide references and the security deposit, and so on.

After the secretary filled out the lease forms, Eduardo signed all three of them and kept one for his own records.

The first two month's rent and the security deposit had to be in cash, the young woman said.

Eduardo said it would be no problem. He took from his pocket the wad of hundred dollar bills that Vianna gave him in the restaurant.

"Six hundred and thirty-five dollars, including tax," the secretary said.

Eduardo took the change and the keys.

The young woman stared at the two men and then at the hundred dollar bills in her hand. Then she looked at them again, no longer able to hold back:

"Tell your friend—he's a foreigner, isn't he?—tell him to be careful. That's a rough spot, really rough. I'm not kidding."

Vianna put her mind at ease. He told her that the other fellow had lived for many years in Manhattan and that he was now a graduate student at Columbia.

Eduardo got the impression that the secretary was still uneasy.

After they left she couldn't help thinking that she had fallen for a scam. *Twenty to one they're drug dealers. After all, they are Latin Americans. Why else do they come to this country?*

Once in the street Eduardo asked where Vianna had learned to speak English so well. He really spoke well, without an accent. Vianna said he had worked for many years as liaison between the Brazilian Army and the American Embassy; that was before he was transferred to Brasília. He had also taken special courses with gringo officers in Texas and Panama.

After a few minutes they arrived at the intersection of Amsterdam and 75th. As they drew near the building, two Puerto Rican drunks who had been sitting on the stoop got up and took off in the direction of Central Park with a jug of Taylor's in hand.

The black kids playing basketball in the lot across the street stopped. They huddled against the fence like do-wop singers.

Eduardo and Vianna entered the tenement. The hall was dark and Eduardo tripped on something. He looked down: an empty can of Schlitz. The walls looked as if everyone who came and went had spit on them and then wiped their hands all over.

"Third floor. Where's 3-F?" Vianna asked.

Eduardo wrinkled his nose, "This is some pigsty."

He opened the door and could hardly believe his eyes.

"Only you, Vianna, only you."

4

Eduardo opens the door and the Black Widow flies in like a rocket releasing a stream of curses and finally sighing relief.

Stella jumps back out of his way and gives a startled cry but Eduardo soon takes control of the situation: *keep your cool, Stella.* He knows he's in a tight spot, the tightest ever. Vianna is certainly up to no good, you can see it in his face. Decked out in black leather from head to toe, his hands trembling, his face unshaved and bright red and the cleats on his boots clanging an impatient beat. *I bet he's killed someone, the sadomasochist sonofabitch,* Eduardo says to himself, realizing he's got to stay real cool, if not it'll be the ca-tas-tro-phe of the year. *Got to stay afloat, otherwise this guy'll bring me down like a lead weight.*

The Black Widow sits down on the sofa and asks Eduardo if he has any whiskey in the house.

He answers yes. He'll get the ice in the kitchen and be right back.

"Forget the ice, I'll take it straight, like a cowboy."

As he takes the bottle and glass out of the cupboard, Eduardo tells Vianna to take off the leather-boy cap and jacket, he must be steaming.

The Black Widow doesn't pay attention and steams away on the sofa waiting for his whiskey.

Eduardo hands him half a glass and Vianna downs it in one gulp, smacking his lips with a grimace and shaking his body on the edge of the sofa.

"Those motherfucking goddamn communist putos de merda. Putos de merda. Damn them. Just wait and see, I'll kill those goddamn communists. Every fucking Cuban. Every one of them. Putos de merda."

Eduardo looks at Vianna's nervous legs and notices that they're trembling incontrollably. Like a Labrador retriever returned from the hunt, he's panting quick, short breaths. He must have rushed down Amsterdam Avenue all the way here.

"Relax, Vianna. Whatever happened can't be the end of the world."

"If I could I'd press the button right this very moment. I'd blast those fucking Cubans right off the Earth."

Vianna continues his litany of curses, whose only connecting thread is his hatred for communists. Eduardo leans back into his armchair feeling a little calmer. He also served himself a whiskey—he'd already gotten over his hangover—and resigned himself to the impossibility of putting Vianna at ease. You can't rush things. Eduardo feels reassured, even more so given that it wasn't a sex scandal that Vianna had gotten himself into, unless, he hesitated, the shock had made Vianna so paranoid that he saw red everywhere, even among gays. Better dead than red. Eduardo starts getting anxious again at the thought that the colonel had been kidnapped the night before. Kidnapped by a gang of Brazilian terrorists based in New York. God only knows how he got loose. But there he was. *How long before we see it in the headlines of the Daily News,* he concludes in a catastrophic bent of mind as the colonel spouts his unending litany of threats. Feeling that it might be better to give into his instinct for caution, Eduardo decides to interrupt the colonel. *Somebody's got to do something and the sooner the better.*

"Vianna, tell me what happened."

The Black Widow wasn't listening.

"Come on, Vianna, tell me. Regurgitating your rancor won't solve anything. What happened? Did it have anything to do with terrorists?"

The Black Widow begins to panic again. His body shakes, blood rushes to his face and the dripping sweat cuts rivulets through the thick stubble.

Eduardo gets up and goes over to take Vianna's leather cap off. Vianna pulls back in alarm.

"Did you say terrorists? Are they after me? They want to kill me, don't they? And you know something about it? If you do, you'd better tell me right away unless you want to lose your job. As of this very Monday."

Eduardo feels angry but pretends he hasn't heard the threat. *It's not worth the fucking trouble. Anyway, now's not the time. May as well humor the Black Widow.*

The Black Widow continues muttering "terrorist" under his breath, hardly moving his lips. The more he mutters the calmer he feels, like a soldier who gets over the first shock of a surprise attack.

We're in for it, Eduardo thinks, *tomorrow we'll be in all the headlines.*

The colonel stands, straightens up and raises his hand (to salute, Eduardo thinks) and takes off his leather cap. He puts it carefully on the coffee table. He takes off his black jacket, folds it, and ill-humoredly throws it on the sofa. Now he's only in his boots, black leather trousers, and black t-shirt. His steel-studded belt gleams as he draws near the window and receives the grayish light of a New York autumn sky. He turns to face Eduardo and apologizes. He's been exaggerating.

"I know you'll forgive me."

Eduardo nods his agreement and recognizes for the first time that Vianna's face lends itself more to his fantasies than to the suit and tie he wears in the consulate. He has the air of a well-bred, manly gladiator who brandishes his recently lost power like a weapon. Behold my glory, behold my impotence.

"I know you'll forgive me," he repeats.

"Did you have any doubts?"

"I did. But not any longer."

Like an actor who retires to his dressing room after the play, tired but free to start on the journey back to himself, the Black Widow's calm face was still smoldered here and there with his subsiding fury. He had overcome it, it had passed like a gray cloud, giving way to the glow of discipline and order.

Eduardo leads him to the bathroom so he can wash his face. He hands him a towel.

Now his well-cared-for skin shines again despite the dark hairs of his beard, which cast a sad shadow over his face.

He asks for another whiskey, this time with ice. He sits down on the sofa feeling less anxious and looks over at Eduardo half-confidently and half-sheepishly on account of his outbursts.

Eduardo takes the initiative and speaks first.

"So what happened? Go on, speak, for Christ's sake!"

"It's all so confusing; I don't know where to begin."

"They kidnapped you and . . ."

"Are you crazy?"

"That's what I thought."

"Well, don't think then."

"I didn't mean any harm."

"Forget it. And please forgive me."

The colonel takes a breath. He has to get it all out in a single burst. Once only, once and forever. He can't hold back the urge that stampedes up his throat and lunges headlong through his mouth in a vomit of words. He coughs and takes a deep breath.

Eduardo sees his eyes cloud over again and asks him if he feels okay.

The colonel takes another breath. It'll come out now.

On Thursday his wife went to Washington to visit an old child-hood friend whose husband had been transferred to the United States. Since she wouldn't be back until Monday afternoon, Vianna decided to spend the night on the town. He went to the apartment on Amsterdam Avenue, changed his clothes and, feeling his oats, went out into the Manhattan night. He went from bar to bar until he ended up at the Spur where he found the guy he was looking for. Alcohol swishing in their heads, reeling from the poppers, and his friend snorted out on coke, they went to the latter's apartment. What a night! About eleven in the morning he returns to his Amsterdam Avenue apartment to change back into his civies. "The door was ajar. I was scared shitless. I wasn't sure if I should go in, they might still be inside. I could get killed." It was better to make some noise by the entrance to scare whomever might be inside and then run down the stairs. From the luncheonette on the corner any suspicious people who went in or out of the building could be seen. "I was going to call you, but I changed my mind." Vianna looked at Eduardo as he said that. He wanted to bolster the sincerity of his intentions and the trust he had in him. "I went back to the apartment fifteen minutes later." The door was still ajar. "I knocked loudly as if

I were a visitor or a neighbor who happened on the open door and was scared. No one came out so I threw the door open."

The colonel stops. His eyes wander around the living room, looking for something on which to rest.

"It was horrible, Eduardo. You can't imagine it. A real horror!" The intruders had written all over the walls with spray paint of all colors.

The colonel stops again. He looks at Eduardo, stares into his eyes.

"No one knows, Eduardo, you've got to keep it secret. I trust you like I've never trusted anyone else." Vianna no longer insisted, he was begging now. There were swastikas all over the place captioned with "Nazi," "torturer," "fascist pig," "gorilla." He just stood there in the middle of the room, stunned by the colors, drawings, and captions. Suddenly he felt like he was in the middle of a battlefield with everyone hooting at him. They were yelling those words at him. They made an infernal racket, nearly breaking his eardrums. And then there was silence again. He ran into the bedroom. They had taken all his clothes, everything: suits, shirts, ties, watch, shoes, credit cards, driver's license, army ID, everything.

Without clothes or documents in this November cold, thinks Eduardo, recalling Caetano Veloso's pop hit "Alegria, Alegria."

"The worst thing is I can't go home in these clothes. I can just imagine what the doorman would think," Vianna laughs for the first time. "He'd probably call the cops."

Eduardo also laughs and almost tells him the nickname the boys who hung out at the 6th lifeguard post used to call him. On second thought, he figures, there's no reason to tell him.

"What now?"

"That's when I thought of you. You're the only one who can help me. I said to myself it's daytime and someone could see me walking around in these clothes."

"You can count on me."

He asks Eduardo if he wouldn't mind going out to buy him trousers, a dress shirt, and a jacket. No one would see that he was wearing boots. Luckily he still had money in his pocket. He was always prepared for his nighttime cruising.

Eduardo says of course, with pleasure, adding that he could go over to Woolworth's on 14th Street. No great fashion there but the clothes'll do. And the quality isn't really that bad.

Vianna agrees it's a good idea.

"One last thing," the colonel adds, "would it be too much of a bother to keep these clothes here for me?"

"I couldn't have these things here, Vianna," Eduardo responds jokingly.

Vianna's eyes beam a thankful, trusting smile.

"Okay, I'm on my way. Just let me put on a jacket; it's getting chilly outside."

No sooner does he close his door than the one next door opens. La Cucaracha hisses out Eduardo's name.

Eduardo approaches the half-open door.

A glowing face meets him and whispers:

"I saw when he entered your apartment," La Cucaracha sucks in her breath and issues it stridently, "Whew! What a man!" as she turns her eyeballs to the heavens.

"Cut the shit, Paco."

"How-I-ennn-vy-you, chico!"

"It's not what you think."

"Come again?" she asks scarcely concealing her self-interest and opening the door some more.

"More queen than both of us put together. She likes to get it in the face. Come all over her face, you get it?"

La Cucaracha wrinkles her face as Eduardo makes off for the elevator.

· · · ·
Beginning: The Narrator

Dung, out of place (said St. Augustine) sullies the house; in its place, it fertilizes the fields. Applying this doctrine to our analogous case, I adopt the words of the greatest of Church fathers, Lord, and affirm that the Jews should be cast from where they sully our house and placed where they can fertilize the fields. . . . May merchants, business, and wealth remain in Portugal . . . .—Father Vieira to Dom Rodrigo de Meneses

The conquest of the superfluous gives a greater spiritual charge than the conquest of the necessary. Man is a creature of desire and not necessity.— Gaston Bachelard

Sometimes when I'm pouring milk into a cup my hand ceases to obey me and goes on pouring even though the cup is full and the white liquid is streaming over the edges of the cup onto the table, soaking the dish towel, sullying everything. I stop—if *stop* is the right word—only when the pot in which I heated the milk is empty, tilted in the grasp of my hand

tilted as if it were the watering can which every afternoon I pass over the plants in the window box that sat in the sun all day long and whose soil never felt completely satisfied with the amount of water I poured over it. I wait for more water to come out of the can, I wait and nothing comes out, and then I realize that the act of watering has ended, even if the thirsty soil of the window box needs more water. I stand there with the watering can in my hand like a jerk and then, remembering the logic of cartoons, I try to squeeze the can, wring the water out of it in case there are any drops left in it.

Sometimes an action, for no reason whatsoever, draws more energy than is necessary to carry it out. The dark, silent order *enough!* does not reach the nerves; it is not transmitted to the muscles and so they relax and the inevitable overflow of energy makes it impossible to predict the outcome of the action that was just begun. If it is not purposely brought to a convenient end, the action suddenly takes leave of the real and the practical and enters the realm of chance.

Something was cut adrift from my will.

Some action had come to exist independently of my will; it was as representative of me as the morning hunger that induced me to make breakfast.

That's what came to mind in 1978

as I entered the metrô at the Odéon station in Paris and saw four street musicians pouring their sounds through the maze onto the escalator on which I descended. The sounds flowed just like the milk that spilled over from the cup into the saucer and from the saucer onto the towel on the table.

The overpowering music waves traveled south, to Porte d'Orléans, north, to Porte de Clignancourt, east, to Gare d'Austerlitz, and west, to Bois de Boulogne. They lengthened or shortened the movement of people descending on the escalators with their tickets in hand and passing through the turnstiles. I noticed that the metrô riders—even those who did not brake their pace, hypnotized by the music that gargled its way through the tunnels on this winter afternoon—moved more slowly with a slightly altered, march-like cadence

like race horses in their laborious daily training suddenly slowing down to an elegant trot as they pass a mare in heat and continue on their way in a seductive gait, themselves seduced, not knowing that they have strayed from the route which their riders, whip in hand, lash them back on to, reining them in so that their heads lunge forward.

I remember the poet João Cabral de Melo Neto once said that norms were given to man, better yet, invented by man, to ensure the satisfaction of necessities;

what the poet meant is that whatever falls outside the norm is a waste of energy, energy thrown out the window of poor results or into the garbage can of good intentions.

Art is not and cannot be a norm, it is wasted energy. It can be anything, for example, an action—here quality has no bearing—that comes into existence with an outburst of human energy; it is then vomited throughout the world of work, the universe of utility, with the audacity and ineptness of someone who, on pouring milk into a cup for the morning meal, lets the greater part of the liquid go to waste on the table.

Suddenly I looked closer at the musicians in the metrô station thoroughfare and noticed that the best of the four was a fat, withdrawn mulatto. He was older than his three jolly white companions. He was playing an instrument that he himself must have invented:

a wash basin, deeper than usual, facedown on the ground with a pole measuring approximately five feet attached to the rim. A thick metal wire ran from the top of the pole to a hole in the center of the basin.

With his fingers the mulatto pulled intermittent, husky bass sounds from the wire. His feet drummed the metal basin in accompaniment. It required balance from his whole body: he held the pole with one of his hands and he poised himself on one of his feet.

The blond saxophonist shook his body like one of those stumbly puppets that we called *GeeGee* when we were kids—a nickname coined in honor of the dictator Getúlio Vargas because we never knew if he would hold onto his power or lose it. He blew a mediocre sound from his instrument.

The short, dark haired clarinetist couldn't keep the beat and occasionally swallowed notes.

The guy on keyboard—a portable Casio synthesizer—paraded from one side to the other in front of the other three as if he were a subway Mick Jagger. Swaggering he belted out a raspy "My Woman."

Everyone was looking at the mulatto, who was in his own world. They swayed to the rhythm that he beat out on the basin.

All the energy concentrated in him burst, escaping from the norms that satisfy necessity.

· · · ·

(I am standing behind the chair on which you are seated. As you write I stoop over your shoulder and read about the spilled milk and the musicians on the metrô. It's December 1982 and you feel that you're ready for a new novel.

You turn toward me and tell me that you despise me now.

I'm taken aback; until today I was under the impression that we were hand in glove, the best of friends [don't you remember my last novel?].

You go on, referring to me now as your first shitty reader. Then you start to complain that I don't help you at all. On the contrary, I'm only good at inhibiting you, making things more difficult than they already are.

"I can't stand you anymore," you tell me. Then you deal me a very low blow by telling me that I'm a useless, rhetorical blowhard, that you've always thought that about me but never had the courage to tell me. But now you're telling me, once and for all, ciao!

You hush for a moment and then add in a loud peremptory voice that if I were an equestrian I'd only know about trotting, nothing about galloping, and what you wanted was to write gallopingly. Trotting is but a tame venture that comes after the gallop.

You get up without waiting for my answer and, as you always do in such moments of impasse, you go to the kitchen to drink water, because it's good for your kidneys, which have been afflicted by uric acid since the seventies. As you drink the water you discover that your nasal passages are congested and you go to the bathroom to blow your nose with two sheets of Charmin. Having cleansed them you now feel your eyes itching because of the smoke left in the apartment by yesterday's visitors. You'll never forgive yourself for permitting them to light a candle when you saw the living room turning into a smoky Parisian bistro like the ones in fifties Hollywood films. Your eyes scream out for the two magic droplets of collyrium.

You return to your desk and continue writing, asking for my help—my lips part in a smile but you make as if you don't notice—you want my help in writing your novel, my help in developing the first chapter of the novel.

So then, I'm not so rhetorical as you said just a little while ago—that's what I want to say but you're already absorbed in memories of Bob Dylan that begin to weave into the circuits of the text you're writing, so I hush because I know that you won't be able to hear me right now.

I sense—despite your request for help—your continued lack of trust in me. It reveals itself in the way you attempt little by little to eliminate the words that your useless rhetorical friend tosses onto the paper so that your intimate experiences—lying in bed next to David one New York summer afternoon—will appear on the paper in all their naked truth.

"Naked!? Have you lost your shame?" I shout like a person who is choking.

Repentently you now feel inclined to save me from death.

You turn to me and say that in truth I am right and that you really don't like autobiographical narratives. Fiction is all bla-bla-bla fakery; and what about the poet? The poet is a quack. Quackery is his trade, quack, quack, the poet is a faker, the fucker, that's right, a jodedor. A motherfucker. A fode-jode-fucker, he fucks just for the pleasure of writing. That's why he's so fucked up. The novelist is a fucker who fucks only to be fucked. El novelista es un jodedor que jode sólo por el placer de escribir, he fucks only for the pleasure of writing.)

. . . .

It strikes me that the mulatto in the metrô plays the bass-basin like Bob Dylan sings or like Buster Keaton acts in his silent comedies.

Maybe Buster Keaton, like Dylan, is also a Jew? Must be. How could it be otherwise?

Jews have the ability to abstract their personality—that is, their temperament, their personal idiosyncrasy, their nervous system, even their heart beat—from everything they do. That's how they maintain that general state of aloofness.

Furthermore, nothing whatsoever that an individual does is significant enough to budge the history of the Jewish race even one inch, nothing will move these historic and eternal people. Nothing is gained, in any event, by personal endeavors to invent them in any way, as an idea, a drama, or a concrete object.

All Jews are professionals—professionals, of course, being the opposite of dilettantes or amateurs.

Beauty means taking the risks discovered in reflection and not acting on the basis of the subject's eccentricities—that is, acting according to one's own will, one's individual conscience.

Every good jeweler is a Jew at heart. Or: every Jew is a good jeweler at heart. Take the art of polishing a precious stone: the slightest intrusion of personal feeling or subjective taste can ruin the perfect form that is sought.

Nietzsche could never understand Jews, hence his anti-Semitism: that is, he couldn't understand how anyone could be aloof in the process of creating a work. (Nietzsche was, of course, the theorist of passion.) Anyone who could write a book like *Ecce Homo* only to ask "Who am I?" could never understand Dylan. He would never understand how Dylan's voice peels off from his body like a bumper sticker. When Dylan sings his body turns into an acoustic chamber like that of any other musical instrument.

Lying next to David one humid New York summer afternoon in 1970 I listened to Dylan's voice hovering in the air like a hummingbird. Like a polished stone or a museum piece, it was forever free from any commitment to the arms, hands, or heart that engendered it. I listened:

How does it feel
How does it feel
To be on your own
With no direction home
Like a complete unknown
Like a rolling stone?

Although the windows were open not the slightest breeze entered the room. And if I didn't know that the words emanated from a human voice, I would have thought that the song hung anonymously in the air like the pieces of a Calder mobile.

Is it possible that Chico Buarque de Holanda is also a Jew? João Cabral can only be from the Sephardic Northeast but Chico is from Rio. Maybe all the roads of colonization lead to Rio. Chico is terrified of spectacle, he shies from lending his body to spectacle; his recorded voice is like a flower cut from its stem and put in a vase to adorn the dining room for a happy Sunday dinner.

There's no feeling in the mulatto musician that leads us to believe he makes music in the romantic sense of the word.

Am I contradicting myself?

João Cabral is right. The work of art is an economy of energy, a means by which the body avoids wasting what it holds most dear. Leisure, not work, is man's highest ideal.

The mulatto plucks and bangs his bass-basin sending musical waves to the four subterranean cardinal points of a cold Paris. He hacks at it as if he were cutting cane with a sickle in the Northeast of Brazil or with a machete in the Dominican Republic, where he probably came from judging by the bass's merengue rhythm. He kicks the basin as if he were pedaling a bicycle back and forth from home to work in the outskirts of any metropolitan area. He wants to cut cane with a rhythm that is productive for HIM, which is to say, that tires him the least. He wants to pedal his bike at a speed that allows body and machine to get in sync for the best performance on his trip.

It's not the body that cuts the cane
it's not the body that sings,
the cane's already cut
the song's already sung,
it's not the legs that pedal
the bike's already pedaled.

All it takes is finding an external, anonymous rhythm—a FORM similar to Dylan's voice resounding in his ears, first and foremost a form—the most economical and perfect form so that this or any other body can express itself significantly for another.

Now I know why slaves sing when they work in their master's fields.

And that must be why the Jews are so economical with their money.

. . . .

(Suddenly you stop writing to show me the preceding passage with the expression of a kid who has broken the cookie jar on top of the table and expects his father, who will arrive any moment now, to reprimand him.

When you pass the sheets over to me it's as if you were extending your hands for the whack of the ruler.

I tell you not to worry—I was reading over your shoulder the whole time as I always do, muffling my ironic laughter so you wouldn't hear it. At one particular moment I remembered a proverb I'd heard in my childhood, "good intentions and holy water will get you . . . ," but you didn't hear it because I held back my tongue

I held back my tongue because it was the only way of determining how far you had the guts to go. And you went pretty far. Congratulations. I admit that I didn't expect you to go so far; you're usually afraid of leaving the beaten path of what you deem solid knowledge. You always said the word "solid" as if you were referring to the weight of a cobblestone; but now you were letting certain thoughts be known that you had buried in the depths of your personal experience. You judged them to be superficial—that is, without the weight of the cobblestone—because they didn't have the supporting documentation of your scholarly readings.

That's why I held back my laughter and my voice: it's doing you good to write like this, to write things that you normally wouldn't have the guts to write or say even to your most intimate friends.

Ah, now you can tell me that I am contradicting myself by accepting subjective values and personal experience in the text without the requisite rhetorical coloratura that I like so much.

So we're guilty of contradictions, huh? So what?—that's what I feel like answering but it seems wiser right now to let you think you've beaten me. I can't always win. But if I did what good would it do me if it's your silence I've won? None. It's better for you to go on writing what you've been writing even if you've contradicted yourself here and there. They're only apparent contradictions anyway, I should add)

. . . .

That's also why Jews are so economical with their money: they plan to spend what's necessary to get by from day to day, one week to another, one month to another.

Capital accumulation is a consequence of the transplantation of the everyday economy of the Jews to Western civilization. For the Jews it consisted of the most organic rhythm for the productive coexistence of man with a stepmotherly nature

ah! the desert, life in the desert, how I'd like to speak of life in the desert . . .

it all became a way of saving, the exploitation of man by man in a society that was becoming increasingly complex and industrialized.

I rebel against that energy which was originally economized for the easy transit of the body through a hostile world. It ended up becoming a form of accumulation. I rebel against it and that's why I look for examples of energy which, like vomit, overflow the world of work and commerce.

In today's society, whether it is capitalist or communist, the only way to rebel against regimes of work, against the praise of work at any cost, against competitiveness or meritocracy is to create an art based on the waste of energy.

That's how I discovered that saving becomes accumulation in favor of the privileged and how accumulation becomes ostentation and requires—for its survival as such—the work of others for its own benefit.

Marx was able to denounce capitalist accumulation because he knew, from within his race, of an economic reason that had no form of surplus value, that worked for the survival of each and everyone, with no discrimination.

Usury is the form by which the leisured economic body of the Jews was grafted onto Western civilization.

This evil was not Jewish in its origin; it was Jewish in its transformation. The evil was Christian. It was the ostentation of the one. Equilibrium is never an evil. The West has a predilection for spectacle. That's why it needs such enormous quantities of money which, in turn, stagnate in the form of luxury. The West likes spectacle, it created the society of the spectacle. But spectacle is always lucre.

(In a corner of the sheet you make a note to remember to draw a parallel between the ostentatious urban architecture of Venice and the utilitarian urban architecture of Amsterdam. Both cities were planned and built with the same money in the same period, although the styles are diametrical opposites.)

Art spurns the display of luxury, it rejects any and every accumulation which seeks power through exhibitionism. Art is not spectacle. Machado de Assis, how right you are: the character who observes Itaguaí from the balcony of his newly built mansion, displaying himself before the admiration and praises of his fellow citizens, should definitely be in the loony bin or even in jail.

I think about my father and I understand why. I know that he and the strongbox in his office are behind all the things going through my head now. But I don't have the guts yet to make my way along that path. I'm leaving that for later.

It's not for nothing that the Jews happened to be the most able wielders of usury in the West. They have the know-how, others can only imitate them and often go astray making ostentatious displays of their wealth.

I must find out whether or not Buster Keaton was a Jew. In any case, there is a resemblance between Dylan's voice and Keaton's face.

There is one portrayal of Keaton that I never again saw in the movies.

Bogart.

There were times when Humphrey Bogart looked to me like a serious candidate for following in Keaton's footsteps. But Bogart was an aesthete: he had discovered that aloofness is a profitable device for an actor within the Hollywood movie industry. He had discovered how to wield aloofness in art as a form of usury. He cashed in on it. And he drew high returns. Keaton wasn't a spendthrift. Keaton's acting remained compartmentalized, he didn't communicate with his actor's flesh and blood body,

like one sees in those spiritist engravings in which the soul exits the body and is the only one that acts.

A soul also exits Keaton's body; it is the one that acts in front of the camera. During the most dangerous or tragic happenings the spectators burst into a laughter that nearly topples the theater's ceilings: they see Keaton's body and his acting move off in different directions.

The ship sinks slowly and the sailor Buster Keaton goes on looking through his telescope as if nothing had happened. He's sinking, first his feet, then his legs, his lower body, and he goes on looking through his telescope at a horizon that never takes on the features of hope or disaster, pedantry or sentimentalism,

the opposite of the ultra-sentimental and romantic horizons one sees in Charlie's films.

Charlie makes faces, he doesn't know how to keep still, he moves his foot, his cane, he twists his mouth into a smile, he winks his eyes, wrinkles his nose, blinks now and always to the spectator to build a bridge on the ostentations conveyed by his body. Charlie suffers, he's a martyr, and he takes a beating. But he has hope for the future, he believes in man and anything that makes one weep. Charlie is a Christianized Jew.

Bogart is simply a non-Jew (probably a WASP): he is a thrifty actor, or a Judaized and Westernized actor. He is also the actor of Hollywood ostentation. Aloofness is his trade mark. It's his sex appeal, his glamour. His individualized exhibitionism makes him unique within the star system of the movie industry.

. . . .

(You can't stand my silence any longer:

"What's up, man? Where do you stand on all this? My fatigue, my silence, the lack of substance which makes it difficult to continue my reflections on the Jews?"

I wash my hands and you look at me furiously; you know I'm going to crucify you. I don't answer you directly; that's why you feel threatened by me. I prefer silence and winding paths. It's like . . .

Through my silence I convey to you that it is not very important what I think or feel about your momentary—pause—failure. I smile. What is important is that I wind you up so you can spew onto paper what might silently accompany you to your grave. It's better to hold my tongue than to tell you that I could no longer stand your subjective blundering or that I was getting tired of begging you not to turn to me each time you got yourself into a hopeless jam.

I don't want to intervene in your work! At least not now. I want you to gallop—the word is yours after all—through the prairies of creation like a frenzied cow. An empty head is the price you pay for choosing an adventuresome path.

It seems that you have been guessing all along the words going through my head. Or maybe you understood perfectly the act of washing my hands,

because you laugh in my face and ask me who is more afraid of embarking on the adventure of writing. And you go on laughing as if the full weight of the emptiness were to explode not in words but peals of laughter.

For a brief instant—you give me no time—I try to imagine how the narrator's silent moments of explosive laughter might be inserted into the novel you are writing. The narrator's laughter is after all as important for the novel as his words or as a character's farts. And it's what the reader continually asks about.

Aren't novels really made of boisterous and hysterical laughter!

You go on laughing at me and I continue musing on the falsity of those novels that only convey continuity of action and never the discontinuity of creation.

So as not to lose the war I press you up against the white wall and tell you that I've hit upon a solution to your silence. "It's simple. If you want to go on writing," I tell you, "all you have to do is deal with the strongbox your father kept in his office."

You become livid. You don't know what to say, you lose grasp of your surroundings and feel the blood rise to your head.

I could return the laughter now but it seems to me better to respect this painful moment for you. Your eyes well up with tears. I see you turn your face again toward your desk and)

. . . .

I never got to see stars above Manhattan's skyline. The moon, at times, looming large at the end of the street. But the stars, never.

In cold countries people do not look up at the sky at night. When they do go out it's only to get someplace and their eyes only look straight ahead along a horizontal track. Windows are the most useless things in cold countries.

When people look at the sky it's only because the weather is cloudy and foul and they want to see if it's going to rain or snow that day. It's a precaution I quickly learned to take; I don't like to get all wet from the rain or have my hair covered with snow. Later I'll pay for it when my head hurts like hell. That's the only reason I ever looked at the New York sky when I went out at night. And only on cloudy days.

Can it be that a gaze which advances only horizontally ends up generating a pragmatic view of things?

Is that why people in the tropics—ever looking up with joy at the spectacle of moon and stars, or out of their windows, or staring into space as they walk around—are such idealists and so impractical in their way of life?

This contrast of temperament, between those who look ahead and those who raise their eyes, is already dealt with in one of Plato's dialogues (as I now remember). I once used it to explain Machado de Assis's pragmatism and idealism.

Plato tells an anecdote about the old woman and the astrologer. The old woman always looked—horizontally and straight ahead—

where she was going. That's why she never had any accidents. The astrologer, on the other hand, was always falling into holes and splitting his head open because he kept his gaze on the stars.

I would like to imagine what goes through the astrologer's head when, after falling to the bottom of a well, his desire to look at the stars is constrained by the well wall that surrounds him. It can only be understood as a punishment, in the Dantesque, infernal sense of the word, for all astrologers, idealists, and tropical peoples. They would be obliged to reenact forever, from the bottom of the well, the gesture that got them there in the first place.

(Thoughts like these are too suicidal; after all, I too am from the tropics—you say to yourself after you've written down the passage, well inclined now to forgive all astrologers and kindred spirits in the history of humankind, for theirs is, if not the kingdom of heaven, then certainly that of the depths.

And now as if to offset the violent attack on your tropical compatriots you imagine what the moral lesson might be for the old woman who walks forward victoriously with her eyes warily and horizontally pitched, never seeing the stars and never falling into any holes.)

The destiny of those nations which follow the old woman's example is to believe that the evolution of humanity is a straight line along which mankind marches eternally. There is no possibility of derailment once the order to proceed full speed ahead is given. Ever on-ward, ever on-ward, ever onward, onward, and whistle on the curves.

Americans would walk forever onward, inventing this, perfecting that, reconstructing whatever, always looking for ways to advance knowledge and technology such that the car of yesteryear is outdated today or yesterday's jet doesn't make it as tomorrow's spacecraft. This holds for everything, from an egg basket to the atomic bomb. Americans would never stop inventing or fiddling with what they made yesterday because yesterdays are to be thrown in the trash like old newspapers, even if they were never read. All that matters is that they are not today's.

it matters little whether or not the newspaper was read, likewise the thousand and one everyday things that Americans leave behind or do not consume instantaneously. It all gives the impression that commodities—like time bombs—come with dials already set for the moment when they will disappear. Until then it's enough to look at the dated foods in the supermarkets and if you don't want to poison yourself to death you'd better throw it in the garbage can.

So Americans would only stop looking straight ahead when their own inventions turned against them. That would bring the final and mortal blow to the entire civilization that they seek to rule (and are in fact ruling) by means of fire and steel. And all of this just because they refuse to look at the sky when they go out at night.

We're finally turning the corner of this future day. For the first time man makes arms that cannot be used in war because if they were he'd blow the world apart

and bye-bye, be seeing you, it was nice, that's all folks, just like every Looney Toons finale. It's the end of that pretentious era—as Nietzsche said—when the human animal presumed to be the sole owner of the planet and of intelligence.

Nuclear arms are conceived, invented, and built to be heaped up uselessly at the bottom of an underground storehouse, waiting for the enemy's real threat of nuclear war. And so long as that threat doesn't materialize,

I raise my arms (and eyes) to the sky and let out a sigh. More than ever the meaning of survival at any cost hits me like the poundings of an African Orixá priest and I feel possessed by a life force that normally eludes me,

so, as long as that threat does not materialize, we will all continue to breathe, it matters little if it's the polluted air of New York, São Paulo or Cubatão.

I think about the waste on which the entire military industrial complex was built after World War II. They used up only a tiny bit of their reserves when they dropped two atom bombs on Japan. I think of today's waste and come to the conclusion that the waste that Brazilians have known—lunch and dinner leftovers or not-so-very-used clothing thrown into the garbage—is nothing

in comparison with the military

and non-military waste of the Americans. I remember a Brazilian friend who came to New York—at that time they came to work, earn a few dollars, maybe a lot more, and then returned to Brazil and built their dream house on the seashore—, and rented an unfurnished apartment. At night we'd go out looking for the things he needed to furnish it and we'd find everything in the garbage left on the streets. All we needed was a little patience and a lot of strength to carry these "kernels" on our backs.

It was the ritziest garbage in the world, the richest garbage in a country that has the richest atomic arsenal in the world.

More than ever I'm afraid of a nuclear war between the two super powers and as I write these flashes from New York I feel that the decline of the world, incredible as it may seem, is not the fault of lazy, tropical peoples; on the contrary, it has been brought on by the frenetic headlong rush of the cold countries. And what an irony there is in the tactics of reducing the possibility of nuclear war by increasing stockpiles; the two powers would have us believe that all these instruments of war have been and continue to be made just for nothing, only to put the fear of God in the other guy: watch out! It occurs to me that there must be a general lost somewhere in the institutional nooks and crannies, half-forgotten behind his desk or his own madness, or maybe even wearing the insignias of the Secretary of Defense who, one day, will get tired of seeing so much money going to waste in enormous nuclear stockpiles and will decide to set off the rockets, bombs and missiles as if he were celebrating the Fourth of July.

The general wants to see stars in the sky, stars he never saw in childhood, so he invents them now by setting off nuclear arms in the sky.

3

. . . .

"While you were out a young man phoned; he wanted to speak with you."

"Did he leave a message?" asks Eduardo, closing the door behind him.

"He said his name was Carlinhos but that you didn't know him. Marcelo gave him your number. He said he'd call later." Vianna relays the message as he takes from Eduardo's hands a plastic bag with the clothes he bought on 14th Street.

"Ready-to-wear is ready to wear," Eduardo tells him and adds: "and don't complain, 'cause if you do I'll get pissed."

"Why are you speaking to me like that, Eduardo?"

"What did you say was the name of the guy who called?"

"Carlinhos."

"Carlinhos, Carlinhos, hmm . . . are you sure?"

"Eduardo!"

"I have no idea who he might be."

"Well he said you didn't know him."

"Does he know me?"

"He didn't say and I didn't ask."

"He's a friend of Marcelo's?"

"That's what he said," responded Vianna, feeling compelled to reply because he had answered the phone. "I shouldn't have answered the phone; I thought it might have been you calling me from the store."

"I'm not complaining."

At this point the Black Widow draws closer to Eduardo and whispers into his ear:

"I had the distinct impression that there was someone listening on the other side of the door. Were you waiting for anyone?"

Ricky, Ricky my boy, thinks Eduardo for a fleeting second but then realizes:

"It could only have been La Cucaracha. I knew she couldn't hold out. You've never seen such a gossip."

"Who?"

"La Cucaracha, Paco, the Cuban who lives next door."

Eduardo notices a flash of fright across Vianna's face.

"Oh, he's a good person, an anticommunist, the best they come." He pauses. "He took one look at your face and did he ever get bowled over. He's been prowling the hallway ever since like a hungry roach."

"How do you know?"

"He saw you enter the apartment and decided to wait in ambush until you came out so he could find out who you are."

"He's loco."

"Loca, you mean, a real queen. You came, he saw, you conquered. And now his ass is itching to know you."

The Black Widow smiles.

"If you want, I can ring the bell next door. He'll come running. Lickety-split."

He stands still, wrapped in thought, for a moment.

"The problem is he doesn't look like your type. He's a good little soul. But that doesn't mean he's small; at six-foot-three and two hundred pounds he's a regular Li'l Abner."

The Black Widow goes into the bedroom. He says he wants to change his clothes. It's getting late.

"Vianna, are you going to place a complaint with the police?" Eduardo yells from the living room.

Vianna comes into view at the doorway looking annoyed and feeling foolish.

"I don't think so. It's better . . . ," he starts to say and then stands still holding the plastic bag in his hand. After a moment he continues: "How on earth could I explain the details of the burglary, the place, the motive, and the items stolen, such as my suit?"

"You'd have to think up a good lie."

"And they didn't even touch a hair on my head."

He stands still to gather his thoughts.

"They'll start an investigation and soon they'll discover the sonofabitch terrorists. A tight spot I'll be in, huh. Amsterdam Avenue, between 75th and 76th . . . ," without finishing the sentence, he goes back into the bedroom to change his clothes.

"What about your credit cards?" Eduardo insists.

"While you were out I called American Express and then Diner's," Vianna responds loudly, his voice shaking from the movements he makes to pull his boots and trousers off.

"And your identification papers?"

"Let's not speak about that."

He enters the living room in black underwear and no shirt.

"I feel all dirty and sweaty. Would it be too much of an imposition for me to take a shower?"

"I'll get you a clean towel."

"Don't bother, I don't need one."

Eduardo goes into the bedroom and takes a towel out of the built-in closet. He hands it to Vianna, who is waiting by the bathroom door.

Eduardo moves further into the bathroom and tells Vianna, who is in the shower:

"I'll gather your things and put them away in the closet. Okay?"

Vianna agrees and thanks him.

He picks up the leather cap and jacket from the sofa and the leather trousers from the bedroom. On the bed he lays out the new trousers, shirt, and jacket from the plastic bag. Then he folds the leather getup and places it in the bag. He notices the mesh shirt sticking half way out of the bag.

"I'm going to put the mesh shirt in another bag. Take it home, it's too sweated up to put it in the closet."

"Throw it in the garbage," Vianna yells as he soaps himself.

Once everything is in the bag, Eduardo looks for a high shelf inside the built-in closet. He goes for a chair in the kitchen to stand on and reach the shelf.

As he passes through the living room, he goes up to the bathroom door again:

"That guy's name was Carlinhos, right?"

"He said he'd call you later."

He goes back into the bedroom and dials Marcelo's number. The phone rings on the other end but no one answers.

Vianna enters the bedroom wrapped in a towel.

Eduardo leaves the room. He feels nervous. He starts to put things away. He takes the dirty glasses and the ice bucket to the kitchen. He washes the glasses, putting each one into the drying rack. He throws the rest of the ice into the sink. He goes back into the living room and puts the ice bucket away in the bar next to the White Horse. He puts a record on the turntable and switches it on. Jim Morrison's voice sings "I'm the back door man."

"What are you going to do with the apartment?" Eduardo asks moving over to the bedroom doorway.

"Merda! I had already forgotten about that."

"The lease is in my name."

"That's right."

Silence. Vianna puts his boots on.

"Did you leave the door open?"

"Yes."

"Why didn't you close it?"

"How could I?"

"Isn't it dangerous?"

"There's nothing to steal."

Eduardo retorts.

"Someone might call the police. A neighbor might see the door left ajar and that's it."

"Don't jinx me."

"I'm not fooling around, you know."

"I know."

Eduardo goes back into the living room.

Vianna is ready, all he needs is a shave.

Eduardo asks him why he doesn't shave.

"I'll shave at home," he replies and adds that he has found the answer.

"For what?" asks Eduardo.

Vianna doesn't respond right away. After a while he says the best way of solving the problem is to break the lease on Monday and pay the penalty. Just invent some excuse to that Jewish girl . . . the student got sick and had to return to Brazil. Vianna leaves everything else in Eduardo's hands. For example, find a locksmith. No problem, there are many in the neighborhood. Contract a Latino to paint the apartment. The owner of the bar on the corner ought to know someone. There's also that Dominican who owns the bodega on the next block. He was very friendly with those of us who went to Santo Domingo in '65.

"When everything's fixed, you hand over the apartment."

Eduardo holds back his anger as he listens.

"You should be able to get all that done on Monday. I'll call the ambassador and tell him I need your help. He'll free you up no questions asked."

Eduardo keeps his mouth shut. If he opened it his words would shoot out like bullets at the colonel. Vianna had said everything without looking at Eduardo as if he were giving orders to someone standing beside him.

"I'll be going home now," he concludes. "And remember, mum's the word. I'm counting on you. And you can count on me."

Eduardo goes back into the bedroom. He calls Marcelo, the phone rings but nobody answers.

He takes his shoes off and lies down on the bed fully dressed. No sooner does his head hit the pillow, Stella screams:

"Me-rrrr-da! Me-rrrr-da!" the piercing cry of someone who has cut her finger on a sharp razor or who has accidentally broken her favorite china (that's how she feels).

She just lies there looking at the hopelessness of the situation.

She'd like to get some Mercurochrome or glue but neither one nor the other could cure the pain she feels. She lies there motionless without shutting her eyes, without opening her mouth. The only thing that breaks the stillness is her steady breathing, intentionally snorted so loudly that it reverberates in her ears. She listens to the sounds of her own breathing as others might count sheep. The sound doesn't stop nor does its intensity abate. Clarity is the only excuse for letting the day go on.

2

Eduardo and Marcelo studied liberal arts together at the National University. After graduating in '63 they didn't see each other again.

Eduardo knew that Marcelo had decided to stay at the National University and study for an academic career.

He knew that Marcelo wanted to continue his studies in France but preferred getting married. He didn't know to whom, nor when. When he found out, Marcelo was already married.

He knew they separated soon afterward.

And he also knew that . . . —now this was a fabrication of those wagging tongues that abound in Rio. Eduardo didn't put a lot of stock in that. In any case, he'd eventually know whatever was to be known.

Marcelo knew from conversations that Eduardo sent everyone and everything at the National University to hell—studies, professors, and fellow students. It was all a crock. A waste of time.

He found out Eduardo could hardly remember his name. Still and all, he said to himself: "I don't know about him, he's probably just going to fall through the cracks."

He found out Eduardo said he didn't have to forget French because he had never learned it.

He found out he studied English at the Brazil-U.S. Institute in Copacabana and that he even dressed like a gringo.

Later he learned that Eduardo dressed like a hippie with long hair and bracelets.

He found out Eduardo worked in a tourist agency at the Copacabana Palace Hotel. It was at that agency that Marcelo went looking for him one day to get a cheap plane ticket, and that's when he discovered Eduardo had gone to the United States.

They got together again in New York after five years of not seeing each other.

Standing in front of him at the passport counter, Marcelo told Eduardo he had phoned his house in Rio before coming to New York. The maid answered half-stuttering and passed the phone to your father who said rather curtly that you were now working in New York, at the consulate—which I already knew. He didn't want to give out your address.

"That's why it took so long for me to find you; I thought you'd had your fill of Brazilians."

Eduardo turned to Maria da Graça and asked her if it was okay to take his lunch hour twenty minutes earlier so he could chat with his friend who had just arrived from Rio.

Marcelo smiled and made a good impression; this made it easier for Maria da Graça to say it was okay with her, but he should ask Terezinha who had the next shift at the counter. Terezinha agreed and got up from her desk, looking wide-eyed at Marcelo, his smile the signal that there was easy fishing in those waters and all she had to do was throw her net quickly.

Da Gloria, the third of the Graces, was away on vacation in Maceió, Eduardo informed Marcelo. Can you believe it, the poor girl can't stand the heat of New York summers.

Eduardo winked conspiringly at the other two and added:

"You should meet her, Marcelo. Maria da Graça was just telling me before you arrived that da Gloria was named cultural attaché for New York." He took a breath and went on speaking in Stella's exclamatory registers: "It's going to be paradise!"

The others tittered: "Oh that Eduardo, he's so. . . ."

"Go on, Eduardo, scat," said Maria da Graça, "before we all get fired. One after the other."

"Let's have lunch, it's on me," said Eduardo when he and Marcelo rejoined at the entrance to the consulate.

"We'll split it," Marcelo proposed, "I also get paid in dollars. You think you're the only one?"

Marcelo said he'd been hired as a lecturer in Brazilian literature at New York University in the Village. Things were getting pretty bad at the National University since he had been transferred from Antônio Carlos College. He heard about the opening at NYU through a friend in New Jersey. He applied and was given a two-year appointment until the department found a substitute for a Professor Fernández, who had left for a position at a Midwestern university. "And with twice the pay," Marcelo added, "that's why people play musical chairs from one university to another."

They went out onto the sidewalk but were not met with the usual blast of hot summer air that scorches your face as your body passes through the revolving door. The Atlantic breezes that sweep over Fifth Avenue sweetened the sun-drenched days at the end of August. It was as if Buckminster Fuller had put a geodesic dome over Manhattan and everyone enjoyed a perfectly stable, air-conditioned environment in and out of doors.

Eduardo walked down Fifth Avenue in suit and tie without the discomfort of perspiration. Marcelo wore jeans and an Indian cotton shirt still bearing the imprint of carioca summers. His sandaled feet bore witness to his easy adaptation to new customs and to the Village, where he lived.

"Why'd you let your beard grow?"

"Why not?"

"Well, for one thing, gringo women don't like beards. They're liable to think that you're some kind of dirty communist. They may even suspect that you're one of Fidel's spies."

"I'd have to be chewing on a cigar. Boy, how I'd like to suck on one," Marcelo kidded Eduardo.

Eduardo got the message.

"I was told your marriage fell apart. Tell me about it."

"Only if you reassure me you've got a fatherly ear."

"Don't you think I've got one?"

"You didn't use to."

"I got it with age."

"Was it age or life?"

"Life, I think."

"So, your tastes have changed," Marcelo said ironically.

"No, times have changed."

"And now you only like poor forsaken youths in need of a father . . ."

"Anything else around here to be had?"

"How should I know? You're the city slicker."

"Look who's talking."

"Me? A poor broken-hearted stranger foundering on the waters of the Hudson . . ."

"Boy, you certainly didn't fail speech and diction at the National . . ."

". . . crying out for a little help from his friends. Help!"

"Well, are you or are you not going to tell me about it?" Eduardo retorts.

"Only after you tell me where all the hot spots in New York are. And I want all the details."

"Sorry, you've got the wrong department. My line is different from yours."

"Are you so sure?" Marcelo insinuates.

Eduardo pretends to be shocked.

"You too? Well, welcome to the club."

"And aren't we the world champs?"

"In futebol, you mean. Only in futebol."

"Or libertinism . . . and the lack of freedom . . ."

"Now hold it there. You know I'm an official in the employ and service of repression," Eduardo bantered.

"I know, always rubbing elbows with the military attaché," Marcelo reparteed, stroking Eduardo's elbow with his own.

Eduardo grew pallid, stopped in his tracks, and turned to Marcelo:

"Now how the hell did you know that?"

"Oh, come on Edu. You're not getting paranoid on me, are you?" Eduardo's violent reaction made Marcelo nervous. "It's no big deal. One of his cousins in Brazil told me all about it. You know what it's like; you tell someone you're going to travel: By the way, do you know so and so? You don't? Well, you've really got to meet him. He's a friend of X, and you know X. Look him up, look them both up, don't forget, they're really good people, they can show you around, help you out."

Eduardo calmed down but the conversation had withered.

They walked a bit in silence. Eduardo showed the first signs of coming back to life when he pointed out the restaurant where they were going to have lunch, on 53rd between Park and Madison.

"French cuisine," Eduardo specified, meeting with Marcelo's approval.

The maître d' was Brazilian and knew Eduardo, who went there whenever he had guests. He gave them a good table.

"Ten minutes later and we'd be stuck at the bar for at least half an hour."

When they took up their conversation again it was friendly and cheerful, with all the carrying on of before, only now they were sitting down looking over the menu. The clouds had dispersed over their horizon, it had only been a squall.

Marcelo reflected that he had done the right thing in dissociating Eduardo from the military attaché in his conversations with the other members of the organization. "Eduardo a spy? You've got to be kidding or you've all gone nuts." *Judging by his reaction,* Marcelo said to himself, *he's not going to take too well to our stalking the colonel. And here I was thinking it would be easy to tip him off about the possible danger. I almost let the cat out of the bag like a jerk.*

If he warned Eduardo, he ran the risk of betraying he was in on everything. Eduardo's relationship with the military attaché in and out of the consulate was interpreted as political and ideological complicity. Both were thought to be working for the National Intelligence Service or for the covert forces of repression. Marcelo, on the other hand, was part of an urban guerrilla group under formation in New York. To save his friendship with Eduardo, Marcelo opted for another plan. He'd ask another companheiro, a third party in this whole story, to help out. When the moment was right, this companheiro would warn Eduardo.

This time Marcelo never got around to confiding in Eduardo about the reasons for his separation. Eduardo insisted on several occasions during lunch but Marcelo always managed to evade the questions. He did so good-humoredly so Eduardo wouldn't feel too intrusive when he raised them again.

A few days later, when they met for the fourth time, Marcelo opened up. Eduardo had already forgotten that he had once shown any interest in knowing how the marriage came to an end.

Marcelo had to remind him that he had expressed interest.

The floodgates were lifted and the roaring mass of water rushed out, its force nonetheless compressed into a delicate and sinuous torrent that immersed Eduardo in a reserved and quiet mood. At last they had recovered the good friendship of their college days. They went barhopping in the Village two Saturdays in a row and, failing to score, on the third they went up to Eduardo's apartment for a nightcap.

"Chrissie was from the North, you know the type, Eduardo, a woman who believes you get married only to have kids. It's not her fault. It's in the genes and it just plays itself out. Her grandmother was like that. Her mother too. And her daughter will be the same. You should have heard the family conversations at her home. But all that motherhood talk didn't get me into the mood. If there's one thing I can't stand it's procreation. I don't want to reproduce myself in this world. No way. I can get along with women alright so long as we're just playing. I'm not like other bisexuals I've known; they prefer to fool around with men and fuck with women. But me, when it comes to threading my lath into their cunts I lose all interest. My rod drops to half mast and I have to pull out. Then it gets so soft I could spread it like butter on a slice of bread. If possible, I retreat and get the team off the field. Quickly and with no compunctions, no regrets. When we were just going out everything was great. Those were the best years of my life. Coming from the North, she would only put out after getting married. I didn't insist.

It was okay with me, I told her. It was enough to make out in the movies, kiss on the sofa, the street, the park benches, under lamp posts, against the neighbor's wall. All over Tijuca. Making out all over the place. And a little finger fucking, that was okay too. I could handle that. But then came marriage and that's when . . ."

He pauses.

"The honeymoon was going just great until one moment when we were in the heat of things and she asked, no she begged: 'Give me a baby, my love, please.' What a dis-as-ter! You can't imagine. I asked her right then and there if she was taking the pill and doing whatever else she had to. That's when the fly hit the soup. I refused to have any more of it. The more she offered, the more I rejected it. It went on for two years, the same shit for two years. Marriage was a two-year hassle. I was always worried that she might stop the pill just to have a kid. She was always wanting to fuck and I wouldn't hear of it. Finally the lack of trust wore us down. Poor girl, it wasn't her fault. After all the making out before marriage she could only expect much more. You can imagine the rest of the story."

He pauses.

"That damned sentence, 'Please give me a child,' if only she wouldn't have said it we'd be together now. Everything else between us was fine. The problem was I couldn't trust her anymore. Chrissie was going to get her child at my expense and without my even noticing it. She was going to betray me. And something strange was coming over me, if I so much as looked at an empty bottle it broke. When I bought beer at the corner store I always had to leave a deposit for the bottle. There wasn't one return bottle left at home. When I came home one day I noticed the vase was empty. She probably didn't get a chance to buy fresh flowers at the market and threw out all the withered ones. So there was the vase, empty and pleading to be filled with flowers and water. I stared long and hard at the vase sitting on a chest in one corner of the living room. It appeared to be looking back at me and laughing, laughing its ass off in my face. Well, there was nothing else to do. Bang! onto the floor. It was going to be pretty hard to explain that: a vase sitting innocently on a chest in the corner of the room. I thought up some tall tale. We had a cleaning woman who came once a week. I had told her that I couldn't understand why she threw all those empties in the trash. I told her it was dangerous, that I had almost cut my hand when I went to bundle the trash in a newspaper to throw it down the incinerator. I would sit there and look at Chrissie watching the evening soap. She too looked empty. She wanted me to fill her up, she asked me to fill her, who knows with what, with come, with a kid, with fucking, with my cock, with anything and everything imaginable. But she never filled out; it seemed to me that her life, her light, her glow were dying out. That I was bad for her. I even told her she was wasting her youth on me. She didn't understand because she said that she wasn't losing anything, she was, on the contrary, gaining. One night, when she convinced me there was no risk, we had a last go at it. The last, glorious fuck. We went at it like crazy all night. In the morning I looked at her face and it was all lit up like one of those blinking neon signs in the middle of the night. The gas had been turned on and her face shined, it glowed."

He pauses.

"Happiness, for her, was being full. Full of my cock, my tongue, my saliva, my love, my come, our kid. So I did with our marriage as I had done with the vase: bang! onto the floor."

3

The doorbell rings.

It's Paco.

"Did he leave?"

"Yeah, thank God."

Standing in the doorway Paco's face is glowing, his eyes sparkling with curiosity.

"Aren't you going to invite me in?"

Eduardo excuses himself. He's not all there right now.

"You tired?"

"A bit, but that's not the problem."

Eduardo asks Paco if he'd like to sit down. Would he like to have something to eat? Paco says no thanks, passing his hand over his belly, he's just had lunch.

Eduardo didn't know he was hungry. He realizes it now and tells his friend.

"Well there are some leftovers in my place I haven't put in the fridge yet. Want some?" asks Paco.

Eduardo accepts but asks Paco to do him a favor. Would he please bring the food over. He's expecting a call any time now. It's pretty important.

Paco comes back with a pot of moros y cristianos and ladles him a plate full of the rice cooked in black bean stew. He garnishes it with tostones—fried plantains or plátanos, as Latinos call them—on one side and chicharrones—fried pork rinds—on the other.

"I'll never be able to finish all this."

"Oh yes you will, and right now! You need more nourishment, chico, just look at your scrawny, famished face."

Eduardo eats the food under the watchful gaze of La Cucaracha who wishes Stella were there to talk to her. *That man in black and evil has killed Stella,* Paco says to himself trying to understand the misfortunes of his friend who just sits there impassively chewing the moros y cristianos and the chicharrones almost unwillingly, like someone convalescing from an operation who eats out of instinct rather than desire. Paco doesn't know what to say so he accompanies Eduardo's chewing in silence.

Eduardo chokes on something, coughs, and pushes the plate to the middle of the table. That's his way of indicating he's had enough.

Paco goes to the kitchen and brings him back a glass of water.

Eduardo thanks him with a smile but declines with a shake of the head.

"¿Qué te pasa, chico?" insists Paco, who forces the glass into Eduardo's hands.

Eduardo yields, grabs the glass and raises it to his mouth. The water refreshes his throat.

He gets up from the sofa and walks toward the bedroom.

Paco follows him.

Eduardo sits down on the bed and pulls his shoes off.

Paco observes him from the doorway fascinated by the distance the other creates around himself, acting as if he were all alone in the apartment.

Eduardo lays down on his back, staring (Paco observes) into the infinity of white ceiling that backgrounds the metallic ring around the white bulb.

Paco would like Eduardo to succeed in visualizing his desires. His bulging, unhappy eyes lead Paco to conclude that the vision is denied. Paco walks to the bed and sits next to Eduardo's outstretched body. He raises his right arm and slowly extends it to Eduardo's head. His fingers comb through Eduardo's ringlets, writing the adventure story of two friends on a treasure hunt; as they approach the treasure it slides over into intangible regions. Their two sluggish, traveling bodies lost in search for a place to rest as the only alternative to continuing a useless journey full of pitfalls. Paco twists Eduardo's curls around his fingers.

Eduardo shuts his eyes, his breathing becomes calmer and his body is gradually rid of the tremors of emotional uncontrol.

"Ay, chico, qué lástima, what a shame!" Paco whispers reassuringly.

Eduardo opens his eyes and looks at him.

Paco smiles back feeling satisfied that his friend decided at last to shorten the distance.

Eduardo unfolds his arms and extends his left hand to Paco's mouth as a way of asking him to keep silent.

When Paco has understood the request the telephone on the night table begins to ring.

Eduardo disentangles himself from Paco's hand and hoists up his body until his back rests against the headboard. He lifts the receiver.

"This is Carlinhos. You don't know me, Eduardo. Marcelo gave me your number. I'd like to speak to you; it'll only take a moment. Is now a good time or do you want me to call you back later?"

"Now's okay."

"Do you know someone by the name of Valdevinos Vianna?"

Paco sees Eduardo smile and is moved. *Stella has come back,* Paco says to himself.

Eduardo is smiling on account of the name. *So that's why,* he thinks, as if he had just found an object he never thought of looking for because he never even guessed it could exist.

"Hey, you there, goddammit! Do you hear me?"

"Hold on, buddy."

"Well, do you or don't you know him?"

"I do know a certain Vianna but I don't know if his first name is Valdevinos."

"Is he the military attaché at the consulate, your colleague?"

Paco sees Eduardo's face take on a saintly, beatific glow. *He's saved,* Paco thinks.

"Valdevinos . . . ," Eduardo smiles again, causing Paco's eyes to get moist with emotion. "Valdevinos . . . , that's why no one ever calls him by his name. Colonel Valdevinos."

"Hey, this is serious, dammit!"

"If you knew the guy, man, you'd be laughing too. More than me."

"I know him more than I'd like to, not personally but from afar. You I know more up close."

Eduardo doesn't want to go on hearing this any longer, he wants to hang up and he does. Afterward, waiting, he becomes apprehensive. *Oh God, please don't let me be misunderstood.*

Paco sees Eduardo waiting but he doesn't know why. The phone rings again. *It's now or never,* Paco thinks as Eduardo lifts the receiver at the first ring.

"Sorry. It was an accident."

"Listen good to what I'm going to say because afterward it's me who's going to hang up on you."

"I'm shaking in my pants. What's up?"

Carlinhos does not take up the familiarity:

"Valdevinos is a marked person."

"I know that."

"How do you know that?"

"I guessed. Now cut the shit. Get serious."

The other changes his tone of voice and carefully spells out his words so there will be no doubt that he's the one giving the orders:

"You'd better not see him anymore. Avoid going out with him."

Eduardo hears the phone click.

"Hello? Hello?" All he hears is the dial tone. "The sonofabitch hung up."

Eduardo slides his body from the headboard back to its former position.

He tells Paco he sees a razor. A razor opening and closing against the porcelain opalescence of the sink. It opens and closes like a pair of magic scissors cutting paper without a guiding human hand. Suddenly the razor is grasped by a strong hand at the end of a long white hairy arm unattached to any body. The razor takes flight like a bird with shining black wings sparkling in the sunlight. The lamp casts its light from behind the man's head, behind his soapy face, two eyes and a black mustache peering through the foamy whiteness. The razor glides along the sudsy skin of the face and descends like a rail guard. That's it, he hears the distant whistle of the train, the same whistle that he heard during his vacation in Minas Gerais. The whistle warns that it is passing through. Trains kill. Trains go by. The razor disappears.

"What a relief!" says Eduardo to Paco. "I see running water, coming out of the faucet and running down the drain. I also see the shiny blade of the razor emerge from the jet of water."

Eduardo says the throat is in the mirror. It's in the mirror so it can't be a real, living throat. It might be a photograph of a throat. "But it's not a photo," he says, "because its skin moves every time someone swallows something." The razor gets very close to the skin as if it were about to open up a slit.

He tells Paco it's my hand that grasps the razor and tries to cut a groove in the throat in the mirror, just like the Amazon Indians do to collect the latex that saps from the grooves they cut into rubber trees. He sees a little bowl filling up with a whitish substance. He says it's latex, but then corrects himself, it looks like foam which flows over the edges of the bowl. Milk boiling in an aluminum pot.

"Ow!" he screams in pain and says he burned his hand. "Someone asks me," he says, "why I would put my hand in boiling milk." Eduardo would like to see a weeping face but he doesn't succeed in bringing it into view. He makes an effort, even asks for Paco's help but the face doesn't appear. All he sees are the faces he's making at Paco, who gets scared. He tells Paco that if he saw tears running down his face the damned vision would finally appear. All he can see is the razor opening and closing against the pink marble of the shelf. It opens and closes without any human guidance, like the shiny black wings of a bird in flight. Eduardo extends his arm to grab hold of it, he tries to grab hold of it but he fails.

Paco tells him it's a mirage; it'll pass soon. The razor doesn't exist.

Eduardo doesn't believe him. He sits on the bed with his arm still outstretched. He stands up in an attempt to grab the white bulb attached to the ceiling.

Paco steps onto the bed and guides his friend's body back to a resting position.

"I'm seeing it," says Eduardo, "I'm finally seeing the face I wanted to see."

Paco smiles and puts his hand on Eduardo's forehead; it's burning, it might be a fever.

He sees the face wafting through the room like a decapitated head falling through the air. He sees the face but he can't make out its features. It's an anonymous face with external contours only. All its features have been erased to conceal its personality.

Eduardo tells Paco I see a man's face but it's not the face of a person.

The hand at the end of a long white hairy arm reappears holding several colored crayons. It throws them down and they hover in the air ready to be used. The hand moves over to the face and begins to color it in. Everything proceeds quickly.

One after another eyebrows and eyes appear. The hand uses colored crayons but the colors of the face are still black on white, unchangeable like those of a design or a sculpture. The hand draws the nose and nostrils. Eduardo says this is not the face he wanted to see. "It should be an adult face," he says and asks Paco to notice the wrinkles on its forehead and shadows beneath its eyes, the eyes of a drunk. Its mouth appears. Eduardo repeats it's not the face he wanted to see. Then hair and ears. The hand and long white hairy arm disappear but the crayons continue to hover in the air. Eduardo now sees a hand covered with suds; no, it's not covered with suds, he corrects himself, it's covered with gauze. The hand takes a crayon and colors in the eyes. It takes another crayon and colors in the face. It takes other crayons and goes about finishing the job, at a quick, manic pace. The face is alive. It blinks, breathes, sees, and tries to say something. Eduardo makes an effort to make it out. He hears:

". . . didn't do . . . anything . . ."

He listens more attentively. The hand grabs the red crayon and closes the mouth. The face remains still again but is now colored as it was not before.

"Hand me the razor," Eduardo says to Paco.

Paco doesn't understand.

"I asked you to pass me the razor." Said loudly the order is clearly heard this time.

"I can't. The cat ate it," Paco responds.

"What happened to the cat that was here?"

"The dog ate it."

"And the dog?"

"The wolf ate it."

Paco lies down next to Eduardo.

"Where's the wolf?"

"The mouse ate it."

"And where's the mouse?"

"The cat ate it."

Paco bends his head toward Eduardo's face, mentally reciting *Caperucita, Little Red Riding Hood, the youngest of my friends, went into the forest looking for firewood.* He looks at his friend's face, up close, and feels relieved. *To gather dry firewood.* He puts his hand through

Eduardo's hair. He raises his voice: "¿Decidme niños, tell me my children, qué pasa? What bad news has been received at home?" He dries the drops of cold sweat forming on Eduardo's forehead. "Everyone went into the forest in search for her but no one found her." Paco fixes his eyes on Eduardo's. "They say an evil wolf ate her." Paco kisses him on the mouth. He let's out a scream of horror. It's not Eduardo whom he's kissing; he's kissing his own image in the mirror. Frightened, he shuts his eyes and shakes his head sideways as if to cast off the image. He loses his breath. He reopens his eyes and now he can't figure out when or how Eduardo's body disappeared. It evaporated from the bed before his very eyes. He looks all around the room, above, below, beneath the bed. He can't see a thing. He's afraid. He thinks Eduardo might have been kidnapped.

"The sonofabitch comunistas hijos de puta, it must have been them. Those fucking communists. Fueron ellos. They did it. Damn them."

If they kidnapped him, he would have seen someone come in. They would have made noise. No one came in. No one made noise. Eduardo wasn't kidnapped. He just disappeared, vanished. Feeling more sure of himself, he gets off the bed. He leaves the room. He leaves the apartment, closing the door behind him.

From the doorway of the bathroom, after vomiting into the toilet the Cuban food he had for lunch, Eduardo sees Paco leaving the apartment, banging the door behind him. Eduardo doesn't feel strong enough to run after him to find out what happened. *I'll stop by later*, he thinks. His head buzzes and the sour and bitter aftertaste in his mouth is just enough to kick up another round of vomiting from his rebellious stomach. He manages to control his nausea, breathing heavily as he paces around the coffee table in the living room. He goes into the kitchen, takes an Alka-Seltzer and lets it dissolve in a glass of water. He drinks it. The effervescent water calms his stomach. He returns to the bedroom and lies down on the bed.

Eduardo falls asleep.

4

When Eduardo wakes up Stella is already raring to go.

"Move, man, come on," she says to herself before taking a feline leap off the bed.

She wants to go out, take a walk, have fun, breathe in the cool night air. After all, no one is made of stone. *What a shitty day!* she attests, *a little fun will calm the spirit. If not, my pretty little mommy's head will blow up.* For sure she's going to go out looking for Ricky. She'll find Ricky and they'll go off and have a good fuck. That'll calm her spirit.

"Ricky is probably short for Richard. Richard must be his name. Oh Richard, dear Richard. Since you haven't called I'll just have to go out and look for you. You won't mind, will you?" she says smiling as she brushes her teeth and looks at her chafed skin in the bathroom mirror.

He never called. He ended up not calling. He still hasn't called. But maybe he did. If he doesn't call today he'll call tomorrow. In case of doubt it's better to think positively, that's right, it's better that way. "A luta continua, on with the struggle, Stella. Fuck if you can and if you can't use your hand." She makes faces in the mirror to help dissolve her torpor and to get a move on. "The future belongs to the man who takes it in his hands."

"You just can't lie in bed all day; people who stay in bed never get anywhere." It's not difficult to guess where Ricky might be, unless . . . "Now don't be cynical, Stella. Unless . . . He found someone richer, more generous, better looking. But a whore's a whore, a slut's a slut, and a faggot's a faggot. Okay, gentlemen, raise the ante and play your game. With the disaster that's in store for us, now's not the time to count pennies," she says walking back into the living room and sitting on the sofa like a futebol player on the bench deep in thought. That's the only way to gather her thoughts, quieting down and keeping her mouth shut for at least ten minutes. If not, she's a goner. After a few minutes Stella jumps up:

"Merda, I still haven't spoken with Marcelo," she says as Eduardo heads back for the bedroom.

He dials Marcelo's number.

Marcelo answers.

Eduardo says angrily:

"Marcelo! Who's Carlinhos?"

"Oh, so he already called you?"

"He sure did and he made all kinds of threats. (He changes registers, mimicking Carlinhos's voice:) 'For your own good, Eduardo, you'd better stay away from Colonel Valdevinos. Don't go out with him, Eduardo. The colonel is a marked man.'"

"That's right, man, you got the message."

"What do you mean I got the message!? Fuck you, I'm not just going to take this lying down."

"Come on now, Edu, don't get hotheaded. Remember, keep a cool head."

"What! The other guy wants to bash my head in and you tell me to keep a cool head. I don't understand you, Marcelo."

"What's to understand?"

"That's just great, Marcelo. Now look here: I'm walking down the street all cool-headed and all of a sudden bang! bang! two shots in the heart. (He changes registers again, now imitating La Cucaracha:) 'Do you like flowers?' 'Yes, I do.' Bang! bang! 'Tomorrow you'll have them.'"

"I'll tell you another one, if you like: 'What's your name?' 'Eduardo.' Then . . . bang! bang! 'What did you say your name was?'"

"Don't play with fire, Marcelo. Come on now, spit it out, if you're my friend tell me the names of the people involved in this. Who is this Carlinhos? Why did he call me? How does he know about my friendship with the military attaché? Why does he want to do him in?"

"Forget it, Edu. It's too complicated and . . . too dangerous. I'm probably saying too much as it is. How do I know Valdevinos isn't there listening in. He might have bugged your phone. You never know with the likes of him. You . . ."

Eduardo slams the phone down.

Marcelo calls him back.

"Stella's hysterical today."

"And who wouldn't be?" (Pause.) "I'm sorry, Marcelo, I didn't do it on purpose. It's your friend Stella, she's got her nerves on edge. Forgive her, come on, don't hold it against her."

"She's hysterical because she wants to be, because she's an ass, a neurotic bitch. After all, no one wants to do her any harm. On the contrary."

"Oh yeah, what do you mean? What's this all about?"

"We're not going back to that old story."

Silence. Neither says a word.

"Forget it," Marcelo insists.

"After all that, how could I forget it?"

"You can, Edu, you can if you want to."

"You're a sadist! Stella got up on the wrong side of the bed today. She had to put up with a sadist during the day and now another sadist at night."

"All right, just to show you I'm not a sadist, why don't you come out and take a walk with me. I'm also fed up today; I spent the whole afternoon in a boring conversation with Professor Aníbal. The guy's a real drag! You can't imagine."

"Who's this professor?"

"Don't you remember? He's the guy who wrote that history text. I think you've never again opened up a book after leaving National University."

"You're right, brother. I'd rather shake my booty. That business of sitting down all day reading, that's not my cup of tea. That's over with."

"Over for you, speak for yourself."

"Don't be so old-fashioned, Marcelo."

Marcelo mocks Stella:

"Get into the groove, cruise, get laid, turn on, tune out, far out. Hey, that's what it's all about, that's living, man. Know what I mean?"

"Fuck you! You're really trying to kill my day. First you have that asshole Carlinhos who I don't even know call me and threaten me. And now you make fun of me. Cut the shit, Marcelo, cut it. You don't know what you're getting into with Stella. She'll squeal and tomorrow even the provost at NYU will know who you are, Mrs. Marcelo Carneiro da Rocha, better known as the mankiller Marquise de Santos. What did you think, that I didn't know about your carrying on with that German aristocrat who came to Rio for carnival?"

"Boy, you're really on a roll today."

PART TWO

. . . .

4

. . . .

"Door's open. You can come in."

Marcelo, making his way along the eighth floor corridor, heard the precise enunciation of a voice dropped to a baritone; it came from inside the apartment, on the other side of the closed door. Marcelo's presence in the building on this afternoon had been communicated to Professor Aníbal by intercom. The way the doorman treated him indicated that he had already been alerted to the two o'clock appointment.

Obeying the order, Marcelo carefully opens the door.

Professor Aníbal greets Marcelo from his wheelchair. His smiling face has the crafty look of a diabolic Jerry cautiously gauging the advance of a daring Tom.

(*I had no idea that Professor Aníbal was* . . . , Marcelo says to himself on seeing the man seated in front of him.)

Before extending his arm for the handshake, Professor Aníbal hastily drives his wheelchair to the door and closes the vertical series of locks.

"You'll have to excuse my caution but in New York you can never be too careful. You can't fool around when it comes to burglary and mugging. Fortunately in Brazil we have chosen *ordem e segurança.*"

(*"Order and Security!" He's got a knack for our fascist slogans. He's not as old as I thought he was. Judging by what he writes you'd think he was a frail old man. From behind he does look* . . .)

"I'm all alone at home today. My wife went out to do the weekly shopping."

(very frail. His deep voice is a shield for his useless legs and his wheel-chair. Should I offer to push his wheelchair? When I knocked, the door opened and it was all pleasantries. Inside it's all burglaries, muggings, a thousand chains and a thousand locks! The doorman called him on the intercom and he must have rushed to open all the locks while I was coming up on the elevator. "The door is open, you may come in." The sonofabitch is full of tricks. This guy's going to die of old age, if he ever dies. Should I offer to push his wheelchair? He knows how to manage on his own so let him push himself around.)

Still in the foyer by the door, Professor Aníbal makes a perfect U-turn in his wheelchair. Finally, he stretches out his arm to Marcelo and in a less pretentious voice tells him:

"It's a pleasure to welcome you to my home. I had already heard of your presence in New York. Word gets around pretty quickly. It's like living on a fazenda in the backlands of Brazil. There's only twenty of us, if that many, in this area. So whenever anyone comes over it's like having one of the family."

The professor gains control of the situation and goes on giving orders:

"You can hang your overcoat on the coat rack. The apartment has central heating."

(Should I jump into the game? Should I tell him this is no overcoat, sir. It's a Japanese jacket, you can't get any cheaper, bought on sale at Macy's Bargain Basement. I should have at least put on a white shirt and tie. With these people you never know. The situation required it. Oh well, let's see if we can't make up for not wearing a tie: I'll wear a smile and dab a little grease on my words:)

"It's very hospitable of you to receive me in your home. It seems that professors here receive colleagues and students only in their offices at the university. Lucky for me to meet up with such generous Brazilian courtesy in this asphalt jungle."

(Plop! I fell into his game like a skater on the ice. Bad luck but it's too late to do anything about it. There's no turning back.)

"No need for thanks. As I was saying, there are about twenty of us in this city and that makes it possible for human relations to be more cordial than usual. More affectionate."

Aníbal casts a professorial glance over Marcelo and continues:

"But let's not be so hasty to criticize the Americans; it's such an unfortunate habit of our leftist compatriots. They see everything except their own defects. We have a lot to learn from the Americans. They respect privacy and if we do not have the cultural temperament to do likewise we should at least admire them for their ways."

(*Should I change the game, turn the tables on him? I don't know if I can manage it. I'll play along.*)

"I didn't mean to criticize the Americans. I was only expressing my joy at reencountering our own ways. Sir, you could have . . ."

"I'm not so old . . . you don't have to be so formal."

". . . could have received me in your office at Columbia. But you didn't. You invited me to your home. I was only recognizing your Brazilian cordiality; I wasn't criticizing the Americans."

"I'm glad. I wouldn't want to be disillusioned so soon. It's an unfortunate characteristic of Brazilians abroad to point out the faults of others and to close their eyes to their good points."

"What do you mean?"

"The majority of Brazilians who come here see the best of the United States and think it's bad and when they see the worst they think it's good. They see things topsy turvy and that's why they end up aping the worst. Only the worst, the trash of American society."

(*Is he referring to my long hair, my Indian shirt, my white sneakers?*)

"With such blindness on the part of our compatriots," the professor continues, "we end up importing what's bad and not what's good. We need more education; we have to be more discerning. We lack civic sentiments. We still live like the savages of Caminha, dazzled by the cheapest foreign beads and totally insensitive to what's truly important in the history of humanity."

(*They close the country down at Galeão airport and now even here in the Village. It's that same old customhouse tradition that not even Dom João VI was able to eliminate when he transferred the court from Lisbon to Rio.*)

Suddenly the professor becomes aware that they have been talking in the foyer and that it must be quite uncomfortable. He puts on an expression of surprise and says:

"But you're standing and here I am sitting down. Let's go inside. You first, please."

He guides Marcelo into the living room as if by remote control, keeping close behind in his wheelchair.

The living room of this modern building is spacious and completely windowed on both sides, the living room proper and the dining area. Neutral-color curtains substitute for or permit one to glimpse an autumn-gray New York. The icy rain, almost as icy as sleet, plops onto the warm glass and stretches out in spiderweb-like spots. The windows look shattered. The furniture in the living room is chaotically arranged and it strikes a jarring contrast with the orderliness of the dining area. Totally out of symmetrical arrangement, the armchairs are placed next to two small tables and a larger one in the center.

Marcelo sits down in the armchair pointed to by the professor. He raises his eyes and sees the wheelchair moving to its parking place. Once stationed in its proper place, the arrangement of the furniture becomes quite symmetrical.

"Very comfortable. Your apartment is very comfortable. Everything in its place."

Professor Aníbal isn't listening; he continues the conversation where he left it.

"As I was saying, Brazil is a country of outturned eyes, our gaze is always aimed abroad. We lack any sense of self-recognition of our legitimate values and that's why we don't have our own identity or maturity. We're like an adolescent who doesn't yet know who he is and is always looking for role models outside his home while all he had to do was look to his own parents' generation."

(*Your blessing, father. May God bless you, my son and . . . judgment, may He give you good judgment! Be careful whom you speak to, especially foreigners. Flee from bad company as if it were the devil himself! You'll never be able to say that your father didn't warn you, you ingrate.*)

"From abroad," the professor continues, "Brazilians only bring rebelliousness and even vengeance toward their elders. There's no respect for the voice of the past or of experience. What Brazilians import only wreaks havoc on our budding culture that we have worked so hard to create."

(*With all these Persian rugs on the floor, prints by Albers on the walls, porcelain and crystal displayed on antique furniture, even I would lock the doors with a thousand locks and fend off rebellious youth at any cost. Should I go back to the topic of his comfortable apartment? Or should I praise rebellion?*)

"Those prints are by Albers, aren't they?"

"They were selected by my wife or by her decorator friend. I would prefer blank walls. I am too accustomed to print, to the contrast of black letters on white paper; colors make me uneasy. And the brighter the color the more it distracts me, the more it provokes abstract meanderings. (*Abstraction is out of the question. Power is always concrete and verbally expressed.*) Take music. It is also abstract. I prefer to read, to spend my time reading. Words induce action. Painting and music are arts of leisure, they are for the lazy. And the spiritually indolent are legion. I feel I am wasting time when I go to a museum or when I am moved to listen to a record."

"Me, I feel I am wasting my time when I read. Words, especially those words deemed literary, couldn't be further from my everyday interests. Words don't help me live, only to transcend . . ."

"I know about you younger generations, accustomed to loud music . . ."

(*I won't let him interrupt me like this for no reason. Be still, you sonofabitch. It's my turn now.*)

"Music enlivens the body with movement, it rolls through us as if it were massaging our muscles from within. It gives us rhythm. The rhythm of a body in movement gives us greater pleasure and profit in our everyday activities than the pachydermal rhinocerotic act of reading for hours on end. Rhythm is essential because it moves us to act according to drives which, although not rational, are immediate and necessary like those which impel us to satisfy hunger and thirst."

The professor observes Marcelo silently, fidgeting impatiently in his wheelchair. His index finger taps insistently against the padded armrest of the wheelchair, like a clock ticking away the seconds. He begs forgiveness for the unpardonable lack of courtesy: he had forgotten to offer his young colleague a drink. His wife isn't at home and she's the one who usually attends to these minute but all the same very important matters. Without her he's capable of acting like a savage.

"Hardly the hospitable host that you spoke of before. As soon as you knock on the door your typical American host greets you with a "May I offer you something to drink."

The professor drops his voice to a baritone again and repeats the phrase in impeccable English, feeling quite satisfied with his repartee:

"May I offer you something to drink?"

"Not right now, thank you. Perhaps later."

(What's with this guy? Is he trying to show off his English? Well, he's been here a long time, since Jango Goulart took power. I'm beginning to feel imprisoned in this armchair. Should I get up?)

"May I look more closely at that print?"

"Of course, please do."

Aníbal doesn't move his wheelchair.

He listens from afar to Marcelo's comments with evident disregard, like a husband who impassively puts up with the conversation between his wife and their dinner guest.

"I like Albers. His prints remind me of Lygia Clark's work. But I think Lygia went farther in her "Creatures" series, mixing Albers's geometric precision with the organic sensuality of Bellmer's dolls. Albers never got away from three-dimensional games on a two-dimensional surface. Lygia discovered the hinge-like duplicity that activates her flat surfaces with the viewer's aid. Afterward the eyes can appreciate the combinations that were achieved. That each participant achieved."

From his position by the coffee table, the professor feigns disinterest in Marcelo's train of thought. He fixes his eyes on an imaginary point on the ceiling as if it were more important. Everything else is circumstantial and thus lacking in interest.

"First of all, Lygia requires the viewer's touch," continues Marcelo; "vision comes afterward. The sensualism of bodily contact with the work of art and of desire with its object make it more comprehensible. The ideal is for all five senses to consume the work of art simultaneously."

And turning to the professor, he adds:

"I would like to write a poem, a book in which the most important thing is to understand by means of touch. In which the reader must take the words in his hands and feel them as if they were viscera, the body of his lover, the tensed muscles of another. The words would have to be flexible, malleable to the touch of the fingers, just as before, in classical poetry, they were flexible and malleable in the unexpected grasp of the mind. The polysemy of poetry would have to take on a viscous form. There would be no difference between picking a word off the paper and lifting a ball of mercury from the table."

"Tsk, tsk, my dear young man, everything you have said is totally futile! Don't waste your time. Centuries upon centuries of tradition have bequeathed us the book just as it is, and the act of reading just as it is. Isolated acts of intellectual rebelliousness and anarchy are either stillborn or the aborted issue of an ailing and sickly mind. (*He's getting heavy now. Easy, man. Maybe I should ask him where all his collegial cordiality went?*) The best artists are those who channel with propriety their reactions to the history of culture. Otherwise, their acts would last no more than twenty minutes and poof! they would dissolve into thin air like soap bubbles. They would only last twenty minutes because no one understands them, no one incorporates the act into their life experience the way people have historically incorporated great books through traditional reading. That reading which, as you said, is achieved by the grasp of the mind."

"A courageous artist makes no compromises with tradition, with history, or with the bourgeoisie who eternally seek to protect their own history. Courage has nothing to do with the durability of its products for the benefit of others."

"If it is not their durability for the sake of others, then what is their social usefulness?"

"To make it possible for anyone to say that he can be courageous and daring if he so wishes. Anyone. Poetry can be made by all or none. The world would be better that way. Anyone would be capable of a daring act so long as it was not undermined by good sense. When each and every person had acted, that would put an end to the difference between creator and reader. Everyone would be a creator, working the materials of life and art in a feast of grand affirmations. That is our future. Or our utopia."

"That is anarchism."

"If you say so, but it really isn't."

"So now you resort to paradoxes."

"It's not a paradox," Marcelo retorts heatedly. "If you, sir, want to call it anarchism there's nothing I can do about it. Nothing, absolutely nothing. It's your right. It's your mouth and they're your words, not to call them ideas. But anarchism it is not. Why should the forms of social relations, of the social contract, have to be mediated by political parties, by their leaders or by a central state? Why should people, when they come together in community, have to hold back their differences? People can also come together through their individual actions."

"That would spell the end of the division of labor, of professionalization. People professionalize in order to serve their brethren, to be useful to the city, to the nation, to humanity."

"When I speak of daring I am not excluding the exercise of one's profession. But it must not be exercised in a mechanical way or like an upstart rookie who plays his money on the field but keeps his body off court. Any profession requires the whole person, body and mind, training and tact, discipline and pleasure, all integrated in the desire to carry out the task at hand. I get the impression that today, in capitalist societies, people study to become doctors only for the money. Or they decide to study this or that so they won't have to work too hard."

"The society you want would be made up of tense people who would tire out quickly," the professor warns.

"That is what you think, sir."

"Am I allowed to think like this?"

"You have a right."

"Thank God you don't dress up in the little red dictator's clothes . . ."

"My clothes are loose, multicolored, and faded. Green uniforms tailored to size and stiffly starched are only good for fat . . ."

"Are you insinuating . . ."

"Me? Never."

"What makes me uneasy in anarchism, and anarchists, is their desire to impose a model behavior on each and every individual. Their authoritarianism takes the guise of a boa constrictor in the act of digestion. Their utopia is for those who already have full stomachs and live with their head in the clouds, enjoying the shade and the fresh water."

"It's exactly the opposite."

"What? The opposite? Wasn't it you who said that everyone must be capable of doing courageous things? And if someone couldn't, what would you do with him? Send him to a crematorium? You would like to destroy weak individuals once and for all, sweep them all from the face . . ."

"Weak individuals do not exist in and of themselves," Marcelo interrupts. "An individual may be sick but that's another kettle of fish. Weak individuals are produced. They're the products of our . . ."

"You're the ones who won't allow weak individuals to live. Hitler lurks behind each and every one of your theories, behind your utopias. And you've got the nerve to say we're the Nazis. We have compassion for people; we take care of them so that they won't die of scarcity. That is the function, the only legitimate function of the state: to protect the citizen who is incapable of making a living with dignity or who is incapable for other reasons."

(*I know your kind, you old fraud. You swindle, you prohibit, you arrest, you beat, you torture, and you even murder. All that for the good of the common citizen. It's the strong who need to protect the weak; that's precisely why you get stronger and stronger.*)

"And what are the results?" the professor asks. "Marighela incites the weakest to rebel against the state, using weapons that they have no idea how to handle. They would like to turn the nation into a vast slaughterhouse, massacre everyone in the public plaza. Leftist terrorists have to learn that you don't put an end to misery in Brazil by sending the poor to the slaughterhouse. We don't need massacres; we need social aid programs that . . ."

"I see: the poor are lambs who should go on being lambs protected by a few wolves. Is that what you mean?"

"You distort my . . ."

"I don't distort anything. I mean to demonstrate that weak individuals exist only in the dictator's consciousness just like the lamb exists in the wolf's. The weak exist only to be made weaker, more useless to society, to become useless and declared incapable of exercising their citizenship by voting or making decisions. That's how the strong get stronger, more powerful. Even the most charitable, why not, get stronger. It's only the leftovers, and what leftovers! which the powerful distribute to the needy."

"You speak of Christian charity as if it were some kind of hypocrisy."

"That's what that kind of charity is, isn't it?"

"You are all hypocrites. Tartuffes hiding behind misery, just waiting to take power by feigning that you don't want it."

"We're the hypocrites!?"

"You don't know how wrong you are!" the professor says, suddenly changing registers, adopting a paternal tone of voice. "That is the danger of such cities as New York or Paris. The young come here. They are ignorant. They expose themselves. They don't analyze what they see. They lack a critical sense. And they become the owners of the truth, a truth that is nothing but a sad joke. That's why it is necessary to lock . . ."

"To open," Marcelo yells.

"To lock," the professor mimics him.

"To open all doors, eyes, ears, mouths, each and every bodily opening. Everyone should come here and see how American blacks are treated. They have a rich white state that accepts as many blacks as there are in its welfare programs. Let there be blacks! Let there be charity! Black laziness is the invention of white politicians who don't want to see black workers, first-class black citizens. Because if blacks ever got strong they would challenge the power brokers in Washington. God forbid! Let's keep them poor and we can lavish them with our pity."

"You're the one who is calling them lazy. To me they're just a bunch of rabble rousers. Especially those who take advantage of welfare just to feed their addictions . . ."

"That's what it's for . . ."

". . . so they can shoot up on every corner and hatch kid after kid. They discovered a loophole in this generous welfare system and learned to mine the personal guilt of white people."

(An old geezer who speaks like white trash is probably not even reading the good old liberal writers of the moment. Some erudite historian!)

"And the worst thing," the professor continues, "is that blacks are teaching their tricks to the new ethnic groups arriving now, like Hispanics. The American dream of making it on your own has gone down the drain."

"Oh, so our dear professor would have Hispanics go through what blacks went through just so they can claim the benefits of welfare. Only by suffering slavery should they be eligible for the generosity that derives from the white man's sense of guilt . . ."

"That's not exactly it, but it's close enough. Blacks at least contributed something through the slave labor of their ancestors. The mistake is to want to make a profit overnight. In other words, the checks blacks write are covered. The problem is that no white society, no economy, Western or otherwise, can foot the bill for such a large social sector and survive. Hispanics think they can just come here, play the victim for the Americans, and cash in. But they're cashing in at the expense of blacks."

Marcelo feels tired. He wants to speak about the situation in Latin America and yet feels disinclined to do so. A silence falls over them that makes the professor uneasy and leaves Marcelo with no desire to go on.

Marcelo looks at the shattered windows and sees the stormy nightfall enter the room.

The professor notices that the room has gotten darker. He turns on the lamp on one of the tables. He looks at Marcelo as if it were the first time since he arrived.

The professor's gaze doesn't bother Marcelo. The image that comes to his mind is that of a body lying on a hospital bed with a nurse beside it carefully removing the pajama top to apply the daily dressing.

The professor's gaze undresses him. It begins to bother him.

He puts his hand on the top button of his Indian shirt as if to assure himself that he is inside the apartment. The gaze bothers him. He fixes his eyes on the gray skyline outside in an attempt to forget the atmosphere that surrounds him inside. Finally he hears a question:

"You're the son of a wealthy father, I assume."

"You assume incorrectly; I'm not."

"If you're not you act like one, so there's no difference."

(*He's really a reactionary, authoritarian sonofabitch. No sooner does he look at someone does he classify him. Somehow, by some error, we fell under the spell of his reason, we took the wrong bus and now there's no way of jumping off in the middle of the road. And all this because truth is always on his side. There's no problem. Just keep going straight ahead. See you later, alligator.*)

"All children of rich parents," the professor continues, "are incapable of understanding that economic success is the result of an entire life dedicated to work. Born with a silver spoon in their mouth, they think everyone also ought to have one. Even without working, without proving they deserve to be rich."

"So that's how you justify everything, even new forms of more charitable slavery. Every new immigrant in the United States, in order to satisfy the cruel American dream, first must prove that he accepts slave work without rebelling . . ."

"It's not a question of slave work, you are distorting everything again. What I mean is that the conditions that make personal economic success possible are completely defined by work. Nothing else. Any society that doesn't hold to the equation this much work equals that much salary will just, pardon the expression, sink into the mire. That goes for the wealthiest societies. That, by the way, is the problem with this society."

"And what if the terms of the equation were unequal?" Marcelo asks.

"That's what unions, social security, and welfare are for . . ."

"Are you saying that unions should only preoccupy themselves with the equation this much work equals that much salary?"

"That's right."

"And they should have nothing to do with politics?"

"Nothing. You yourself saw the chaos that it all brought to Brazil during Jango's regime."

"The entrepreneurial class is the ruling class. What else is there to say?" Marcelo concludes mimicking his interlocutor's voice.

"It's the haves that govern."

"And the have nots must obey."

"Socialism is the invention of rich kids who feel guilty about their parents' wealth," the professor says as if he had the formula ready on the tip of his tongue from the beginning of the conversation.

Marcelo looks at the time on his wrist, *it got dark so soon*, he thinks. He's afraid the conversation got too heavy and that it's better to pull the team off the court before they get into a scuffle. That's a no no, he remembers Falcão's warnings.

The professor looks at him from the corner of his eye, visibly preoccupied by the silence. He smiles an everything's okay with me smile. And what about you?

Marcelo tries in vain to guess the reason for the smile. He can't think of one but there's got to be one. Why does the professor provoke, insult, and then make amends? He's sure of one thing: the provocation has got to have a specific purpose. The question is which purpose. Maybe because the more he provokes the more the other will reveal himself. *The more I'll reveal myself,* Marcelo concludes silently and apprehensively. The invitation roused his suspicions so he decided to come but armed to the teeth. Falcão told him to accept the invitation but to keep his mouth shut. At the beginning of the conversation he measured his words but after a while he began to express his views sincerely and clearly. *I blew it.* Marcelo realizes he's there to fill in a gap in the professor's knowledge. That's why he was invited. Little does the professor know that he is also filling in a gap in our organization's information. Tit for tat. Stuck in his wheelchair and limited by the information received from his conservative friends in Brazil and censored newspapers, Professor Aníbal has little idea of what the other side thinks of the current situation. Marcelo smiles at his conclusions, leading the professor to think he has finally returned his smile as a signal that the truce has been accepted.

The professor asks him if he is happy with the courses he is teaching at the university.

Marcelo responds that it's too early to tell. The two systems are so different and he's only been teaching here for a month and a half. Too little to form an opinion.

Does he have a heavy load?

The normal, Marcelo responds. Three courses.

Does he have any advanced courses?

No. One language course, a civilization course, and a kind of literary appreciation course. We read four plays included in an anthology edited by Wilson Martins and Oscar Fernández. Three courses overall.

Does he have good students?

Marcelo can't tell yet whether or not they're good. They are hardworking. They make a real effort, that much he can say. It's too bad that NYU isn't on a campus. He had been told that campus life in the United States was idyllic. But NYU is too much like the Brazilian university system in that it's a commuter college completely integrated into the cityscape.

The professor tells him the administration is working on transforming the university into a campus school.

The doorbell rings.

"It's probably my wife. I didn't hear the intercom. Excuse me."

Marcelo is startled when the chair starts moving again. He had forgotten all about the professor's legs and that he was sitting in a wheelchair.

The professor wheels himself to the foyer, retracing his carefully plotted path amid the furniture.

Looking at him from behind, Marcelo is reminded of the great centaurs of history. He is saddened by this pathetic picture of the defender of the Brazilian ruling classes. No legs to walk on, hoveled in an apartment as if it were a trench, afraid of any and every likely and unlikely enemy, surrounded by his books, his Persian rugs, and the delusions of grandeur of others. The only act he seems suited for is making superfluous inquiries at the door, barking his questions as if he were a colonel or a sentinel:

"Is that you Leila?"

Marcelo listens to the question, uttered in his magnificent baritone voice. He can't hear the woman's voice. He hears the successive opening of locks; they sound like little canons going off. A celebratory volley of canon shots to greet the person arriving. He didn't get such a reception on his arrival. The door was closed but the locks were already open. Finally he hears the brief click of the latch when it is retracted by the turn of the doorknob.

He hears somebody panting. Exclamations about the cold, fatigue and how nice it is to be back. And the ostentatious smack of a kiss, like a firecracker going off in the air.

Leila.

5

· · · ·

No one will leave here without hearing the melody
from our mouths; pleased and enlightened
he will move on.—Homer, THE ODYSSEY, *Bk XII*
(trans. M. Odorico Mendes)

Everything is perversely anachronic, muses Professor Aníbal that
same Saturday night. He sits like a snail in front of Leila, who men-
acingly hovers round and round him like a butterfly. He is at his
desk in the center of the study which is covered on all four walls,
from floor to ceiling, with overflowing bookcases. Leila bobs and
weaves around her husband like a boxer trying to find an opening
for his combinations, for a solid, devastating knockout punch. She
is very agile in her movements, fierce and furious, gesticulating until
she breaks into a flood of words and screams:

"You miserable weak idiot!" she screams, arrogantly and defiantly
raising her head and tossing her black hair back. "You bastard!" she
continues screaming, trying to catch her breath. She puffs out her
chest like a bird ready for flight. Her voice quivers, overcome by
emotion:

"You wanted a woman to play cat and mouse with, didn't you?
That's what you take me for, isn't it? You got what you wanted
and here I am a dummy, I fell right into your trap. Look at me,
the dummy! If only you were a real man. Boy was I stupid, a real

dummy! I should beat some sense into my head." Leila smacks her
face, which is already distorted by emotion. The blood rises and
colors it red. "Look!"

Leila sits on one of the edges of the desk and buries her face in
her hands. She crimps her fingers, tenses the muscles and nerves
of her arms, and turns a burning, threatening face to her husband
who just sits there lost in the solipsistic labyrinths of his untethered
imagination.

"One of these days there won't be any left of your honey pie. It's
just a matter of time. Go ahead, just sit there with your books like
a good little professor; one of these days when you open your eyes
I'll have already flown off to Brazil. Waiting will have its reward.
She who laughs last laughs best."

Aníbal sits quietly, his body immobile and impassive in its chair,
his sloping shoulders conveying not disheartenment but relaxation,
his hands folded over his lifeless legs, his eyes staring decisively into
space. On this autumn Saturday night, as so many times before,
Aníbal went into an absolute and nirvana-like state of intellectual
retreat. It was in such moments that his mind formulated the principles of his thought. If it were up to him, those sexual farces should
never end. They were the tonic he needed to penetrate further into
the understanding of humans and the world, he needed them for
his most intimate and academically uncompromising reflections. In
moments like these he was the only one hard at thought.

One day he wrote on a piece of paper:

"The commonplace is integral to man. Take the metaphor of the
pearl, which many judge to be ridiculous and worthless but in truth
is very much the opposite. The search for originality at any cost
leads to the loss of any sense of the absolute."

He was not able to set aside what was personal and ungeneraliz-
able in his principle. He continued writing but now to justify his
unease among his peers:

"Why is modern man afraid of thinking the great topics? Modern man, in contrast to Atlas, cannot bear such great weight on
his shoulders. That is why our epoch—characterized by a barbarian
and derivative imagination—will go down in human history as the
most mediocre. Irremediably. As the white man began to disburden
himself, tired of bearing the weight by himself, barbarism began to
impose itself everywhere. Modern man deviated from the path to

the absolute seduced by the provisional and the minor. He didn't learn how to endure great pain, much less how to treat it. The slightest sign of tragedy on the horizon sees him drop the sails and change course away from the voyage toward knowledge. He yields to any sentimental plea. He's a puppet in the hands of destiny. Even today's history sides with the tears of the victims and do-good feelings of piety. It totally avoids the stoic and sublime destiny of man. I can't stand humility."

Leila gets even more excited in front of her silent and impassive husband. Attempting to bridge the distance between them she gesticulates like a silent movie actress in a Greek tragedy, opening and closing her arms with the same noise she makes in opening and closing her mouth. When she hushes it's to show Aníbal her yawning mouth and her razor-sharp teeth. Then she rims her scandalously red-lipsticked lips with her tongue, posing like a streetwalker calling to her Johns. She runs her hands over her breasts and her face, smearing her makeup and staining her blouse as she brings her hands back over her breasts. She takes off her shoes and throws them to a corner of the study, bull's-eye, knocking over the books on the bottom shelf of the bookcase. She takes off her stockings and raises her skirt, showing off her sexy black-lace panties. She rolls the stockings in her right hand like a ball of yarn and stretches her arm out into her husband's face. She stops halfway and draws her arm back close to her body. Then she lunges into a sensual dance, barefoot and tousling her black hair with her hands, moving her body to a silent lascivious music. She cries out louder, rebelliously demanding that she isn't a show animal, a potted flower, a doll, a book, or a sheet of paper. No, she's made of flesh and blood—she pinches herself all over—, a woman made of flesh and blood, she repeats, who will not settle for a man who only looks from a distance. It's not good enough to look, you understand? What I want is a cock, a big hard cock (she measures it between her outstretched palms), "do you hear me?" I want to kick my legs open and fuck, to fuck and scream, right now, come on

Unperturbed, Aníbal thinks: *Man gains nothing in the practical realm, at best he is reduced to his animal condition. Manual labor must be understood to be degrading. To judge it degrading is the necessary condition for man to redeem himself—in his historical destiny—from the animal within him. The decline of Brazil began when we failed in trans-*

forming slavery into another system as productive and as profitable. We were too hasty in yielding to foreign pressures and forces; that is why we failed. We didn't know otherwise.

Leila stands in the line of the professor's blank gaze. Dancing like a mermaid, she takes off her blouse, rolls it up as her hips keep swaying and throws the little bundle onto the desk. Now she's dressed only in her bra. She lowers her breasts for a better view and turns her head, mouth open and panting, eyes burning and nostrils shooting flames. She walks over to Aníbal, shaking her index finger and protesting it won't do you any good to make believe you don't see me, don't hear me dancing in front of you babbling like a madwoman, trying to seduce you. You think I'm crazy, ha! Leila bursts out laughing: "I was the crazy one when I married a nut like you!" She spits on her husband, hitting him in the face from a distance, and goes on saying that now she is well and sane. "You, you're the one who's crazy. Only you, Mr. Softee!"

Leila shakes her index finger in front of his open but blind eyes, her words assaulting his open but deaf ear drums. Aníbal thinks *God didn't have to imagine the world to create it. God made the world without thinking. Hence the chaos of a humanity conceived without God's intelligence. It was conceived through the labor of God's divine hands, that's true, but without the creative intervention of the mind. If God had only thought harder before . . .*

in her seductive and repellent advances toward her husband Leila doesn't even manage to graze her fingernail along the white skin of his untouchable face. Seeking to have an effect on him she moves like a sleepwalker toward one of the bookcases, walking backward so she can keep her eyes fixed on Aníbal. This bookcase holds books sent to the professor by the authors and review copies, all of little value to him. Swirling like a gypsy, Leila backs into the bookcase, turns her body, and opens her claws. Keeping her gaze on her husband as if she had eyes in the back of her head, seductively and aggressively, tenderly and violently, with hands like a fairy and a witch, like a seamstress and a butcher, Leila throws open her arms and legs and presses her whole body against the bookcase as if it were another body, humping its inert matter, feeling the protrusions and recesses of books piled high. Then she takes the books one by one and throws them on the floor to the cadence of her dance. Suddenly she grabs a book from the floor and starts ripping its binding, turning toward her husband, showing him the pages she is ripping. She licks a wad of torn pages; the more she rips the calmer she feels. Finally she tells him that it's no use making believe you don't see me, I know, I know you see me. "Look! This is what I should do," as if twisting his delicate Cornish hen neck, just like this: she tears out a chapter from the book and sticks out her distended tongue. She laughs and dances, swirling around on top of the books. She rips off her skirt and continues in her sexy black lace panties and her black-lace bra. She squats, smearing her cunt all over the books, coming back over them with her ass. Squatted over the books, contorting her body, it's as if she were hesitating to dive into a pool of water. She turns again toward Aníbal and threatens to piss on the books, shit on them, piss and shit on them. They're worthless, not worth the piss and shit.

Despite all this, Aníbal hasn't even blinked. He continues sitting still, blind and deaf to everything except the bookcase with his favorite books: philosophy and history classics finely bound with red leather spines and engraved with gold leaf lettering. He looks at the books framed in their black varnished case, and thinks: *Where are the heroes of our time? They are the men in white labcoats who work day after day, year after year in a laboratory, their imagination ruled by the desire to postpone the death of man. Oh, what depths of degradation we've fallen to! Where are you hiding, Ulysses! Those men in white labcoats would save man from death by injecting, cutting, amputating, adding, substituting. To conquer death in order to save the common man who deserves nothing and would be better off in an early grave. The common man who is nothing but a dead weight on society. The day man invented the microbe in his laboratory was the day he dealt his greatness the coup de grace. The new heroes, the heroes of our time do not deserve epic treatment. They are worth very little, not even the small change Sweden annually grants them.*

Leila is still kicking about on the floor. She squirms out of her panties and bra and lies on the floor adopting poses on top of the books. Languid and nude, her legs stretched out and her nipples hard, she takes a book and rubs it slowly along her slit. She drags it up her body to her breasts and on to her neck and finally to her mouth. She kisses it, bites it, sticks out her tongue and licks it, sucks on it and looks fixedly at her husband, waiting for some word, for any sign of life. As her passion abates she comes to herself, as if the desired outcome of her passion had always been a drawing closer to herself, seeking in the pleasure of her own body a continual release of her well waters.

Meanwhile Aníbal thinks: *All of man's efforts have only resulted in making the Earth even uglier*

Leila pisses on the books strewn about the floor

his work has only repeated God's work, His insensitivity: manual labor without imagination.

her urine streams like a rivulet among the books on the floor, finding its way along the recently polished floor of the study, welling up around Aníbal's desk

All work is useless, it serves no purpose.

when she's through pissing, Leila puts her hand on her cunt, grabs her clitoris and sticks her hand in

It would have been better if the world had only been thought, if man still existed in a paradisiacal state and the Earth—this one, ours—were but the product of the imagination. Man would be a creature born of the imagination of the first man, not of God's insensitivity.

Leila stares hard at her husband as she squeezes her nipples with her left hand. She pinches them hard and then caresses them lovingly. Then she balances her breasts in her hands, offering them up for show. Suddenly her hands are at her cunt opening up her labia. "Look!" she shows Aníbal, inciting her husband with her open red mouth, look, you fool, look, she sticks out her tongue as if to lick the air. She contorts her body, contracting her legs and dragging her ass over the piss-drenched books

The imagination of the first man would compensate for God's mental laziness.

Leila gets up and walks slowly into the professor's line of vision, onto the backdrop of his favorite books, obstructing his sight. There she goes into a kind of sex show, her right hand in her cunt and her left hand caressing her hair and neck. Her transparency takes on opacity

and Aníbal sees Leila taking shape before him, he sees her naked body, Leila caressing her hair and neck and masturbating like a degenerate after tearing up his books and pissing on them

"Look, you fool, don't be timid. Give me your hand, go on. Put your hand on it; see how good it feels. Hmm! You don't know what you're missing." Leila moves closer. The desk is between them. She extends her arm like a bridge, the tips of her fingers coming to a stop just short of grazing his face

Aníbal's cock begins to throb

Leila notices that Aníbal's eyes have brightened. "Come," she tells him, "come," even more possessed. She begins to yelp like a bitch in heat, the movement of her hands taking on a frenetic urgency.

"Stop right there. Don't move!" she orders Aníbal, whose eyes are on fire

His eyes are shining, Leila says to herself

with his eyes on fire, Aníbal takes his hands off his legs. They come to life around his cock which throbs beneath his drawers.

6

. . . .

I

Leila is not so much a woman but a wild mare. Untamable and yet tame. She was born in the backlands of Minas Gerais and went to boarding school with the nuns at the Colégio Santa Maria in Floresta.

2

Aníbal was not able to attend the gymnasium with other kids his age. While in grammar school he was stricken by infantile paralysis. Fearing pernicious masculine reactions to his illness, his father enrolled him in a girls academy run by nuns. Blessed was he among women. A fruit among women.

3

Leila took her special sensitivity for detecting smells from the backlands to the boarding school at Santa Maria. Smells that inebriated her mind with endless memories: like the unsettling taste produced by breathing in the dust kicked up by the rain. It peppered her nasal membranes like the handful of flour that a baker throws over a ball of dough that is still moist. Or the stench of a pigsty (pigs wallowing in the fetid mud), the reek of billy goats (peacefully tethered to the backyard corral), the fetid fumes brought by the evening breezes that ruined the tranquility of an outdoor hammock snooze and forced Leila to move closer to the rose bushes.

4

Every morning Chiquinho pushed Aníbal's wheelchair to the academy run by nuns and at midday, when classes were over, he would return to take him home. Chiquinho, pickaninny son of an old washerwoman at Paes Leme, started pushing Aníbal's wheelchair when he was twelve. He was laid off just before his employers moved to the capital. He was then sixteen. Chiquinho never saw Aníbal or his family again.

5

Some nights when Leila couldn't fall asleep she would surrender herself to the Lady-of-the-Night perfume that wafted up from the garden to her window in the boarding school. Mixed in with the perfume was the smell of mangoes, guava, bananas, and even the imported apples that came boxed from Argentina. The boxes were kept in the pantry until Christmas day when her father opened them and the smell of apples invaded the living room, the whole house, the street, and the entire city. Leila moved inside a perfumed cloud; it was like the dense fumes of the Lady-of-the-Night perfume which would envelope her later. The fumes created a lush, inebriating, sweet atmosphere like that of the apples. It entered through her pores and left her body suspended, oblivious to all events and stories. Now her body had become a compendium of memories of sensations. On rainy nights she felt the humidity so close that it was like drops running over her body, streaming like sweat. And the fresh evening breezes would break the night heat and bristle her skin and hair; the change of temperature would goose-bump the skin on her arms and buttocks (it was like the touch of flat hands). And then the intolerable heat would leave her body wrapped in a viscous layer of greasy sweat. So intolerable was the grime seeping into her skin that it was the only thing that could wake her out of the perfumed torpor and make her run to the bathroom and shower. The sudden noise in her daughter's room would startle her mother, who would yell out Leila's name to make sure that it was she who was carrying on like that at such an early hour: running to the bathroom and washing, with such insistence and suds, the greasy, sticky fat that coagulated on her flesh.

6

Chiquinho asked why don't you play with your toys? Aníbal wouldn't respond; he'd just sit there staring ahead at the point toward which Chiquinho pushed his wheelchair. Chiquinho said if they were mine I'd play with them all day and all night. The houses would shake up and down as Aníbal's wheelchair went over the cobblestones, Chiquinho trying to find the flatest trajectory amid the uneven rows of stones and the potholes. Aníbal felt he was being pushed dangerously close to the shaking houses. He asked Chiquinho to push slower so that he might have more time to appreciate the world's loss of balance and the oncoming earthquake. Chiquinho responded angrily that he couldn't go any slower, a car might come rushing down the street and your father warned me that you can't be too careful when crossing streets. Aníbal tried to prolong the presence of the houses shaking in front of him as if they were reflected in a pool of water concentrically rippled by the stones Aníbal threw just to see the houses and the trees sway and contort like dancing bodies. The houses, too, moved like a row of dancing bodies to the rhythm of the jumps and starts of the wheelchair as it was quickly and artfully steered by an apprehensive Chiquinho.

7

Leila liked to take walks in the countryside by herself. She said I'll only go as far as Mariana's house. "Okay, my child, you may go. But don't be late for lunch. It's your turn at the head of the table." She walked along the main road, turned left and then left the path and walked on the tilled red earth. She took in the smell of horse and ox dung and piss that acridly penetrated her nostrils and made her walk faster in search of who knows what, perhaps the smell of sweet-grass ruffled up by the wind and mixed with the smell of the riverbank and cow dung. Gradually she slowed her pace, coming slowly to a stop and then finally sitting down on the ground. ("How did you get your dress all dirty like that? It couldn't have been while you chatted with Mariana. You two . . . I don't know.") And she laid down on the ground and just stared at the sky, the white clouds, the blue sky, more white clouds, elephants and barking dogs, smiling faces, tigers, no, panthers, snowscapes . . . The burning smell of nature kneaded her body as if it were being massaged by a thousand expert hands. After kneading her body the acrid smell cast it back on the ground like old Nhô Campeiro when he flipped his stogie onto the ground after chewing on it hours on end as he sat on the porch bench. Crouching, Leila would creep up to Nhô Campeiro's knees and glue her face to his legs to get a better whiff of the sorrow-laden, frothy smell of the saliva-fermented cigar lying on the ground. She got all dirty just to take in the cigar smell exhaled by Nhô Campeiro's clothes, hands, and skin.

8

Aníbal asked Chiquinho why don't you study? Chiquinho answered I don't know. Aníbal: "What do you mean you don't know?" Chiquinho: "I don't."

"Doesn't your father send you to school?"

"No."

"Don't you want to go?"

"I do and I don't."

"Well, do you or don't you?"

"I don't know."

"You wouldn't have to push my wheelchair."

Chiquinho doesn't say anything.

"Do you like pushing my chair?"

"My mother said I should."

"She asked you or told you to."

"I don't know. I think she told me to. She said it would be good for me, in the years ahead."

One of Aníbal's classmates approached him and asked if he would help her cheat on the geography exam. She hadn't studied.

Aníbal didn't say anything. He only warned Chiquinho to watch out for the steps ahead.

The girl told him he was hateful and then turned her head and body away, walking off quickly and leaving the two behind.

Chiquinho pulled the wheelchair up the steps to the school without hitting one single bump.

9

Early on Leila lost the desire to be with other girls her age. For her, conversation was something stupid, infantile, a waste of time. Empty chatter. No one listens to anyone. When you converse you only say stupidities, stupidities all the time, never anything that makes sense, never anything really important. When you speak to your parents you lie. When others speak to you they also lie. So why bother talking? No one says what goes on in their head, what they feel or desire. If I want something I can't say what it is. If I do I won't get it. Even to herself Leila said very little. "A quiet girl," her mother would say, assuming that she probably preferred to confide in her girlfriends in the city. Her father had lost track of her existence; he only wanted her to go to the capital to study. "You're wasting your time in the Colégio Madre de Deus," he said over and over again. Leila felt she could change her life in Colégio Santa Maria, she didn't want to waste her time any more. There she would really be able to talk to her schoolmates. It's only in the provinces that people engage in empty chatter.

10

Chiquinho wanted to know if Aníbal had a cock, if a cripple's cock could also get erect and hard.

11

Lying on the ground by the riverbank, her body permeated by the wild smells of nature all around her, Leila passed her hand along her vagina and felt a pleasurable sensation.

12

"You're very lucky, Aníbal," Chiquinho said.
"Lucky? Why?"
"All those girls around you all the time. They adore you. They treat you like a prince. And each one is prettier than the next."
Aníbal's head swelled with self-pride.
"The one with the dark hair, meu deus! She devours you with her eyes."

"Margarida?"

"That's right."

"She's a dummy."

"If she's a dummy, then I'm twice a dummy."

Aníbal told Chiquinho he was in a hurry. He had things to do at home before lunch.

"If I were you I'd make a pass at her."

"Watch out, Chiquinho, look where you're pushing the wheel-chair. You almost broke one of the wheels."

"Didn't you say you were in a hurry?"

"Yeah, but not such a hurry."

"I'd rub my hands all over her little tits. Then I'd press a couple of kisses on her lips, kisses that would leave her breathless."

"Is that all you can think about, Chiquinho? Sex?"

"I'm not made of stone, am I?"

13

Leila couldn't understand why she had to go to school, attend class, write in her notebook, buy books, read, underline passages, learn, take exams, be promoted to the next grade. She didn't understand but she also made no effort to. She went to school with the same detachment as when she had breakfast or lunch. It was just another obligation to take care of between breakfast and lunch: school, where she learned the national language, arithmetic, geography, and history. She learned, got good marks, was promoted to the next grade, and listened to her father say that Colégio Madre de Deus was a waste of time. She came to believe everything she learned was worthless and only what she would learn in the capital was worth knowing. It would be different. And Leila continued her drills, studying for exams, being promoted from one grade to the next, all without the faintest idea why. What purpose could it all serve?

14

"I'll let you see mine, but only on one condition: that you let me see yours first," Chiquinho said to Aníbal.

"I'll show you mine afterward," Aníbal insisted.

"It's no good that way."

"You're so suspicious."

"I know you, Aníbal."

"Just a peek to see if mine is like yours," Aníbal insisted somewhat apprehensively, perhaps even timidly.

"I know it's only a peek. But I also want to see yours. Show me yours first."

"It's no good like that, Chiquinho. I thought you were my friend."

"I am."

"So, then, let's see it. Come on, Chiquinho."

Chiquinho opened his zipper and took out a dark little sausage, all hard and erect.

"It's shaking," he said.

Aníbal looked at it and couldn't believe his eyes.

"It's so slender."

"And yours isn't?"

"It gets fat when it's hard."

"Okay, I showed you mine, now it's your turn," Chiquinho said as he brought his hands to Aníbal's zipper.

"Get your hands off!" Aníbal shouted angrily. "If you touch me I'll call daddy."

15

Leila had noticed the city pharmacist's stare. Leaving the counter and standing by the door he would compliment her, staring open-mouthed and smiling at her little breasts beneath the fine cotton blouse; undressed by his eyes, they stood erect like rosebuds, the tender nipples embossing the fabric. Leila had no idea she was being followed by the pharmacist, completely spellbound by the little breasts that seemed to scream out to be caressed and squeezed. This time, when Leila came to the riverbank, laid down on the ground, and opened her nostrils to the dark and dense atmosphere that transported her to a place without people, without talk, without houses and streets, only green smells and the sounds of running water, this time she suddenly sensed a different smell. She turned around and saw the pharmacist half hidden behind a tree stroking an enormous hard thing that protruded from his pants. His eyes opened wider when Leila, entertained and puzzled by what he was doing, turned toward him, and then he stroked the thing harder and harder until it turned bright red and he snorted like a horse, almost neighing and losing his breath. All of a sudden a liquid squirted from the thing and Leila laughed. Blessed be her laugh, he thought.

16

Aníbal could rattle off by heart the names of every port in the Americas. He would enumerate the names from north to south or from south to north, from the Atlantic to the Pacific or from the Pacific to the Atlantic. He could even recite the list hopscotch-style, giving the names from the extreme north and south, from one side of the Atlantic and the other of the Pacific, until he reached the middle and the two halves met.

17

When Leila got up to get a closer look at the thing, the city pharmacist got afraid and ran off. Leila tried to but couldn't make any sense of that white labcoat flying across the woods, running away from the riverbank, and finally reaching the dirt road in the distance. Leila looked to where the thing had squirted its liquid. She squatted and put her finger on the wet ground, *it's not piss,* she thought. She grabbed a handful of the sticky earth and thought *toads and lizards,* but she wasn't repelled. She sniffed it and thought *okra.* She walked to the river and washed her hands.

18

Aníbal asked his father: "Dad, I'd like to go on retreat during carnival this year."
Dad: "Don't you think you're taking all this too far, my son? You really don't have to, you know. Stay at home and take advantage of your time off. Relax."
"But I want to do more, Dad."
"I don't think I know what you mean."
For Aníbal everything was as clear as a country scene after a rainfall.
"It's the spiritual effort that counts. Both the body and the mind have to be maintained in ideal condition."
"What effort are you talking about, my son?"

The spiritual effort of the one in contrast to the wants of the many. Few people isolate themselves from the world of sin and flesh. But they are the ones who count, who can bring salvation. The concentrated will of the one can redeem the evil of the others. The convent on the mountaintop is the place of God and of the Spirit on Earth during the three days of orgy below."

Dad moved good-humoredly over to the wheelchair in which his son sat and pulled up a chair and sat in front of him:

"Now don't get angry, my son, but I have to have a heart to heart with you. Don't you think you're taking the nuns' words too seriously? That's their business; they elected to be God's servants. You didn't. You have another future. I've always wanted you to be a lawyer. Have you thought about defending noble causes before the justice of men? Of course, a justice inspired by God, because without Him, without His divine inspiration, man wouldn't know how to use his intelligence."

Faced with his father's lack of understanding there was nothing for Aníbal to say. He had a spiritual and social mission to undertake and by golly he would. No matter what the cost. A mission much higher than the one his father had just proposed. Next to it his father's didn't amount to anything. He had a mission which he thought he could accomplish with his father's acquiescence. It didn't work out the way he planned. Now his father was an obstacle. Whose side was his father on?

"I'm the one who doesn't understand you, Father. What side are you on?"

"Side? What side? Me? I don't know, everything you say is Greek to me."

19

Leila didn't like animals. They make too much noise. The sounds of nature were much more harmonious and pleasing without animals. Dogs were a plague. All dogs should be hanged. Just like that! One morning two enormous, strong hands descend from the sky and twist neck after neck of any barking dogs. The birds' song, now that's another thing. You can go right up to them, if you like. It's different. But when a dog barks he instills fear. Not the little birds; they're there to please. In Leila's house music was almost never heard on the radio. Her mother didn't like it. The maid liked it but wasn't allowed to play it. Her father listened to Brazil Hour and The Esso Reporter. The radio was kept in the living room as if it were an ornament. It was only turned on after supper. Leila didn't like to see her father so engrossed and pensive listening to the radio. She was jealous of the radio and its voice. One day she sneaked behind the console and broke one of the tubes with a knife. It only took a light tap. That night the radio wouldn't go on. Her father pulled the console from the wall and saw the bits of broken glass on the floor and the broken tube. He turned to his wife and said: "This tube must have exploded. It's easy to replace."

20

"It's for you, Aníbal," said his mother as she handed him the letter that had just arrived in the mail. It was his first ever. Excitedly he read his name and address on the front of the envelope. He looked at the postage stamp. Then he read the initials of the sender on the back: M. R. C., *they're Margarida's* he said to himself. She had gone to her cousins' house in Belo Horizonte for the holiday. Aníbal wheeled himself to his bedroom. He opened the envelope and read that Margarida missed him a lot but really liked life in the capital. Her cousins laid out the red carpet: mornings they went to the Minas Tennis Pool, the largest in all of South America. And the water, you'd have to be there to believe it, was so blue; on account of the chlorine, that's what gave it such a pretty color. Do you remember the Praça Raul Soares, where the Eucharistic Convention was held? It has an illuminated fountain that's just breathtaking. Before that, she had already been to Pampulha, where the mayor has an immense artificial lake under construction. She also took an excursion to Ouro Preto, a historical city. Aníbal would like it there. Going up and going down the slopes you'd swear you could still feel the movings about of the Inconfidentes during their aborted revolution in 1789. Evenings she and her cousins would while away the hours chatting. They were very intelligent and lively. She felt like a farmgirl compared to them. No one had told her that she dressed like a hick, that's how she thought of herself: a hick. Too bad Aníbal wasn't there too. He'd really like meeting her cousins, especially Leila. She was yet another cousin who had been sent to Belo Horizonte to board at the Colégio Santa Maria. She was different from the others. Talking to her was like talking to him, Aníbal.

21

Leila kept a doll in her closet, a Christmas present from when she was still a little girl. The doll lived in the closet and Leila only took it out when she was really, really angry. She would take it out and yank off her two little legs, her little arms and finally she'd cut off her little neck. Then she would throw each member to a different part of the room. Only the trunk of the doll's body would be left in her hands. It was a rag doll and so it never felt anything when it was stitched back together. It was a new doll again. But with only the trunk in her hands, Leila's feelings would change; suddenly she felt bad, very bad, and began to cry. Now look-a here you silly goose, you won't gain anything by crying. Crying can't solve anything (she'd say to herself). A flood of tenderness would come over her, leaving her liable to beg forgiveness from the person who had made her angry. She would then gather up all the parts of the dismembered doll and lay them out on top of her bed to see if she could put it back together again. The doll's eyes didn't show any pain. Its face remained expressionless, whether Leila caressed it or abused it. Eyes and face expressionless, its mouth was always closed. No need to speak, you won't gain anything through words. Even if the doll were to scream, rage, cry, or kick its legs, its mistress would go on yanking off its little arms and legs and severing its neck.

22

Ricardo was the only friend his own age. Chiquinho wasn't really a friend. He was a servant. A servant and a fool. Chiquinho ceased to exist on the day he insisted on seeing Aníbal's weenie. Aníbal could no longer stand to see the little pickaninny before him. Only behind him, wheeling him about. *That's what he's paid for anyway, not to have conversations with me,* Aníbal would justify himself. Ricardo would come to visit Aníbal at least once a week. Aníbal's mother was pleased by little Ricardo's visits. There was a levelheaded kid. A good kid, very different from the others nowadays who only wanted to make trouble. She would have the maid prepare lunch and she herself would take the tray to Aníbal's room. Ricardo had the habit of interpreting expressions literally. This didn't displease Aníbal. *A dog's life:* human beings who walked around on all fours. They don't speak; when they open their mouths it's only to bark. Aníbal himself would add to this game: people who speak only in monosyllables, bow, wow, wow. *To skip a page:* to close one's eyes and take a leap over an obstacle made of words. *To make a racket:* to thread a net onto an embroidery ring. Aníbal disagreed: it is the business deals of the racketeer. *To get the check:* when the teacher put a check on your homework. Aníbal laughed. Ricardo was nothing like Chiquinho. He had a healthy and spiritual head on his shoulders. He wanted to be a professor when he grew up.

23

"You've got a knack for math, my dear." That's what Leila's mother said every time she looked at her report card. From the first grade and on, numbers and their combinations never had any mystery for Leila. Arithmetic problems were mere trifles and she always made fun of the teacher when she resorted to using objects and things in the room to make her explanations clearer. Some people, when they read a novel or see a movie, can predict the upcoming sequences before the author lays them out on the page or the director on the screen. Leila had the same capacity to predict upcoming math lessons. She never had to take notes in class. One after another, her teachers tried to dispute her solutions. But faced with perfect scores on homework and in-class exams they had no alternative but to button their lips and admire a girl who showed absolutely no enthusiasm for their endeavors. Leila had no friends among the other kids in her school. Whenever her mother threw her lack of friends up to her, Leila simply made up names and specific situations. "Hmm, I don't know her. Who did you say her mother was?" Leila just went on inventing things with a convincing passion as her mother grew more and more dismayed that her daughter mixed with such humble people and frequented the poorer areas of the city. It was part of Leila's strategy; that way her mother, gossip that she was, wouldn't be too eager to inquire further. Leila's mother was under the impression that Mariana lived in a pigsty because Leila always came home from visiting her with her clothes dirty.

24

Chiquinho was a fool. Aníbal had him coming and going; if he wanted him to go suck on soap or plant yams he'd do it. Sometimes he'd even tell Chiquinho to go to the corner and see if he, Aníbal, was there. Chiquinho grew sad at the constant hostilities and humiliations and gradually began to lose his volubility and spontaneity. He even left off maintaining and cleaning the wheelchair. Aníbal would get ornery when it was time to go to school and refused to get into the wheelchair, into this filth no thank you. His mother would come running out of the bedroom with a damp flannel cloth and polish and Chiquinho would bend over, humiliated, to give the wheelchair a once over. Aníbal, meanwhile, sat on the bed and dictated the things he had to do. Impatiently, the mother urged: "Make haste, Chiquinho, Aníbal can't miss his first class." Chiquinho didn't know whom to attend to first. Between the two of them Chiquinho just felt awful. On the way, the left wheel got caught in a pothole and Aníbal was thrown over the side. Not even God's intervention was going to keep this war from exploding. They were in front of the school and Aníbal began to yell at the top of his lungs and beat the defenseless Chiquinho who was trying to set the wheelchair right side up again and put Aníbal's heavy body in it. Aníbal demanded that his father be called to school when classes let out. It was an accident. No, no, no, it wasn't. Come now, my son, these things happen. But he did it on purpose. He did it out of malice, he was taking vengeance for I don't know what, the monster. Aníbal's screams and indignation carried.

25

Leila liked to chew leaves. She liked the bitter green taste of chlorophyll spurting in her mouth, soaking her saliva and dirtying it. Her teeth pressed on the shredded and balled-up veins, solidified into a small white wad which she spat onto the ground.

Nhô Campeiro chewed his stogie.

26

Aníbal sat in his wheelchair in the center next to the old parish vicar, who was also seated. Everyone else stood on a little footstool, arranged in the shape of a flower cut in half or an open fan. The photograph was taken in the churchyard with the portal as a backdrop; it showed a group of new Marian congregationalists. Each wore a blue ribbon and a silver medal with the effigy of Mary in all her splendor as mother of Christ. Aníbal was a faithful devotee of Mary. He was afraid to speak directly to God. He didn't dare ask Him why he had brought this punishment on him because he feared that it would be made even worse by God's vengeance. God could make him lose the movement in his arms. He chose Mary to intercede on his behalf. Mary, the Compassionate, pray for us who turneth to Thee. Ever since he was stricken he had developed an antipathy to Christ. He was just like him, also punished by God. Aníbal made Mary the third person in the Holy Trinity. Dreams, premonitions, visions, illusions, his imagination produced infinite images of him getting up from his wheelchair and walking again. He would walk directly to Mary who waited with open arms for him a few steps away in all Her infinite bounty.

7

. . . .

I

A little after ten Marcelo rings Eduardo's doorbell as they had agreed on the phone.

"Who is it?"

"It's me . . . Marcelo."

"Come in, the door's unlocked."

Eduardo quickly positions himself behind the door, next to the hinges. That way he won't be seen by whomever might enter.

Marcelo calls out Eduardo's name, wondering where he is, in the bedroom?

No sooner does Marcelo walk in than Eduardo leaps from his hiding place, surprising him from behind and grabbing him in a stranglehold:

"I'm going to kill you, you fucking sonofabitch traitor, faggot filho da puta motherfucker."

Totally immobilized by Eduardo's surprise attack and his forceful hands, Marcelo, choking, stammers:

"Let me go! Get your fucking hands off me! Have you gone crazy, Edu?"

"I'll let you go when you've told me everything. Tit for tat. Okay? Now promise! If you promise I'll let you go. If you don't . . ."

"Tell you what?"

"Are you going to promise or not?" Eduardo's hands draw tighter around Marcelo's neck.

"Okay, I promise." His face totally livid but relieved, Marcelo takes in a deep breath, his neck still in the grasp of Eduardo, who got carried away trying to make the scene as realistic as possible.

As Eduardo relaxes his hands Marcelo shakes off the weight of Eduardo's body from his back. He rubs his neck and complains:

"You really hurt me." Then he runs his hands through his hair and smooths out his clothes.

"You've really gone nuts, girl. Just like a hysterical queen from Cinelândia. Not even Madame Satã in the golden days of burlesque at Lapa could have outdone you."

"Madame Satã is your mother, you son of a bitch!"

"Oh, stop it, Edu, I can't put up with your campiness now."

"Well, excuse me! Don't you think you've got it backward? If there's anyone who can't be put up with it's you, Marcelo. I mean, you're the one who got me into this mess. One of these days they'll decide to slit my throat and you won't even bother to call me."

"I sent Carlinhos to warn you, Edu. But you wouldn't listen. You thought it was all bullshit, that we were playing with you. But you were warned. It takes a real friend who looks out for you."

"And you couldn't call me and say something like: hey Eduardo, they're going to come down real hard on the Black Widow. But no, you had to go and send me this guy Carlinhos that I've never even met before."

"What would you say if I told you that when I first got here from Brazil they were planning to come down even harder on you? You didn't know that, did you?"

Eduardo, suddenly afraid, calms down like a small child petrified in bed at night at the slightest sound.

"And you also didn't know that I got you off the hook," Marcelo adds.

Eduardo turns his back on Marcelo's gaze and walks to the window. He opens a little crack in the drapes and looks down on the lighted asphalt street teeming with Saturday night's traffic. A light mist rising from a recent icy drizzle envelopes the lampposts in a mysterious aura.

"They thought you were a spy that had infiltrated the group on Colonel Valdevinos's orders."

Eduardo smiles on hearing the military attaché's name for the second time that day.

"Did you say spy?"

Marcelo draws up close to Eduardo and gently puts his hand on his shoulder.

"S-p-y, spy, that's right, Eduardo. I think it was Carlinhos who first suspected you of helping the military repress us."

"You're not going to bring that faggot up again!"

"Carlinhos is the busboy in the restaurant where you and the colonel have lunch every Wednesday."

"How do you know where I have . . ."

"We have ways of knowing, Eduardo."

"How? I didn't tell you anything."

"It was Carlinhos, if you really want to know. Every Wednesday, the two of you, all alone in the corner, huddle together at the same table whispering secrets. What else could they think?"

"And what did they think?"

"The obvious, Eduardo. That you're a spy. After all, you were also rubbing shoulders with the Brazilian exile community in New York. You were getting friendly with everyone, with Mario and the other Eduardo, the guy who works in the movies. What else could they think?"

"Well, they thought wrong!"

"And that's exactly what I told them. And here you are accusing me of betraying you."

"As if I didn't have a reason," Eduardo turns and looks straight at Marcelo. "Why didn't you tell me before?"

Eduardo lets the drapes close behind him. His face, offset against the pattern of the drapes, looks like one of those faces on most-wanted posters hanging in the post office.

"I tried, I really tried, but it didn't work."

Eduardo stares wide-eyed at Marcelo.

"You can't imagine how many messages," Marcelo arches his fingers in quotation marks, "they planted on you to pass on to the colonel."

"Messages?"

"Yeah, mess-a-ges, Edu. God, you'd think you lived on the moon."

"So they made a fool out of me."

"You or them, Edu, it's all the same. I don't know who ends up playing the fool after all is said and done. You? Them? Everyone? Who knows? In any case, it's too late to worry about that now."

"Too late, my ass. I'll get it all straightened out, just you wait and see."

Marcelo's voice sounds harsh for the first time:

"That's not a good idea, you hear. And watch out, listen carefully to what I'm going to tell you, Eduardo, lis-sen ve-ry care-fully, don't, you hear me, don't you even think about tipping off the military attaché about all this."

"Oh yeah? That's exactly what I'm going to do. You'll see, you'll all see."

Eduardo walks from the living room into the kitchen to get ice. *He's not being very fair with me,* he thinks. He can't forgive Marcelo for not having warned him personally about the plot to kidnap the military attaché, above all because it involved him. *Well, he wasn't totally unfair. He did tell them that I wasn't a spy. But he's not really a friend. La Cucaracha was right. You can't trust these commies, you just can't.* By the time he's filled the ice bucket, he has convinced himself that he can't trust Marcelo. *And here I thought I was going to be able to open up to him. What a fool, I was a real fool.*

"I thought you were never going to offer me that whiskey only Stella knows how to prepare."

"Do I have a reason not to offer it?"

Eduardo takes the whiskey bottle from the bar. *He's so steady, so sure of himself, so calm. He's probably guessed by now that the Black Widow was here, changed her clothes, maybe even that the apartment on Amsterdam Avenue was in my name.* He decides to feel Marcelo out for what he knows. *Come on, Stella, it's your turn now,* he thinks as he takes on a different tone and different gestures.

"Ohhh, you wouldn't believe what a cra-aazy afternoon I've had."

"Cut my whiskey with a little water, will you. I already had two before coming over."

"Ohhh, so you're cheating on Stella, are you? I didn't know you had o-thers stashed away!"

"They're friends, Stella, only friends."

"Carlinhos, maybe?"

"That's right. Carlinhos and a couple of other friends."

"Oh, so you were giving your reports?"

"Are you referring to our finances or the hits for the month?"

"Hey, I'm not fooling around, Marcelo. I'm talking about Operation Black Widow, the reports on the operation."

"You're right again." Marcelo deliberates for a moment and then says: "How did you guess?"

"I didn't guess. I was informed."

"Valdevinos told you?"

"Let's say he did."

"Eduardo, you're playing with fire."

"Oh, yeah? My knees are knocking, I'm so scared I'm going to wet my bed tonight."

"You mean you know they ransacked the apartment on Amsterdam the other night?"

"'Pig,' 'fascist,' 'torturer,' 'informer for the Americans,' 'CIA agent,' 'enemy of Brazil,' should I go on?"

"That'll do." Marcelo doesn't know what to think. "Is this where the Black Widow came at lunchtime in her S & M getup?"

"She sat right there where you're sitting. She looked a bit more nervous and sweaty than you. She also needed a shave."

"I didn't think you were such good friends."

"Inseparable."

"So you know everything."

"The whole kit and caboodle, Ev-ery-thing."

"Was it you who bought the clothes for him on 14th Street?"

"You've got it."

"You frighten me, no, you surprise me," Marcelo corrects himself.

"I have the right, don't I?"

The phone rings in the other room.

"It's for you, Marcelo," Eduardo shouts.

"I took the liberty to give your number to . . ."

"Carlinhos?"

"Yes, to Carlinhos."

Eduardo returns to the living room while Marcelo yesses and nos curtly.

I bet I know what's up, Eduardo thinks when he sees Marcelo's face contorted for the first time.

"They already knew it was you."

"What now? Are they going to put a tail on me? Bomb my apartment? The consulate? Are they going to kidnap me or send me anonymous letters saying they know I'm a CIA or FBI agent, or God knows what?"

"Cut the shit, will you, and listen to what I'm going to tell you. They're convinced that you're innocent, that you're not involved in anything. That's what they called to say."

"I'll bet it was Carlinhos who discovered that I'm innocent. Let me see if I can guess how: He figured it out from the tapes of our conversations in the restaurant. Am I right?"

"That's probably it." And Marcelo immediately adds, "They asked me to . . ."

"They asked you to what?"

"They gave me orders to . . ."

"To kill me?"

Marcelo remained silent, eliciting Stella's sarcastic remark:

"Choose your weapon, rapiers or firearms."

"The orders were to have a talk with you, to inform you of the current situation in Brazil and in the world. They feel that you just don't know what's going on and that if you did you might even be useful to the cause. They trust you, Edu."

"And me, why should I trust you all?"

2

When Marcelo Carneiro da Rocha, alias Caetano, came to New York to teach he also had another mission. He was to join a recently formed group of guerrillas led by Vasco (an alias). Early in 1969 a group of guerrillas came together around Vasco. Most of them were Brazilian students already living in New York. Some had jobs there and a few were artists who moved to New York for all kinds of reasons.

Vasco, who had attended a meeting of the Organization of Latin American Socialists together with Marighela in Cuba, entered the United States by way of Canada with a false passport. He stayed several months in Montreal, grooming his already excellent French to pass for Canadian; that way he wouldn't raise any suspicions on crossing the border. His mission in New York was to establish ideological and financial relations between Brazilian guerrillas and the subversive minority movements in the United States. His main contacts were to be the Black Panther Party, led by Defense Minister Huey Newton, and the Farm Workers Movement in California under Cesar Chavez's leadership. He was also interested in the Young Lords, a recently formed group of Puerto Ricans from Spanish Harlem led by Felipe Luciano.

The Cuban leadership was impressed with Vasco's plan, which was also endorsed by Marighela, according to Vasco. He would be able to send information to Havana from the Panthers and Chavez without the FBI and the CIA suspecting anything. The Cubans took great care in furnishing him with convincing ID papers. It was important that even the Cuban contacts in the United States remain ignorant of his existence, read the communiqué which he used as a letter of introduction. Otherwise, spied on as they were, Vasco's name would soon be added to the data banks of Yankee imperialism.

The group began to take a more formal cast only after many meetings of the "Brazil-U.S. People's Fraternity." Meetings were held in a Protestant church on 46th Street between Ninth and Tenth Avenues. Fearing that its cover might be easily infiltrated, the group soon gave up the masquerade of a "People's Fraternity." Worse still, the very existence of a formal association would become a liability when the group decided to move to action. Claiming that there were too many legal and financial difficulties, the "fraternity" was dissolved in one last quarrelsome meeting staged for the purpose of scaring off the easily intimidated and the potentially troublesome. In the future, the small core of activists (no more than eight after Vasco's rigorous selection process) would meet in different locales to be announced shortly before by telephone.

Luck had it that the encounter with the North American groups took place in the most inconspicuous manner. Leonard Bernstein, the conductor, following the example set by other progressive friends, decided to give a party to raise money for the "Panther 21 Defense Fund." They were still in jail, held on charges of "conspiring" to bomb five department stores in Manhattan, railroad terminals, a police headquarters, and even the Bronx Botanical Garden. (The bombings, of course, never took place because the group was apprehended before putting the plans into effect.) The American justice system demanded a ransom—bail, in legalese—for the release of each suspect. Leon Quat, defense attorney for the "21," got Felicia and Leonard Bernstein to agree to make their Park Avenue duplex available to host the fundraiser that would attract American showbiz celebrities who sympathized with the black movement. It seemed like a good occasion for an enlightening dialogue between both parties; people of good will would be able to get a direct line on the Panthers' view of things without the usual distortions of the print and electronic media.

The Bernsteins had a delicate problem on their hands: how to throw a cocktail party for eighty people without hiring help. Black Americans, the most likely to provide this service, were out of the question; it would show a lack of respect for the guests of honor. The problem was solved when an agency they called suggested hiring a caterer who employed Latin Americans. Carlinhos found out about the job and tipped Vasco off, who got the contract.

Setting a mood conducive to establishing contact during the party was a breeze for Vasco; the camaraderie struck up between the guests of honor and the help made it even easier. Vasco made his way to Don Cox, the Panthers' field marshal, identified himself and passed him a note for Huey Newton sent by the Cubans. Cox told him he'd see what he could do; it would take a few days because Newton was on the West Coast at that moment. In any case, Vasco should meet them at The Red Velvet Lounge on 125th and Broadway in a week. Newton himself would not be there, no need to worry. They exchanged passwords.

Whether or not it was justified to extend the Latin American revolution into the United States is a debatable question today. The Cuban revolution was only the starting point, according to Marighela in a 1967 speech given during a visit to Cuba where he formally withdrew from the Brazilian Communist Party. This view is recorded in documents such as "Letters to the Central Committee" (dated August 17, 1967) and "Answers to the *Pensamento Crítico* questionnaire" (dated August 8, 1967). In none of these documents, however, is there any mention of Vasco's mission or the minority movements in the United States. Without these motives, it is hard to justify taking the revolution into the United States.

Whether these events require rewriting the history of the sixties and of the guerrilla movements legitimized by Cuba is too early to say. Reliable sources, however, have put forth this alternative version, most probably circulated by Vasco himself. They claim that the Cuban leadership asked Marighela to put a lid on the tactical incursion into the United States; that would keep the repressive Yankee forces in the dark and also make it easier for Vasco to work as the go-between from Castro to the gringo rebels.

According to other, less reliable sources, Marighela thought twice about getting the Brazilian guerrilla movement involved with the American New Left. The example of such undisciplined individuals in matters of drugs and sex was certainly not conducive to transforming his ill-trained Brazilians into a crack revolutionary corps. Vasco was thus "under any circumstances prohibited" (Marighela's exact terms) from associating with white student activists. Their idea of revolution, in this version of things, was limited to hedonism and libertinism.

The Panthers, of course, were another story. Their struggle required systematic revolutionary training. They were involved in an all-out battle against the repression of blacks against the deep-rooted racism of Yankee society. They also demanded a plebiscite in black communities, to be overseen by the United Nations, in order to ensure a relative freedom from outside coercion, especially that of the two hegemonic political parties.

Whatever the story, Vasco's influence on Marighela's thinking requires a careful analysis. One thing, however, is crystal clear: Vasco was more in tune with the cosmopolitan spirit of the period than Marighela, who always had a narrow view of things, despite the fact that his ideas were inspired by a foreign model, the Cuban revolution. He was obsessed by two goals: to make revolution in Brazil and to change the centralized structure of the Brazilian Communist Party, period.

In Vasco's opinion (according to Caetano's recently published memoirs), had Marighela not gone to Cuba he would have been sacrificed early in 1967 by the Party. His criticisms of the central committee were becoming an obstacle to the basic survival tactics of the left in Brazil, especially after Castelo Branco's departure from office. His comrades disparaged him for his rampant individualism and fanatical reverence for Che Guevara; they alleged that his idea of revolution boiled down to putting himself at risk.

Marighela's familiarity with the Cubans—particularly the publication of his "Letter to the Central Committee" in the Cuban press—saved him from any reprisals from the Party. The first sentence of the letter—"I am writing to inform you that I have decided, here in Havana, to break with the Central Committee of the Brazilian Communist Party"—is very significant in linking his defection to Havana. It was a way of shielding himself after being expelled from the Party. Everyone knew this but the letter went beyond a mere symbolic gesture of self-justification. In the first place, it was a way of saying "hands off"; in the second place, it was a way of flaunting his newly found prestige: you know who I am by the company I keep.

Ultimately, the meeting with the Panthers did not lead anywhere. And with the Farm Workers Movement, he never even got as far as setting up a meeting. The rendezvous with the Young Lords took place under similar circumstances as with the Panthers, in the house of another socialite, Ellie Guggenheim.

The Panthers were going through some very rough times. Fred Hampton was assassinated in his own bed; the cops alleged self-defense. Maybe. And the imprisonment of the "21" in February of 1969 put an enormous strain on the financial resources of the Panthers. Add the high cost of American justice and the situation was disastrous.

The most Vasco was able to get out of his meeting with the Panthers was an introduction to a small group of underground white radicals. They contributed to the coffers of the Brazilians—the former "People's Fraternity"—by donating the proceeds from a bank heist in the Bronx. At the time, the Panthers were divided on what their relationship to Cuba should be. The Cuban model of political action and the unparalleled figure of Comandante Che were beginning to lose their aura. The constant clashes with the police and the complex labyrinth of the American justice system —used brilliantly by the forces of Yankee repression in order to "democratically" contain the progress of black people—forced the Panthers to adopt a line of action more in keeping with the American Way Of Life if they hoped to win even the slightest bit of sympathy from the public.

It was in this difficult period that the Panthers began to cite passages from the Declaration of Independence, emphasizing such democratic propositions as the right to hold plebiscites, by which they sought to elude the corrupt electoral politics instituted by the major parties. They also questioned the selection of grand juries composed predominantly of white upper-middle-class Americans who had little understanding of the Panther cause. At this time, too, they organized day-care centers and opened community schools that might serve as models for a new educational system.

When it became obvious that the strategy of infiltration conjured up and put into effect by the Cubans could only fail, Vasco took it upon himself to move the wandering group of Brazilians in a direction more to their interest. He organized reconnaissance missions with the objective of determining which Brazilian officials in the United States were or had been in the service of repression and torture in Brazil. This was a decision much applauded by guerrilla groups like the MR-8 who sent Vasco a communiqué through Caetano offering their solidarity.

But the direction of the group took a completely different turn when Falcão (an alias) arrived in New York. By the end of September Vasco had lost the leadership of the group, which adopted a direction more in keeping with the strategies and modus operandi of Marighela. Falcão had impeccable credentials. He had participated in arms heists from an Air Force warehouse; he was one of the leaders who took part in the VAR-Palmares meeting in Teresópolis; he was the lieutenant commander of a guerrilla group in Niterói; he had taken part in five bank heists and two supermarket robberies in Rio de Janeiro; before he went underground, he had been an agitator on many campuses, helping to plan strikes, protests, and insitutional insubordination.

Falcão was also one of the guerrillas freed in exchange for the American ambassador Elbrick. In Mexico, he successfully executed an operation planned in Brazil; it consisted of obtaining a false U.S. passport and joining a group of northern braceros disaffected with Cesar Chavez's political proselytizing; they were on their way to work tomato fields in California. He got off the bus in Chihuahua, met the braceros the next day and in a specially chartered bus crossed the Rio Grande from Juárez to El Paso. Once on American soil he sneaked off into the night and caught a plane to New York.

Vasco gave him a complete briefing and he immediately set out to plan his first offensive. Carefully designed and executed like clockwork, it wasn't meant to score any great victory, only test the group's cohesion and readiness for action. The operation consisted of terrorizing the military attaché, who was known to have collaborated with the military dictatorship, according to information which Carlinhos had obtained.

3

That was an epic binge this afternoon. And how we needed it, it was absolutely indispensable. A toast to the Black Widow, alias Valdevinos Vianna, alias Colonel Valdevinos Vianna, illustrious officer (trumpets blare) of our honorable National Guard and not least Queen Emeritus of the cruising spots of Copacabana, Paris, Amsterdam, London, Manhattan, and other alluring places. A toast to the glory of the soft-assed, cocksucking faggot. These thoughts go through Eduardo's sleepy head as Marcelo brings his tedious political-revolutionary harangue to a close. He perorated like a scholar while Stella kicked about on the sofa, no longer able to restrain her impatience and her desire to go cruising around the Village. The syncopated samba beat of her heart makes her want to get up and fly out, find Ricky:

We'll fly down to Brazil.

You bet! But Marcelo has a long tongue tonight and doesn't stop rolling out the virtues of urban and rural guerrillas in Brazil and Latin America. He talked the whole night long while they compulsively downed whiskey after whiskey. At one point Marcelo asked Stella if she had heard about the kidnapping of the North American ambassador in Rio. Just to bust his chops, Stella asks:

"When was that?"

And Marcelo answers:

"Hey, it's no fun if you get like that, you're fucking drunk."

"*We* are," Stella corrects him. "We both are, me on whiskey and you on words."

Stymied, Marcelo swallows hard.

"Come on, Marcelo, a toast, chin-chin, a toast to our petty pus-il-lan . . . to our pus-il-lan-im-ity, whew!" Stella clinks her glass against Marcelo's and goes on: "We've got to think up a good ending for this film on the Cuban Revolution in the Americas. Let's see, we'll cast it with classic Hollywood stars: Alan Garfield in the lead role, who else could do it? And (ta-ta-ta ta-tum) Lana Turner, that treacherous redheaded doll as Fidel Castro's sister Juanita, the black sheep of the family, corrupt denigrator of revolutionary heroes . . ."

"I'm trying hard as all hell not to make you feel bad and here you are trying to demoralize me."

"Come on, Marcelo, chin-chin, a toast to the blessed ignorance of men. And now chin-chin again, another toast, this time to Ricky's cock and gorgeous ass." Again she clinks her glass against Marcelo's, who is doing his best to contain himself while Stella Turner, her hair tousled over her forehead, very much in character, asks Marcelo:

"Is silence made of gold?"

And Marcelo responds:

"Yes. And if you keep your mouth shut no flies will enter."

"That's for sure, man, but if you want your whiskey to ooze all velvety down your throat . . . ? Can't you feel it oozing down, Marcelo? Eduardo grabs Marcelo's hand and puts it to his throat so he can feel his Adam's apple rising and lowering as he drinks.

"God help me, vade retro, Satan, I'm allergic to Brazilian faggots, you're so pretentious," says Marcelo referring to Stella's faggotries. By now he had given up on following through with the orders to indoctrinate Eduardo so he'd spy for them at the consulate.

("The colonel would suspect anyone but him," Falcão concluded once he had been informed about the special relationship between Eduardo and the attaché and about his friendship with Marcelo. "As a passport official he's invaluable to all us exiles.")

Marcelo, on the couch, sits up straight.

"I'm going to have another, the last one," Marcelo gets up and totters over to the ice bucket and whiskey bottle on the coffee table. With an unsteady hand, he serves himself a drink. Eduardo says:

"Now who's stinking drunk? You're wrecked. You know, I've always wanted to see you in action, your gold-green flagpole erect over my country 'tis of thee." (Stella looks straight at Marcelo without concealing her interest in him.)

"If you've got it, flaunt it, if you don't, wag your tail," Marcelo retorts as Stella dumbdivinely winks her almond-shaped eyes. She draws up behind Marcelo and embraces him like a boa constrictor, making him lose his balance and drop his glass, which smashes on the floor.

"It's your fault, you faggot!"

"Don't worry about it, Bastiana comes tomorrow to do the cleaning," she says, still clinging to Marcelo who gently manages to disentangle himself from her grip and sit down again on the couch.

"I'll fetch you another glass in the kitchen," Eduardo says, standing up.

"It's okay, don't bother, I've had enough."

"Okay, don't get excited, dear!" Stella says sternly and adds: "We can still go for a walk in the Village. I want you to meet Ricky, the Eighth Wonder of the World, James Dean brought to life again by Nicholas Ray, a timid cowboy lost in the big city." Eduardo hands Marcelo another glass and he fills it with whiskey and ice.

"We killed the bottle."

"Don't worry about that, I've got another one stashed away."

"Working in the consulate has its benefits, huh?"

"That's right, it's better than running about playing the under-developed guerrilla. Beat that," Eduardo laughs so hard even he is startled.

"He who laughs last laughs best."

"Yeah, but if you're six feet below it doesn't count."

"Anything is worth it if it doesn't stunt your soul."

"That doesn't count either, it's blackmail," Eduardo bristles on hearing the lines of Fernando Pessoa's poetry which they used to recite back when they studied literature at the National University.

"Ahh, the problem is that I'm tired of being a man," Marcelo continues.

"I've always depended on the kindness of strangers."

"Et un jour j'ai assis la Beauté sur mes genoux et je l'ai trouvée amère."

"The cock's crow, dark and topmost fruit of this tree, is otherwise a mere accompaniment of dawn."

The two stop to muse in silence.

"This is the last one, Eduardo, then I'm going straight home. Professor Aníbal and Stella are too much for one day."

"Take it easy, girl, take it easy!" Stella admonishes him, this time a little less harshly. "We can still go to the Village. You have to meet the poor man's James Dean; for twenty dollars you get it all, a night of love and everything you've ever wanted. He's your type too," Eduardo insinuates, attempting to convince Marcelo to accompany him: "he's a real WASP, blond hair, blue eyes, a rare find in this land of Jews, blacks, and Puerto Ricans."

"You'd better stop that racist shit; keep bad-mouthing the oppressed and I'll tell Carlinhos."

"Me, a racist? Look who's talking! You can't see a pair of blue eyes without drooling, like a baby in need of a pacifier. And then you come to me with all this shit about the Panthers and the Young Lords. It's all bullshit; deep down the only thing that'll satisfy you is a nice pink cock couched in blond tufts of pubic hair."

"I'm starting to think that Falcão is slipping: if he knew Stella personally it wouldn't have occurred to him that we could turn her into a spy at the consulate."

"What's that you're muttering?"

"Oh, nothing. I was only thinking out loud."

"I can just guess: how to kidnap an ambassador in ten easy lessons."

"No. Make that: how to bore yourself silly on a Saturday evening; or better yet: how to act like a vulgar faggot and get stinking drunk to boot," Marcelo retorts, finally showing annoyance at the flip way in which Eduardo has been putting down his organization.

"Look who's talking! Te gusta el bacalao, you're into codfish too, as La Cuca likes to say."

"Can that Cuban queen next door be trusted? Didn't you tell me the other day that she spits and makes the sign of the cross anytime she hears the word communist?"

"If she had been here today, I would have only let her stay if she brought a spittoon with her," Stella jokes, mimicking La Cucaracha's outlandish gestures when she gets upset. "I didn't tell you she's head over heels—like me over Ricky—to-tal-ly snowed by a Brazilian journalist, a real hunk according to her."

"Who is he?"

"You think she'd mention his name? You've got to be kidding, love; her mouth is shut tight like a crab's. But I haven't told you the worst. One day this journalist waited until she had gone to work and he cleaned out her apartment. She told me he took everything of value. 'You have to be understanding,' she said; can you believe that?"

"Did he ever come back?"

"Never. The poor thing spends all her time waiting and trying all kinds of spells to see if he'll return; but he never does."

"Some people really go off the deep end," Marcelo muses compassionately as Eduardo raises his eyes wide open, not recognizing his friend.

"I thought you were going to say, good, she deserved it, the anticommunist bitch!"

Marcelo looks angrily at Eduardo who remorsefully says: "I'm sorry, okay, I'm sorry, I know I was exaggerating. But it does get to be a bit much, you know. First I have to deal with the Black Widow, who gets all hysterical and then with you, who reads me the catechism of Latin American revolutions. It was too much, I'm sorry, please forgive me."

"It was my fault. The problem is that you were accusing me of not warning you and I felt I couldn't let it go until later because then you'd throw it in my face again, that I'm not a real friend. I know my Stella and what she's capable of."

"It won't be easy to disentangle myself from Vianna."

"From who?"

"From Colonel Valdevinos, as you all say. If it wasn't for him I'd still be in Rio. I might have already put a bullet through my head."

"Stop it, Edu, you're getting me down. In a minute we'll both be crying. Maybe I should go to the bedroom for the tissues, you know, it's good to be prepared . . ."

"You don't understand Marcelo. You look at your life too logically and with no regrets. You're married for two years, then you get separated and it's no harder than not drinking for a couple of days; you'll be thirsty a few nights but you know that by next week you can have your whiskey. For me, Marcelo, it's not so easy. You can pose as a young college professor while you secretly want to blow up Manhattan island. I can't hide things like that, I'm different, too sentimental, too attached to people, especially if they're nice to me. I just can't break off with somebody, leave them stranded, unless, of course, they've been a sonofabitch to me or if they're nuts. They've got to have done something to *me;* if they fucked someone else over it doesn't count. If someone fucks me over, you can't imagine how depressed I get, the world comes tumbling down around me, you've never seen a sadder faggot. It was in just such a moment that Vianna came to the rescue; I really owe him one. That's what I was trying to tell you when you got on your soap box about the armed struggle in Brazil. I wanted to tell you all about it but the words got stuck in my throat. I tried but I never got them out, because, you know, I want to be your friend too, I want to understand you, maybe even help you out. You can't imagine, Marcelo, what a drag it is to be sentimental, to always have your feelings festering on your skin like shingles. On days when there's no one to salve my feelings, they start to blister, it's a real torture. I feel all empty inside, and I get resentful and paranoid. It's like a centipede crawling all over your body, you can't sit still, you run from one place to another like a stupid roach and only begin to calm down when you hear a generous, friendly voice. You can't imagine, Marcelo, how bad it is to always be dependent, at someone's mercy. At first I was dependent on my family and now it's Vianna. And I fear he's got something bad cooked up for me, he's going to get me in trouble, I can feel it coming, I don't dare think about it, I can't and I won't. . . ."

Eduardo's voice was starting to crack.

"What can he do to you, Edu?"

"What can he do? Are you kidding? He's just got to lift his finger and I'm fried."

"You mean he doesn't trust you any more?"

"Keep out of this, Marcelo, things are bad enough."

"Later you'll accuse me of not telling you something, of being a traitor, a con artist."

"Listen, I've got to work this out on my own. I'm the only one who can do it; you're too mixed up in your intrigues to be of any help."

"Are you going to tell me about it?" Marcelo insists.

"Let-it-go, Mar-ce-lo, don't in-sist," Eduardo tells him, emphasizing each syllable as if he were a radio announcer.

"Okay."

"Want to finish off the bottle?"

"You go ahead, I'm already sloshed."

"Halvesies?"

"Okay, but don't open a new bottle."

"I don't want to either. Let's go to the Village afterward."

"You go ahead, there's a meeting tomorrow to assess the situation. It seems like we put the fear of God in the colonel, according to his maid. She's a Bahiana who's going out with Vasco."

"Does the colonel know about her?"

"Know what?"

"That's she's a spy in his own home."

"Who said she's a spy? Vasco called her and she gossiped that her patrão had spent the night away from home and returned the next afternoon mad as all hell."

"And what did you have planned for him?"

"I didn't have anything planned for him."

"What do you mean nothing? Don't get all holy on me now, the halo doesn't suit you, you know, gold doesn't go with black hair. Did you ever see a black-haired saint with a halo? The darkest you'll ever see is dirty blond."

"You're goofing on me, Edu. Okay, go on but you should know that we've kept records on the colonel's good deeds. He was sent to New York by the holy office of the death squads. You wouldn't believe me if I told you that he was the one who gave orders to torture prisoners after Castelo Branco died. He's a sadistic butcher."

"Stop it, Marcelo, this is a real downer. You can put your catechism away now, okay?"

"He took special courses in the United States and Panama and brought back new techniques for psychological warfare to the Brazilian military. You skewer them upside down, shock their balls with electric current and give them a real high."

Eduardo goes crazy and now he's the one who drops his glass.

"I'm such a clummm-sy bitch," she cries and goes into the kitchen for another. When she returns she sees the bottle is empty. She looks at Marcelo's glass and asks:

"Want to go halvesies?"

"Okay, buddy."

"We'll go out later."

"You go."

"Don't make any predictions, Marcelo; tonight Ricky won't escape from me, I'm going to take a fishing rod and a bucket. All he has to do is look my way once and he's mine, in the bucket!"

"So you're going to leave me drunk and all alone at the bar, huh?"

Eduardo stretches his arm and caresses his friend's head.

"How could you think that about me? We'll all come back here, the three of us."

"I was never in a ménage à trois."

"There's always a first time." Eduardo takes his last swig and urges Marcelo to do the same. "Okay, down the hatch."

"Here goes."

Eduardo turns off the lights while Marcelo waits in the hallway. Then he closes the door and locks it.

"You should see the fort Professor Aníbal lives in; it has at least a hundred locks."

"I know the type," Eduardo says as he presses the elevator button. "He's one of those who thinks that nine out of every ten New Yorkers is a thief."

"Do you know what time it is?"

"The same as it was yesterday."

"One fifteen."

"Let's walk over to Eighth Avenue and catch a cab."

"At this time only the Anvil is open."

No sooner do they walk into the Anvil than Eduardo spots Ricky accompanying an older man with the air of a proper Bostonian.

Marcelo can see that Ricky suits Eduardo's tastes to a tee.

"Now that's a tasty treat."

Stella unabashedly taps Ricky on the shoulder.

"Hi!"

"Hi, Eddie!"

"How're you doing tonight?"

"All right, and you?"

"Okay, fine."

"May I buy you a drink?"

"Not now, thanks."

Eduardo orders a scotch and soda and pays while Stella says to herself: *He'll make at least fifty dollars tonight. The price of his shares is getting higher. If he keeps it up he'll soon be making a hundred.* After the bartender gives him his drink, Eduardo walks over again to Marcelo.

"You're not drinking anything?"

"I've had enough."

"Enough, my ass," Stella squeals as she goes back to the bar and orders another scotch and soda and brings it back to her friend.

"Saúde!"

"Saúde!"

"Wish me luck, Marcelo, the competition is getting tough, he's got a colonel on a leash tonight."

"He'll get rid of him soon."

"May God hear you, my son, I hope he hears you."

Eduardo sips the whiskey from his glass, leaving the ice cubes tinkling at the bottom. He retraces his steps to the bar and orders another whiskey, pays and looks for Marcelo, who is speaking with another fellow in Portuguese. *It's got to be Patricio,* Stella muses and decides to hover inconveniently around Ricky. *I wouldn't be caught dead tonight with a Brazilian.*

8

· · · ·

Leila picks up the clothes she threw on the study floor and still naked goes into the bathroom to take a shower.

Aníbal doesn't get impatient: he sits quietly in his wheelchair stationed in front of the desk. He doesn't even bat an eyelash when Leila picks up her clothing and leaves him alone caressing the hard stump beneath his shorts. Aníbal's face conveys the emptiness of waiting, as if the span between thought and action were occupied by the space-time of beatitude. In this state, the body, ready and still tense, only exists as an accumulation of energy as yet undirected toward some target. It is like an artificial lake in which the hydraulic potential of the contained water remains inactive until the floodgates are opened. Aníbal's nerves and muscles lie dormant while his mind navigates in empty space. He cannot see anything concrete around him. The bright colors of the spines of the books on the shelves fade into a cloud that invades the room, creating a vast stage that recedes along infinite vanishing points. After Leila's brusque departure only silence inhabits the large room. It is this silence which Aníbal tries to imitate; it provides him with the sensate absence of the sweep of time. In this total, nourishing silence even roses do not wither.

Leila throws her clothes on the floor and goes into the shower stall. She puts on a plastic cap to keep her abundant black hair dry. First she turns on the cold water, feeling the cold spray on her hot, excited body; the shock gradually relaxes her flesh and diminishes the readiness that keeps the body tense, as in a wrestling match. Gradually the harsh gestures give way to the infinitely soft and gentle tonalities that give her face its normal expression. Now she turns the cold water all the way off and turns on the hot water until the water temperature matches that of her body. Stimulated by frustration she feels the rebirth of a feline compulsion swelling beneath her skin. Contact with water makes it recoil, waiting for the moment of its total metamorphosis, when it will lunge onto the streets, its desire livid with the rawness of an open wound. Leila is unable to imagine the rawness and swelling of her desire; she cannot foresee the sudden and unexpected healing when she returns home satisfied. She reacts like a cat, searching along dark alleys, leaping over obstacles, garbage cans, until she lands on her prey, suffocating him with her feline caresses.

Aníbal savors the wait to the hilt; he knows all the twists and turns of waiting, every delight; he had explored every nook and cranny of its terrain, he had lived its drama. For Aníbal, waiting is a form of meditation, a luminous and monotonous Sahara through which the soul travels unencumbered by any obstacles or limits. There it seeks the gracefulness of flowing (the natural flow of a river along its well-trod bed), swaying (the dry leaf's challenge to gravity as it falls into the grasp of a gust of wind), and floating (anything can take flight on the driving power of thought). The body's grace-fulness lies in its ability to cut its earthly ties and fly among butter-flies and birds, seagulls and doves, vultures and hawks. In his ascent, Aníbal experiences this dislocation with no sense of pain or suffer-ing. His body flies through infinity like on a magic carpet which carries him to familiar and unknown landscapes. Unaware whence he comes and where he is going, Aníbal glides through space on an impossible sled.

Leila lets herself be guided by the fragrance of soap wafting in-ward through her nostrils, mobilizing her memory of flowing river water, the sweet and acrid perfume of wild flowers. It is the smell of feet treading over a dirt road and of a body that suddenly comes upon a refuge of flowing river water. She moves from under the shower, exposing her upper torso and with her agile hands she sponges her shoulders and armpits and then lingers at her breasts, making the soap suds foam up over them like a dense white fuzz. She moves back under the water and helps it do its job rubbing her hands over her body. Now she moves to the back of the shower stall, getting totally out from under the spray; she runs the soap through her vagina and across her buttocks and then descends along her legs to her feet, her body taking the shape of the number four as she stands first on her left leg and then on her right.

Descending quickly like a parachutist, Aníbal lowers his body and steps onto the hot Sahara sands. His body walks through the desert and the soles of his feet start to tingle, the hot surface makes them numb, he only feels the prickling of a thousand and one pins and needles. Aníbal remembers that his feet were walking but the more they want to walk the greater the resistance of the sands that receive his weight with the submissiveness of quicksand. Despite the obstacle, his legs are still agile and push his body forward. The dunes become confused with the sky ahead in the soft light of the horizon that remains constant and predictable to the eyes that move and advance in its direction. Only Aníbal's shadow disturbs the tranquil atmosphere of ecstasy in which he sinks his eyes; in that zone light recedes and the anonymous grains of sand lose their sparkle, the image of bright sunlight.

Leila shuts off the hot water and turns on the cold water full blast; she wants to shock her body with the cold. Under attack, her body rises to the occasion and tenses up again for the battle, regaining the armor of her goose-bumped skin that numbs her even as she surrenders to enemy waters. The blast of cold water acts like a time machine, putting Leila back into the frame of mind she was in before she entered the shower. It's as if she had never engaged in the cleansing and relaxation ritual. Leila pushes open the shower door and quickly grabs a towel, enveloping herself in its downy fabric, which she rubs against her body. Her body loses the milky whiteness of its skin as purple abrasions erupt in endless vertical streaks from head to toe. Her body is a rekindled ember. In the adjoining bedroom, Leila dresses hastily, as if she were trying to outpace the slow and graceful cadence of her everyday movements. She dresses artlessly, with trivial and rapid gestures, like those of a soldier who gets back into his uniform after having gotten used to the feel of civilian clothes while on vacation. Leila's uniform molds itself to her curves, highlighting them with the contrast of black cloth against white skin.

Aníbal wanders through the desert like a fugitive from the Foreign Legion, like a Bedouin who has strayed from his caravan. Dom Sebastião, the Infante Dom Sebastião, no doubt wandered through the desert like this after his defeat at Alcácer Quebir. Aníbal wanders like Dom Sebastião, knowing that his entire being is a state of waiting for the precise moment in which the veils of oblivion will lift again to reveal the grandeur covered over by time. He marches back in time and walks pleasantly through the dunes; his soul, cleansed and serene, is regenerated as he overcomes all obstacles. He revels in a joy born of the sand as it molds to his feet; it is as if he were taking a carefree morning walk. Aníbal skips over the sand and stretches out his arms in search of other arms to make a square and sashay to the left and sashay to the right, grab your partner and turn her 'round . . .

Leila stands in front of her vanity mirror; before her there is an entire arsenal of makeup that her meticulous and artful hands put to good use. Her eyes are brought back to life by the crayon that darkens her already black eyebrows and stretches the corners of her eyes to her temples in bold strokes. She blows up her cheeks to make it easier to apply the blush; her cheeks turn red like those of a schoolgirl confiding her peccadillos to a friend. The lipstick kindles her lips in a blaze of red that lights up her whole face; with a wave of the wand, her face takes on all the colors of an all-too-easy and garish seduction. Leila looks at herself in the mirror and knows that from now on she'll be the other woman, the incarnation of the image that Aníbal created for her and which she recreates for him whenever he gives the signal. Leila is a fluid image fastened to the surface of the mirror; she is familiar and yet strange—the woman she'd like to be but never quite embodies, Aníbal once told her. She grabs her fur coat and purse from the wardrobe and ready or not here she comes.

Aníbal succumbs to the desert's pitfalls: hunger, thirst, and fatigue. Unable to take another step, he sits down on a high dune and then stretches his body on the sand. It scorches his skin and he begins to sweat. He looks up and high above all he sees is the burning sun, indomitable and alone in the sky. It's his guide and his subjugator. Aníbal weakens but he would like to react. His body, however, can no longer get off the wheelchair on its own. When he puts pressure on the wheelchair's leather armrests, he discovers that he's tied to the ground, a prisoner of his seat. Suddenly something breaks the silence of his study.

"I'm going out," Leila tells him from the door of the study. She's wrapped in her fur coat, leaving enough cleavage exposed so her milky white breasts can be seen.

Aníbal is brought back from his long voyage in the Sahara; he scratches his eyes as if awakening from a deep sleep. He moves his wheelchair backward quickly, opens the center drawer of his desk and takes out a black case.

Leila turns the key in the door lock and walks to the elevator. She presses the button.

Aníbal closes the drawer and moves back to the table. He opens the case and takes out a pair of binoculars wrapped in red flannel, which he uses to wipe the lenses on both ends.

A heavy fragrance hovers in the elevator after Leila steps out. As she passes the doorman, she draws the fur coat more tightly around her. Noticing that she's very well dressed, he guesses she's off to a party and wishes her a good time. He opens the door for her and she is hit by the humidity of a New York autumn.

Aníbal handles his binoculars as if they were a surgical instrument or a coveted toy. He holds them carefully with shaky, timid hands or fondles them caressingly, drawing them toward his chest. All the while he muses: *Ah, silence. It is only through silence that social rank and relations are maintained. Secrecy is the heart of religious mystery, of all divine power.* After a brief moment, he peers again through the binoculars in his hands.

Leila descends a few steps and walks through the alleyway of hedges surrounding the building complex.

Aníbal rests the binoculars against his breast as he moves his wheelchair to the study doorway. He crosses the hall and enters the living room. The windows are covered by heavy gray drapes. Aníbal maneuvers around the obstacle course of furniture and brushes up against the drapes. He parks his wheelchair parallel to the drapes and brusquely pulls them apart in the middle, covering himself as if he had somehow landed in a lair. He crouches there in hiding.

Leila walks slowly without any hurry. No sooner did she descend the steps in front of her building, than she let go of her body, relaxed her muscles, released her nerves. She put on a wide, phony smile. Having gotten over the feeling of uncertainty that guided her steps, she now poises herself without anxiety; she walks without missing a step, although she also gives the impression that she is hoping for a pair of strong, masculine hands to grab her before she falls to the ground.

Holding on to the drapes, Aníbal moves his wheelchair back and forth until the right wheel touches the window, giving him the best view of the grounds. The haste to accommodate himself leaves him short of breath. It is hot in the space between the window and the drapes, but that doesn't bother Aníbal, who feels as comfortable there as if he were stretched out in bed.

Leila looks more fragile in her high heel shoes; her fur-enveloped body seems weaker now that she no longer draws her coat tightly across her collar. Her arms, now swinging beside her, permit her coat to open, displaying a slender figure whose only point of distress is her bust imprisoned in a tight bodice.

Aníbal, his face glued to the window, no longer knows what to do with himself inside his tent. He still can't see Leila walking all bundled up through the gardens of the apartment building complex. He waits nervously for the shadowy figure to come into view. And while he waits he imagines what he didn't get to see when they were both together in his study. He evokes in his mind's eye Leila's body twisting and turning before him like a serpent in heat, rubbing her own breasts and pinching her nipples. He follows her contorted fingers reaching down along her belly to her labia which avidly open up:

"Look, you fool, look at me, you don't know what you're missing."

"I'm looking, dear, I'm looking, honey; it's you who stays away from me."

"Touch it, stick your finger in, stick your whole fist in."

"You won't let me."

"I won't let you? Are you crazy?"

He sees her face entranced, her nostrils flaring and closing in long inhalations, sucking in his entire being. Suddenly Leila stops, grabs her clothes lying on the floor and leaves.

"Don't leave me now," Aníbal screams, frightening himself as his cry crashes against the window. He looks down again and this time makes out Leila's shadowy figure, crested by a very white face. His hands clasp the binoculars around his collar.

Leila walks in the direction of Bleecker Street but as she arrives at an intersection in the gardens, she stops abruptly, turns around, raises her eyes and searches the building in front of her for the windows of her apartment. She finds them. Where's Aníbal! She looks for him but fails to see her husband in his wheelchair. At best she makes out the metallic reflection of the chrome chassis, struck by a random ray of light. *He's already there,* she thinks, *I can continue walking.* She waves to him and feels safer knowing that someone is spying on her behind her back, that a gaze is fixed on her, that she is no longer walking alone toward Bleecker Street. Someone has taken an interest in her, in her fate, someone high up. The further she walks away from Aníbal the closer she gets to him, ready to encounter him in another's body. With that encounter she will have touched his forbidden body, that protected body up there, unavailable to more common hands, hands that are not his own. *He's following me and waiting for me up there. Only I can join the person who I am looking for with the one that follows me. I feel pressed between the two, between Aníbal's gaze and a stranger's hard-on thrusting into me.*

Aníbal can't hide his anxiety; his nervous hands fumble as he tries to focus the binoculars. Suddenly Leila appears on the other side, tall and splendid against an unusual backdrop of leaves and branches. Aníbal's anxiety subsides, he calmly breathes the stagnant air inside the makeshift drapery tent and leans back against the back of his wheelchair. His breathing recuperates its normal rhythm as he watches Leila in the distance, brought close up to his dazzled eyes and wide smile by the lenses. Leila waves her hand; opening her coat, she lets him peek at her body. Aníbal's hands feel their way to his groin like those of a blind man; the heat rises into his fingers and winds around them as his cock swells as if to match the gigantic proportions of Leila's image in the garden. She turns her back on him, scurrying off into the darkness again like a shadowy figure caught in the wind. Leila walks firmly but with the jerky movements of a marionette. The further she moves the more her figure stands out within the atmosphere that envelopes her. Her figure glows incandescently as she passes under a lamppost. The fur on her coat becomes more distinctive as its dense nap bristles with a sheen that blinds Aníbal. He reaches down and opens his zipper; he sticks his hand into his drawers and fondles his hot erect cock that refuses to stay hidden in his underclothes. He pulls his gaze away from the binoculars and looks down at the enormous, throbbing hard-on offset in high relief against the dark cloth of his pants. As he puts his hand around its huge circumference, he has the fleeting impression that his vision is getting cloudy. As he peels back the foreskin, however, he discerns quite clearly the purple head of his huge banana lunging forward.

Leila knows why she's searching: she received orders to search with all her five senses rolled into one. Propelled by fate, she wanders through the grounds of chance, the grounds of this Village apartment building complex on a dark autumn night. She searches but she doesn't know whom she's looking for. It might be anyone; whomever she runs into will be the person she's looking for, the person she's always looked for. She is not interested in the person, only in the chance encounter. It's enough for that person to stop, look, talk, lunge forward with outstretched hands and lips. She's ready and waiting, as if seated at a dinner table waiting for the host to give the signal to begin. *I look for what I can find, I find what I can't look for,* Leila reflects as she reconnoiters, like a lighthouse, the ground in front of her, breathing in the dull, rusty polluted air whose source she detects in the repulsive saccharine smell emanating from the smokestacks. *You can't smell nature here; everything smells artificial, as if the ground were strewn with fake flowers, beautiful fake flowers.* Leila imagines the bushes overrun by weeds and covered by swarms of pests; bushes laden with fragrant flowers. She breathes in the worn, recycled evening air, mixed with the din of the cars on this Saturday night and infused with myriad heavy metal sounds ricocheting along the street from the cafés on McDougal and Bleecker and from the blaring radios in Washington Square park. Leila knows that Aníbal is watching her and that gives her confidence to continue wandering to the cadences of chance. She doesn't know what Aníbal is doing; she doesn't even want to guess. She stops. Aníbal can't be seen covered as he is by the drapes, but she turns to look anyway. Leila knows he's spying on her with his binoculars, spying on her from his tent. *Aníbal wants me to be free, how can I hate him? Aníbal gave me orders to go out and search for someone, why should I feel remorse? Aníbal knows what he's doing, he always knew what to do.*

Go on, my dear, go on, Aníbal says to himself when he thinks he sees Leila hesitate in the middle of her stroll. If he could, he would run down to the garden and snap his fingers at Leila, standing there like a gigantic statue of black granite, brushing her head sideways against the collar of her fur coat. She looks indecisive. *Not now, Leila, not now.* She stands there absorbed in her own world, forgetful that she went out on a mission. *Don't do this to me, Leila, not now,* sputters Aníbal no longer knowing what to do with his hand around his cock. *Leila, I'm waiting for you to act, don't go back on me. Leila, I'm following you, protecting you, you don't have to worry, you can continue,* Aníbal would like to say to her by telepathy. And she gets the message; Leila takes a step and continues on her way toward Bleecker Street. Aníbal starts to masturbate. His binoculars shake to the rhythm of his body and the image in the lenses goes out of focus and gets fuzzy, like a realist drawing reverting to the underlying cartoon. When the image fades out completely, Aníbal goes into a panic. Leila has left the garden along a path that gets no light from the lampposts, a narrow path bordered by hedges that grow quite high in the summer. Aníbal stops masturbating, frantically looking for Leila's figure. *Where did she go?* When he sees her again, she has already made it to the sidewalk and her figure is less striking against the colorful metallic backdrop of the parked cars. Leila immerses herself in these colors like a swimmer going off into the sea. Aníbal grabs his cock again, gently, and goes on stroking it up and down.

Leila crosses over to Bleecker Street but before she steps onto the sidewalk she pauses to consider whether or not to follow the rush of Saturday night people in the direction of the West Village. She waits until the last of a band of Puerto Rican youths go by and she decides to stay in the area around the building complex. She leans against a car and looks up. *There he is, watching me. I'm only a distant image to him.* She wonders whether she should wave to him. Two girls passing by look at Leila in confusion as she lifts her arm abruptly to wave. Thinking she's waving for them to come over, they slow down, turn their bodies to the right and say

"I beg your pardon."

Leila has no idea why these girls address her. She wraps herself in her fur coat and takes a step back. The two girls continue on their way; "a bad trip," they comment. Leila is not interested in any of the men making their way west. They arrive in groups, walk around in groups, carry on and make a racket in groups, eat and drink in groups, and afterward, on their way home, they belch and throw up their guts in groups. They come out of the subway on the East side and like a rustling gray cloud of locusts, they walk past Leila one after another, like trains on a subway platform. Leila doesn't even see them. She's got her own mission.

Aníbal carefully focuses the lenses on Leila, paying full attention to the gigantic image of her face. He sees her forehead so close up, so near, that he could reach out and touch it with his hand. A nearby lamppost shines its light on her face, allowing Aníbal to discern its every detail highlighted by makeup. Her face is so near his hands, his touch, his mouth; that's what he wants, her mouth, to kiss, in the empty night filled in by the alluring image of Leila leaning against a car. She suddenly disappears behind a barricade of passers-by and just as quickly reappears all alone against the bright color of the car's fender. Aníbal searches her out for another kiss, tongue entwined in tongue, while his hand goes up and down on his cock, his agitation increasing with the syncopated rhythm of his faltering breath. *That bitch won't find anyone to fuck her tonight,* Aníbal begins to get impatient with Leila's passivity just as he feels a burning sensation at the tip of his cock. He puts the binoculars aside and looks down on the chaffing produced by the frenzied movements of his hand. He spits on his cock's purple head to lubricate it and continues stroking it, looking through the binoculars again for Leila's image.

Leila is looking for a man, a man who will lick her face, her neck, her collar, lick her from head to toe, leaving her drenched in saliva, leaning there against the car, to the surprise, revulsion, ridicule, and disdain of the passers-by. A man who, by just imagining her body behind the coattails of her fur coat, will get so hot that his cock will spew come all over his pants, staining their cloth with lust. A man who will caress her with no more pleasure and persistence than someone who opens a door for a stranger. He opens the door for an unfamiliar woman who does not enter but approaches just the same. She approaches but doesn't enter. A man who will desire her even though she desires Aníbal. A man who will not be shocked by her gaze, lost in the distance as if she were keeping watch for the arrival of the police or of phantoms. A man who, in embracing her, will also embrace Aníbal, sitting up there watching with his binoculars and feeling the lust and the shudders of the struggles of lovemaking. Each of Leila's kisses is for two men, her every feeling and even her submission are for two men at the same time. The hand that moves slowly down his abdomen and fondles his lusted-after hard-on, it does it for the both of them.

Aníbal unbuckles his belt and lowers the upper part of his pants and then his drawers. He fondles his balls, freeing them from their prison between his legs. He squeezes his balls, which pressed together react like flint stones. The purple head of his cock lunges forward, throbbing. Now Aníbal clasps his hand around the shaft of his cock and masturbates with real fervor.

Leila, meanwhile, is looking at a tall, bearded blond man wearing cowboy boots and hat. He passes by, casting an admiring look her way. He runs his gaze up and down her body, his lust evident in the sparkle of his eyes.

He doesn't take his eyes off Leila. He continues to walk East but cranes his head backward so as not to lose sight of her.

Aníbal follows the man with his binoculars. *She caught one,* he says to himself as he loses sight of the man, *goddammit,* but is quickly gladdened again as he sees the man returning.

Leila waits and readies herself to cast her net.

The man walks back toward her.

Aníbal gets excited and begins to pant frenetically inside his tent.

Leila puts on an innocent look while her mouth purses in a gesture of desire.

The man slows down as he nears her. *It's in the bag.*

Aníbal: "What the hell are you waiting for? Go ahead, can't you see that she's yours. Move, you idiot!"

Leila feels the man's body next to hers. His eyes peer inquisitively beneath the rim of his hat at the woman on the make in a fur coat in the Village.

She must be a nympho, the man thinks, *but who cares? I've got what she wants and more.*

Aníbal imagines the man as a hawk swooping down on his vulnerable prey. The fragile dove, hypnotized by the piercing gaze of the hawk, does not even dare to flee. She seems to think he will provide protection.

Leila responds by opening her coat. The asphalt cowboy's body is so close she can almost feel it brushing up against her.

"Just walking around?" the man asks.

Leila doesn't answer; she assents with her face and her body, which is pressed against the car.

Aníbal accelerates the rhythm of his hand as he sees

Leila yield to the advance,

tasting the cowboy's boozy breath.

PART THREE

. . . .

9

. . . .

October 19

The doorbell rings insistently.

La Cucaracha's face peers through his slightly open door. He wants to see who is bothering Eduardo so early on a Sunday morning. It must be that hideous guy from yesterday.

Two men stand in front of Eduardo's door. They don't say anything and show not the slightest impatience. They're dressed conservatively in gray suits and striped ties, like Jimmy Stewart in *Vertigo*. They've got heavy wing tips on their feet. They're tall and athletic; one in his early forties, the other in his late thirties. They're not brothers although they look alike; it's not their physical features that makes them similar, it's their manner. They catch on to the curious neighbor spying on them behind the partly open door. They make believe they haven't noticed him.

Not knowing that he's been spotted, La Cucaracha does not remove his foot from behind the door. Who knows what these two guys want in Eduardo's apartment. Poor baby! It must have something to do with that S & M bitch from the other day. That dumb queen in black leather drag must have laid some trap for Eduardo. When Paco realizes that he's been seen, one of the two men, on the orders of the other, walks in his direction. It's too late now to close the door. It might make them suspicious.

"Excuse me, sir. I hate to bother you, but do you know your neighbor, Mr. Silva?"

"We're good friends."

"Great. Do you know if he's in the city?"

"I think so. I saw him yesterday."

"Are you also Brazilian?"

"No, I'm Cuban."

"Thanks a lot for helping us."

Paco shuts the door quickly, responding to ancient fears (*They smell like detectives to me. Poor Eduardo!*) as the younger of the two men walks back to report. They press the doorbell again and let it ring for quite a long time.

No voice or sound comes from the apartment.

The assistant looks at his chief impatiently, signaling that it would be better to return later. The chief doesn't notice; he continues to look at the door in front of him, nothing fazes him.

"He's probably gone away for the last part of the weekend," the assistant suggests.

The other man says nothing and continues to stand indifferently in front of the door, ready to make his customary introduction or to react quickly in case of any disagreeable surprise. He has his right hand in his pants pocket. "You never know what might happen," he always lectures his assistants, "you've got to be prepared for anything, for good things and bad things."

The chief presses the doorbell once again and instructs his assistant:

"Sunday mornings you've got to give 'em enough time," and then he tries to crack a joke to break the monotony of the wait. "Those Latins, you know, that's all they think about," he says without changing his expression to accompany the crack.

The assistant wonders if it would please his chief if he asked whether he meant that they only think about sleeping or about sex. But seeing that his boss has finally gotten impatient, he only smiles silently to himself. He decides to say instead:

"Wouldn't it be better to leave a note under his door?"

"What for?"

"He might be afraid to open up."

"I would have already heard his footsteps as he approached the door."

"But if he's barefoot?"

"Even barefoot. The floors in these old buildings always creak," he lectures the younger man.

"It never occurred to me . . ."

"That's why you can't concentrate enough. You never know."

"Chalk up another one; I've learned another lesson."

"I'm going to ring one more time. It'll be the tenth. I never ring more than ten times. It's my lucky number."

"If no one answers we can return later," the assistant concludes impatiently.

"Do you believe there's such a thing as a lucky number?"

"Is there any reason not to believe it?"

"Yes, yes there is."

The chief rings the bell for the tenth time. They wait.

"You won!" the chief says, conceding the victory. "We'll return later."

"Should we leave a note?"

"Have you gone crazy?"

"You think he's gone on the lam?" asks the assistant sheepishly.

The chief reflects, a momentary doubt wrinkling his forehead. He decides, however, to stick to his decision: "we'll return later and see."

They walk over to the elevator.

From behind his closed door, Paco has tried to keep track of what they've said. He didn't make out very much because his door is heavy and the men were whispering. On top of that, he didn't want to get too close because the two men seemed to be able to hear the beating of a mosquito's wings. Now he hears the noise of the elevator door opening and closing. Then the metallic click of the motor. The elevator went down; they've left.

Eduardo didn't sleep at home; it surprises Paco. Eduardo has always been a homebody and last night he slept out. Paco decides to spend the rest of the morning waiting for Eduardo to warn him about his early visitors. *Should I tell him who they are? I've never seen them around here before, unos desconocidos, chico. They look like they might be from the diplomatic corps but they might also be cops. ¿Quién sabe, who knows? chico. If I tell him he might get edgy, more than he is already. He was all bent out of shape yesterday, pobrecito!* Paco remembers the night they met by the elevator door. In his mind's eye he sees Eduardo's face wrinkling into a fit of tears, sitting on the sofa in the living room. He thinks Eduardo must have a skeleton in his closet. *Cosas de maricones, the trials and tribulations of being a faggot,* he says to himself without too much conviction. If it were so simple and mundane he wouldn't be so depressed. It must be that S & M bitch who knows about his past and now has him in the palm of her hand; she might even be blackmailing him. *Cosas de maricones,* he muses sadly, wondering why faggots make such bad friends. They want to see the other guy dead and buried. If it were up to him, he would start an international club in which they all would feel like sisters, in which a true spirit of sisterhood prevailed. The universal sorority. And all catty, treacherous, arrogant, bitchy, slanderous, condescending maricones would be punished, or even better, they would be expelled for the greater peace and harmony of club members. His fantasy gives way to the actual feeling of being the creator, organizer, and president of the club de maricones. He feels like a queen on her throne, looking upon thousands and thousands of members who give her all the recognition and love she deserves. All of a sudden he laughs at his fantasy. If he told Eduardo about it he would surely say that he had never met such a deficient maricón. Eduardo psychologizes everything. *Oh, I'm such a paranoid, schizophrenic bitch, I'm lacking this or that on account of. . . . What a fool I am to give any credence to such idle chatter.* Paco can't stand maricones who analyze themselves or others. He feels they have three defects.

The first is that they're too loose, too uninhibited, as if you could be a faggot twenty-four hours a day. You lose your sense of convenience. Eduardo says that it's a way of taking on an identity and that it's good. Paco retorts that it's like being possessed by the devil. *Mira esta maricona in black drag, she dresses and parades herself on the street as if it were carnival time.* Has the bitch lost all sense of shame? For Paco, a faggot has to have a sense of modesty, just like any woman who is truly a woman—una hem-bra—must have a sense of decency. Of course, it never occurred to Paco that Eduardo held him up as an exemplary faggot, a maricón with a true sense of self. Paco's life was no longer that of a man or a woman. He had style. Not an individual style, his and his alone, but a style that recuperates and sums up and synthesizes all the inventive gestures and behaviors of an entire class of people. In a conversation with Eduardo, Marcelo said the main characteristic of today's bicha is the constant search for his own faggot style. The difference between bichas and straight men or women is that the latter live already codified lifestyles. Their personal development simply involves assuming one of the styles already perfected by previous generations. That's why,

Marcelo concluded, straight people lose their inventiveness when they reach the age of reason, they speak the language of Everyman. Bichas, in contrast, reach maturity by the constant exercise of free imagination, inventing their own language every day, which is interesting for that very reason alone. Bichas create a lifestyle that enables them to fit successfully into a society of compulsory heterosexuality without suffering psychological damage. As far as Marcelo is concerned, history and the past are of interest only to straight people. Bichas only believe in the present and they root themselves in it as if they were trees, appropriating everything they can and as rapidly as possible in the time allotted to them on this Earth.

The second defect is the most serious for Paco. He can't imagine losing the sense of sin inherent in the homosexual act. Those maricones under analysis have lost all sense of shame; they fuck with as much concern as if they were drinking a glass of water. Once they've satisfied their thirst, it's as if nothing had ever happened. They feel free, unconstrained, they go about life like butterflies roaming through a field. "God, what a tragic queen you are!" Eduardo always tells Paco when he speaks of the profound feeling of sin and subsequent repentance. "It's no tragedy at all, Eduardo, it's the need we all have for religion. Men and women get married in church and have their union consecrated by a priest. Faggots have none of that. Maricones are like prostitutes; they have to seek out a saint to intercede on their behalf." Eduardo smiles as his friend describes all the pleasures of mortification, pleasures as cherished as the pleasures of the flesh. "One of these days you're going to get laid just for the pleasure of mortification," Eduardo jokes at Paco's expense, who gets offended by the lack of respect. "You're an atheist; I can't imagine why you haven't become a communist yet. You should see what it's like to be a maricón under an atheist regime. I can tell you all about it." Paco found it hard to formulate what he wanted to say, which is pretty much as follows: he believed that it was only because of religion that faggots had the little freedom that they did in any country. Whenever he spoke of communist countries it was only to speak of sexual intolerance. Religion makes a country more tolerant because for the truly religious it is not necessary to extirpate sin—the possibility to commit evil—to cut it off at the root. Religious people accept the existence of evil in their lives, so long, of course, as sinners repent. That's how the word mortification functions in Paco's reasoning. Thanks to it, faggots can be reclaimed by the society in which they live. There is no need to throw them in jail or put them in concentration camps. Paco never stopped to consider if mortification was as high a price to pay as confinement in a concentration camp. It isn't a matter for analysis, you either believe or you don't. If people reflect on the matter, it is only to deepen their belief, not to change how anyone thinks.

The third and last defect follows from what was just said. Faggots under analysis are repulsive, they have the habit of explaining everything away, for no other reason than to bring about change, to think things differently, sometimes even contradictorily. With every hour, worse, with every minute they show a different face. They're chameleons. They lack a coherent center. But Paco couldn't guess that his desperate and tragic search for coherence was what Eduardo referred to as his style. Eduardo told Marcelo that La Cucaracha was like a novelist, or in any case that she thought she was a novelist, searching for herself day and night, night and day, like a novelist in search of a character. She's stupid, Eduardo added, but she has found a kind of religious redemption in her own intellectual limitations. And she grabs on to life and pleasure like a man overboard grabs on to a plank. "I'm always teasing her about being the most tragic queen I've ever met. She gets pissed, resentful, full of mala leche, as she says, but deep down inside I envy the way she has organized her life. She has found a system that fits her like a glove. And she does everything without inhibitions because everything goes so long as you repent sincerely for what you've done. She has such an enthusiasm and love for the other that I feel lacking before her. You know Stella, Marcelo, you know what she can do, her cruelties. You know what she's capable of when she gets into her routine. And she lays all that on poor Paco. Stella has no pity; I hate her at times for that."

All is still silent in the fifth floor hallway. Eduardo hasn't shown up and those two scarecrows are about to return. Paco gets impatient and his thoughts turn gory as he goes over the spate of deaths, murders, disasters, and violence throughout the city on Saturday nights. And then he feels bad for letting bad thoughts get the better of him. *Qué tonta, I'm such a little dope! A lo mejor está gozándola, for all I know he's probably having the time of his life right now.* He remembers Tito Puente singing the refrain "A gozar, muchàchos, a gozarla!" in a merengue with bongos and maracas in the background. He's probably on Ricky's leash. Paco smiles, Eduardo didn't talk about anything else yesterday.

Paco waits in vain for Eduardo.

Eduardo is in his room, lying on his bed. He's alone, unconscious as a result of last night's debauchery. He's still dressed, although Marcelo was able to pull off his shoes and his windbreaker, leaving his wool socks and shirt on. Marcelo brought him home after he fainted at the Anvil. The management went into a fit, thinking it was an overdose but everything was ironed out after the bartender said he knew him well and that he could guarantee he wasn't into drugs, only alcohol. All the same, they made all kinds of sarcastic and nasty comments about foreigners. Marcelo just let them go in one ear and out the other. The worst thing you can do on such an occasion is to acknowledge them by defending yourself or counter-attacking. What Marcelo didn't expect was Ricky's reaction; he was the most helpful person there. When he saw Eddie lying on the floor of the bar he ran over and broke up the circle of onlookers so he could breathe more easily. Then he picked him up and carried his one hundred and thirty pounds to a corner of the bar where he put down Eduardo, who muttered incomprehensible sounds that were neither English nor Portuguese.

"I'm going to take him home," Marcelo finally decided when he realized Eduardo wasn't going to come around for a long time.

"I can help you, if you like," Ricky offered.

Marcelo accepted his help for more than one reason. First, however, he asked him if he was going to leave his friend alone at the bar.

"He's not a friend," Ricky answered curtly.

Marcelo got the message, it wasn't his business.

They hoisted Eduardo between the both of them, one arm around Marcelo's neck and the other one around Ricky's. Since they were both taller, it was easy to carry Eduardo, without the extra hindrance of dragging feet.

Eduardo went on making those incomprehensible utterances that sounded like muffled words or simple interjections.

Marcelo gave instructions and Ricky followed them obediently. *The poor fellow has no idea—how could he—that he's the cause of this fiasco,* Marcelo thought as he observed the tenderness with which Ricky helped Eduardo.

"Poor fellow! To drink the way he did he must have some serious problems or hang-ups."

"He does," Marcelo said.

"I was getting to know him yesterday. He's a nice guy."

Marcelo smiled but didn't confess he already knew everything, including the twenty dollars. He might scare off the gringo. He'd think that Eddie, such a nice guy, was also a blabber mouth who used his girlfriend Stella to spread throughout Manhattan the intimate details of their night together.

They hailed a cab.

Marcelo was glad Ricky was with them. What with his accent and Eduardo stone drunk they would have surely brought out the gringo's animosity throughout the ride.

As Ricky pulled him into the cab, Eduardo wrapped himself around Ricky's body and blurted out some words—"Ricky, my love"—that finally made some sense.

"He's saying my name. He's alright now," Ricky said without disguising that he was pleased.

Marcelo got into the cab last and closed the door. He gave the driver the address.

"Ricky, my love, we'll fly down to Brazil," Eduardo insisted, his eyes still closed and his body limp.

"That's what he said to me yesterday. Do you think he really means it?"

"Of course," Marcelo answered; he didn't want to be a killjoy.

They got out of the cab and up the stairs quickly with no problems. Together they managed quite well with Eduardo, who had reverted to spouting incomprehensible sounds with closed eyes.

Marcelo took the key out of Eduardo's pocket and opened the door. Ricky carried Eduardo, still wrapped around him, to his bed.

Marcelo kept a duplicate of the key in his hand and locked the door as they went out.

Ricky told Marcelo he didn't have a place to sleep.

Marcelo asked him if he'd like to stay with Eduardo. He was sure Eduardo wouldn't mind at all.

Ricky wasn't as sure as Marcelo was; he didn't know how Eduardo might feel or what he might do when he came to. He also admitted that he wasn't really Eduardo's friend. He didn't want Marcelo to get the wrong idea.

Marcelo reminded him that he had already said that they had only just met the night before.

Ricky smiled and Marcelo thought that he had to act right away without thinking twice or even once. It had to be quick; sink or swim.

"Do you want to spend the night at my place?"

Paco hears Eduardo's doorbell ring again. It rings insistently, like before. *They've returned.* Paco was relaxing but gets up and pricks up his ears.

It is almost noon and the two men are standing in front of Eduardo's door again.

The older one tells his assistant that nothing happened while they were away. The assistant asks him how he knows or is he some kind of fortune-teller.

"Elementary," says the chief, who had left an unnoticeable thread across the crack between the door and the jamb. The thread was still in place.

The assistant asks him when he put it there, he hadn't seen him do it.

"While you spoke with the neighbor, that Cuban guy."

"I'll be a sonofabitch!"

"Stick with me and you'll learn something," the chief gloats.

The assistant wants to know where he can learn these things, they weren't included in the courses he took. He had learned about all kinds of electronic devices, each more complicated than the last.

The chief tells him triumphantly that he devised his own methods.

The assistant wants to know more and plies him with questions.

The chief tells him it's just a white thread, the thinnest that can be found on the market. He put glue on the ends and let it dry. When it comes time to use it you just lick the ends to activate the adhesive, just as you do with an envelope. "Easy, isn't it?"

The assistant assents envious of his boss's expertise. That's why he went up so fast in the ranks, he reckons.

The chief asks his assistant to hush for a moment.

He hears noise inside the apartment, barely audible noises, then footsteps followed by grumbling and finally a voice. The chief doesn't understand a word even though it is clearly a sentence that he hears. He tells his assistant it must be Brazilian the guy inside is speaking. He concludes that Mr. Silva is not in the habit of receiving American visitors at unusual hours.

Eduardo is looking for the keys; they're not in his pants' pockets, where he always keeps them. He can't remember a thing. He makes an effort. He doesn't know Marcelo left them on the living room coffee table. His hangover is terrible; his headache even worse. It feels as if his skull were going to explode. He can't remember a thing and his curiosity grows greater but there's no time to explore, the doorbell is ringing and he's got to find the fucking keys. God damn fucking keys! He runs his hands over all the furniture because it hurts too much to search with his eyes. Every time he tries to open them his reflexes shut them to ward off the pain in his head. Finally he finds the buggers. He turns the lock, opens the door and jumps back startled.

"Yes?"

The chief reaches into his coat pocket with his left hand and, like pulling a rabbit out of a hat, shows him his badge. He holds out his right hand to Eduardo, greeting him cordially.

"Good morning, Mr. Silva. We're with the FBI and would like to talk to you in private," says the chief in a clear and overly enunciated voice just in case the foreigner doesn't understand English well.

Eduardo looks at the FBI seal on the badge and remains silent. He has no idea what the hell is going on. It must be a nightmare. But then he hears:

"May we?"

The chief conjectures that Eduardo must have slept in his clothes, he's in his socks and still very sleepy. There can be no doubt he's just awakened. He must have really been under to sleep through all the knocking on the door earlier. He also notices it's difficult for Eduardo to open his eyes and that he's very pale. Just out of fear? Not likely. He shows obvious signs of a hangover, he thinks while he waits for Mr. Silva to speak.

"Come in, please."

They walk into the apartment as Eduardo holds the door (actually he's holding himself up). The two agents walk into the living room and stand there facing Eduardo as he takes his time closing the door. He feels more confident so long as he can see Paco at the other end of the hallway.

Eduardo invites them to sit down on the sofa. He excuses himself for the mess, he had a friend over last night for drinks.

The chief asks him if he's alone.

Eduardo says yes.

The chief notices the empty liquor bottle and the ice bucket. Two empty glasses. Another glass or, rather, pieces of glass strewn on the floor. He decides to crack a joke to make Eduardo feel at ease.

"I see you had a good time last night," he says as he tries to come up with a good reason for the broken glass. Nothing occurs to him.

"I need some rest," Eduardo says, hoping they'll get the idea and leave quickly.

"We won't keep you very long," the assistant says, catching the hint. The inopportune remark gets the chief a little pissed.

The chief says it's better to go straight to the heart of the matter and asks a series of questions about the rental of an apartment on Amsterdam Avenue to which Eduardo answers affirmatively.

The chief says he's satisfied with the answers, which are more or less corroborated by what Mrs. Simon, the real estate agency secretary, told him. There are, however, he goes on, a few shady points. If Mr. Silva wouldn't mind helping to clear them up . . .

Eduardo assents.

He rented the apartment but he doesn't live in it. He rented it for a Brazilian friend who was coming to study in New York and needed a place to live. So he pays his own rent? No, Eduardo pays for it. Who's the student? Eduardo quickly pulls a name out of a hat: Mário Correia Dias. The chief asks Eduardo to write down the name. He gestures for the assistant to hand Eduardo a pen and an appointment book open to the month of October. Eduardo's hand shakes as he writes the name. He apologizes, saying he's badly hungover. The chief takes the appointment book from Eduardo's hands and reads the name. He asks what Mr. Dias is doing in New York. He's in a graduate program at Columbia University, Eduardo says as he remembers what the colonel told him. Is he in the city? Eduardo doesn't know. Is he still living in the apartment? Eduardo hasn't seen him for a long time, but yes, he's probably still living there. How else could he survive in a city like New York! So why does Eduardo continue to pay the rent? He couldn't let them throw him out, could he? What is the reason for all this generosity? Eduardo doesn't have to answer if he doesn't want to. Eduardo says he'll answer: his friend from Brazil wasn't going to be able to finish his degree because he didn't have enough money. Anyway, two hundred dollars a month was not so much and he made good money, more than enough considering he led a relatively modest life. The chief's face relaxes and shows a real liking for this Brazilian. He's different from all those other Latinos he's had to deal with, especially those from the Caribbean.

The assistant is already convinced of Mr. Silva's innocence. They're going to have to bark up some other tree, he figures.

The chief still isn't satisfied. He likes the young man and feels he isn't lying. His answers are convincing. His reasons for paying someone else's rent are plausible. But Eduardo didn't ask them why they're there asking him all these questions. It could be because he's still groggy. Worse still, however, is that Eduardo's words don't jibe with the state of the apartment on Amsterdam Avenue—graffiti all over the walls, suggesting the work of terrorists—and the statements made by the Dominican bodega shopkeeper and the owner of the bar on the corner. They both spoke of a loca flamante who lives in the apartment, a fiftyish queen who might be anything except a poor student. "They've got money," said the bodeguero, "the older one's got a brand new car and he always shows up in expensive suits; he must be a senior executive at a large company. But you should see him when he goes out at night, dressed to his teeth in black leather, like in those filmes porno para maricones. He's probably off carousing in some bar in the Village." The owner of the bar said the guy showed up Saturday morning looking very nervous. He was decked out in his S & M duds, you know, all that black leather stuff. He went out of the bar to make a call at a public phone booth on the corner. The assistant asked the owner of the bar if he could recognize the guy if he saw him again. He said yeah, sure, he's been hanging around the neighborhood for more than a year.

The chief decides to change his questioning tactics, focusing on Mr. Dias's identity. He asks how old he is. Eduardo says he's not sure but that he's about his own age, twenty-five or twenty-seven. Does he have older friends? Eduardo doesn't know. Perhaps a rich executive? No, Eduardo doesn't know. The chief informs him that a fiftyish executive type has been frequenting the apartment. *The colonel,* Eduardo says to himself, *they must know all about him,* and tries to hide the insecurity that is overtaking him. "I don't know anything about him," Eduardo insists as the chief plans his strategy to get information on the principal reason the New York Police Department called the FBI into this case. He asks Eduardo if he knows whether or not Mr. Dias is involved with any right-wing political groups in Brazil or the United States. Not as far as Eduardo knows; but certainly the chief must know more about such things than him. The chief asks if he knows the apartment has been broken into and turned upside down. What? It's been broken into? We don't know for sure—this time it's the chief who answers, giving a detailed account of the state in which they found the apartment Saturday night. Eduardo pretends to know nothing and appears to be startled. The chief is sorry to have let the cat out of the bag but since he did he figures it will be better to go on giving the young man more details. The head honcho in Washington was quite alarmed when he found out there were Portuguese words scrawled on the walls of the apartment; there had been serious run-ins with American personnel in Brazil. Eduardo tells him he must be referring to the kidnapping of the American ambassador in Rio. It was a group of young Brazilian guerrillas who did it. The chief confesses he didn't know about it and thanks Eduardo for the information. He says a full report must be on its way to his office. What the chief didn't tell Eduardo is that the head honcho was most concerned by the fact that it was a senior official of the Brazilian Consulate in New York who was living in the apartment. That's why the telexes he got throughout the night had "TOP SECRET" written in the top margin. He also figured there were good reasons for getting him involved in such an apparently minor case.

The chief tells Eduardo he's going to let him get some rest. "You've been very cooperative." But as he goes out the door he tells Eduardo he shouldn't leave the city; it might be necessary to speak with him again. As far as he was concerned, though, Eduardo wasn't implicated, although, of course, there was the matter of his having been the one who signed the lease. And if it turned out to be a case of international terrorism, well, then, you know, the people in Washington can get very heavy.

As soon as they're gone, Eduardo runs over to the telephone and dials Vianna's number. Vianna himself answers.

"Two FBI agents were—" he doesn't get a chance to finish the sentence because the colonel hangs up. All he hears is the dial tone, adding to his already considerable confusion. "Sonofabitch!" he curses and is ready to shout himself hoarse with every other curse he knows when he hears his doorbell ring. "Coming, coming. Just a minute."

It's Paco looking like he just came from a funeral.

Eduardo excuses himself profusely but he just can't ask him in right now. He's got to make an important call.

Paco asks him why the cops came to see him.

"What cops? Have you gone nuts, ¿tú estás loca, chica? Those guys are investigating a visa forgery. Everything will be straightened out tomorrow. Why don't you stop by tonight, we can go out to eat. My treat."

Paco doesn't believe him but figures it's better not to inconvenience his friend. He says good-bye and adds if Eduardo needs anything, he'll be next door. Eduardo can count on him.

Eduardo calls Vianna again. *Let's see if he's got the balls to hang up on me again.* The phone rings once, twice, and continues ringing without anyone answering . . . *Those agents are going to call Columbia to find out who this Mr. Dias is and they'll be back in no time. Sorry, buddy, Mr. Dias doesn't exist. Want to try something else? . . .* the phone is still ringing. Eduardo hangs up; what's he going to do now without Vianna's help? *It's Vianna who knows about guerrillas, counterespionage, the FBI and all that shit. That's his problem. They're already onto his case, they know he's Brazilian. You can't fuck around with an accent and that guy in the bar will recognize him for sure when they show him a picture. It's his problem. Me, the most they can accuse me of is lying. You're a liar, Mr. Silva. What did you say his name was? Mr. Dias? A graduate student at Columbia? Ha, ha, ha, Mr. Silva is joking with us.* At this point Stella takes over and makes Eduardo go into the bathroom, brush his teeth and wash his face. *God, you've got a face like a corpse.* Eduardo notices he's walking around in his socks. *How did I get home? Holy shit, I must have been dead drunk! Marcelo must have brought me home, or maybe it was Ricky, the bitch, running around with that Bostonian*—that's the only image Eduardo can remember from the previous night at the Anvil; everything else is enveloped in a dense fog.

While brushing his teeth, Eduardo decides to take a nice hot relaxing bath. He's all strung up, quickly losing his grip and in danger of going off the deep end. He's got to stay alert, really alert, because he's really close to losing it all. That fucking faggot Vianna. Well, the shit's going to hit the fan, Eduardo's not going to take the fall for anyone.

He steps into the shower, breathing a sigh of relief under the lukewarm water; he lathers himself all over with the bar of soap. He makes an effort to empty his mind, he doesn't want to think about anything. He concentrates on the shower, letting the water spray his back and then his neck. Gradually his muscles begin to relax and his headache to subside.

He decides to call Marcelo and dries himself hurriedly with quick towel strokes. Calling Marcelo is the best way of compensating for Vianna's rejection, that dirty traitor, opportunist, bloodsucking motherfucker. *He hung up on me, well we'll see about that. He'll get his too. Stella doesn't go back on her word.* As he grabs the robe from the hook behind the bathroom door the telephone rings in the bedroom.

Vianna's voice surprises him and before he can say anything, he hears:

"I'm in a public phone booth. Don't mention my name, your phone might be tapped. Listen carefully, now. I want you to hang up when I tell you. I'll be able to determine whether or not your phone is tapped by the sound it makes. Don't get all worked up, I'll call you right back."

After a little while, the phone rings again.

"Nope, it's not tapped," says the colonel triumphantly. "That means the investigation hasn't gotten into high gear yet. So much the better, we can use the extra time."

Eduardo tells him excitedly all the details of the FBI agents' visit and interrogation. He only omits the part about their already knowing of the existence of some well-off fiftyish guy often seen coming and going from the apartment. He's got to keep an ace up his sleeve. He also tells him it was that ugly Jewish bitch at the real estate agency who told the cops about them. He knew she was no good as soon as he set his eyes on her ugly face. By the time Eduardo wraps up his account he is nervous, shaking out of control, saying this time no one's going to save his ass. He doesn't have any idea what to do, what he's going to say to the agents when they come back and tell him there's no Mr. Dias in graduate school at Columbia.

"Eduardo, listen to me. Calm down! The worst is over, you can relax now. Don't get carried away by your emotions. Keep a level head and don't lose courage. We've still got a winning hand."

The colonel's admonitions have a sobering effect on Eduardo, who internalizes them quickly. He's another man now.

"Okay. Now we've got to make a plan. Listen carefully because we won't get another chance to. If you've got any doubts, you'd better air them now. We've got to get all details straight, as if we were synchronizing our watches. Got it? One second off and everything can blow up in our faces. We can't afford to fuck up and we won't. Think positively, Eduardo."

But Eduardo starts to lose his recently acquired confidence as soon as the colonel describes all the difficulties and risks they run.

"Listen carefully to the plan. When the agents return, which they will, there's no doubt about it, because they're not going to swallow all that shit about your student friend or be taken in by the picture of generosity you painted for them . . . Well, when they return, just admit that you're guilty. It's better to admit your guilt straight away or they'll try to break you down. They'll play cat and mouse with you until you can't take it any longer. I know their methods. Just admit your guilt, tell them you were contacted by an agent of the SNI, explain that it's the Brazilian secret service, and that he asked you to cooperate in a sting to capture a group of Brazilian terrorists in New York. Tell them that as a consulate official you really couldn't refuse, that you're really a victim of your own good will and innocence. They understand that shit, most of their plainclothes agents are placed in consulates and embassies. If they don't work for the FBI, they're with the CIA. If you follow my plan, Eduardo, the worst that can happen is they'll bother you a bit. It won't amount to much, no pressure or anything like that, not even psychological games to catch you contradicting yourself. Don't worry. They'll just hassle you a little."

When the colonel finishes, Eduardo remains silent. Eduardo's weakness starts to worry Vianna. When somebody doesn't answer right away it's usually a bad sign. Vianna tries again:

"Eduardo, Eduardo! Say something. You've got to admit that it's not a ridiculous plan. It'll work, you'll see."

"I don't think I'll hold up."

"Sure you will, you can do it."

"I know myself, Vianna, I know what I can withstand and what I can't."

"Think positively!"

"Next time they question me I'll break down, I know it. You don't know how skilled they are, playing good cop bad cop, closing in on you the whole time."

"Sure I know. I know all their games. All you have to do is stay one step ahead of them."

"But what step, Vianna? They're quickly catching on to us. You don't know how many things they've already discovered. They're uncanny."

"I know, I know. I know exactly how they go about things, their techniques, their tactics, the leaps, attacks, and withdrawals. I know it all like the palm of my hand. The problem now, and listen good, Eduardo, the problem now is to get ourselves off the hook by putting them on the scent of one of their own colleagues, the SNI agent who's working undercover. It's for that agent that you rented the apartment, got it? He contacted you at the consulate. Just wait and see, a week from now you'll be freer than a bird."

"Or in prison like a caged bird."

"If you don't stick to the plan."

Eduardo doesn't say anything. Vianna knows he has to insist, it isn't easy to be convincing without the use of force. If that weren't the case, his life would have been quite different. Eduardo starts to get short of breath; it's a bad sign. He's inhaling noisily, he might be crying. Vianna also knows he has to wait, be patient yet persistent. Wait until the crisis blows over. But he just can't let his name be implicated in any of this. Worse than the reaction at the consulate or of his military peers in Brazil, worse than anything imaginable is the reaction of his colleagues in the American intelligence service. He remembers the time one of Johnson's advisers was caught with his hands in the cookie jar in a YMCA steam bath in Washington, just a few blocks from the White House. No one is more intolerant than the Americans, the exact opposite of the British. It's beyond them why the English allow so many faggots into the secret service. Five'll get you ten they're all commies. And since the Americans can never be sure they take all kinds of precautions. Gringos will overlook anything—alcohol, women, handicaps, even drugs—but faggots, never. All faggots are commies. If you're found out, there goes your career; forget about your contacts in the States. You lose everything. Better get the ball rolling.

"Vianna, I can't handle this on my own. Please don't leave me."

"Hey, I'm here, no? Am I not making plans so nothing will happen, so everything comes out right?"

"Vianna, you've got to help me."

"Hey, I'm helping you, no? What else can I do? You can rest assured that as far as the consulate and the Brazilian authorities are concerned, you've been working in my service all along."

"I couldn't care less about that. I shit and piss on what they might think about me. What worries me is I know I won't be able to go through another interrogation. I'll run away if they come again, I know myself."

"Oh no you won't."

"Oh yes I will."

"Hold on, Eduardo, cut all that stupid talk. Be a man!"

"Easier said than done, especially with those two pachyderms pressing me against the wall."

"If you want to save yourself you've got to take advantage of the confusion; you've got to wheedle, fudge, and finagle. You get all hysterical, I can't understand you. You lose your wits, you fumble, you don't know what you're doing, you get tongue-tied, you even shit in your pants."

"That's right, Vianna, bull's-eye."

"Okay, so then resist, concentrate, be firm, don't let yourself be intimidated, get rid of all negative, self-destructive thoughts. Act!"

"I'll try, okay? But on one condition."

"What?"

"That you find some way of getting me out of here, send me back to Brazil, anything."

"That's the worst thing you can do, can't you understand that?"

"Hey, I don't care if it is the worst, the best, or whatever. It's what I want, and right away. That's my condition, take it or leave it."

"Listen Eduardo, when I say it's the worst it's because I know it's the worst. I don't want to see you get hurt. On the contrary, I'm looking after your well-being. Do you think the FBI hasn't alerted the secret service in Brazil? Of course they have. As soon as you land in Galeão airport, wham!, they'll grab you and never let you go again. The secret service in Brazil is no joke, take my word, they'll really fuck you over. They're not like the Americans. Did you forget there's a civil war going on in Brazil?"

"That's what I'm afraid of."

"You've got nothing to do with that, so why worry? (He pauses.) So we're back to scratch. Eduardo, you're innocent, in-no-cent, you hear me? That's why my plan will work, it has to work. If you weren't innocent it wouldn't work."

"That's what worries me. I want to be sure I have a way out in case something goes wrong, that's the reason for my condition. Vianna, you'd better start finding some way of sending me back to Brazil. Pull some strings for me."

"How? You don't even have diplomatic immunity. You're just a clerk at the consulate, a hired office worker."

"I want to go back."

"That's worse."

"I want to go back, I want to go back, I want to go back, back, back, BACK!"

Vianna can feel the danger coming upon them so he decides to play hard. Enough of this childishness. He takes a deep breath,

"Go back to what? Come on, tell me."

"I just want to get out of here, out of this hell."

"Get out and go where?"

"Back to Brazil."

"Where in Brazil? Go on, tell me!"

"Home."

Vianna mercilessly seizes the occasion.

"And you have a home in Brazil?"

"That's right, I do. I've got a father, a mother, I've even got a maid, Bastiana."

"Eduardo, as far as I'm concerned you can lie through your teeth, I really don't care. It's your life and it's your madness too. Do what you want with them. But you can't lie to yourself, boy. If you do you're only hurting yourself."

"What are you getting at? I don't understand what you mean. Go on, tell me."

"I'm the one who doesn't understand you. Do you think I'm some kind of moron or something?"

"Moron? You? Con artist I'd say."

Vianna recognizes the last ditch insolence welling up again within the beast as it's led to the slaughterhouse. Enough playing around, now he's going to go for the jugular.

"When's the last time you heard from your father? Have you received any mail from him since you got to New York?"

Eduardo doesn't say anything. As he loses control of himself he can't figure out where Vianna's going, where he's taking him. Vianna goes in for the kill.

"When's the last time you heard from your mother? Have you received any letters from her?"

"None," Eduardo answers automatically, almost in a whisper. "None." Then he adds: "She hasn't sent anything, nothing . . ."

"You see, Eduardo. Why would you want to return? You don't even have a home."

"Just because they haven't written to me doesn't mean they no longer love me."

"Your getting closer, getting hot . . ."

"Are you trying to say . . ."

"I'm not the one who's trying to say anything."

"If not you, then who?"

"It's not me, so figure it out."

"Who, then?"

"Your own father, Eduardo."

"My father?"

"If you want to call Sergio your father that's your business, but I don't know what he would . . ."

"Are you suggesting . . ."

"I'm not suggesting anything, I'm telling you he's not your father."

Eduardo is speechless.

Vianna realizes he has to tone it down. He overdid it and now the young man is breaking down. A very bad sign.

"Eduardo, you can count on me. I know what you're going through. I didn't want to hurt you, I still don't. But you didn't seem to understand I'm your best friend. I had to bring you back to reality. That's all, you understand, don't you?"

Not a word.

"If I hurt you, please forgive me. But it's better you found out. If it weren't today it would be tomorrow or the next day. It's better this way. Now you won't waste your time dreaming about Brazil, you can put your feet back on the ground."

Still not a word.

"If Sergio doesn't love you anymore, that's his problem. I still love you. You're the son I never had. I got you out of a scrape once and I can do it again. You can count on me, Eduardo, you have a friend you can lean on. Don't you see that?"

Vianna hears a click and then the continuous monotone of the dial tone. He calls Eduardo again. The phone goes on ringing and no one answers.

Eduardo puts the phone back on the cradle, slowly and as if in a trance. He doesn't want to hear anymore, he doesn't want to say another word. He's no longer interested in that call. He cuts it off like one turns off the gas after boiling water for coffee, like one turns off the faucet after a bath. There's no longer any possibility of establishing communication between him and Vianna. Words are now superfluous, exaggerated, abusive. Only feelings count and now they've become totally disengaged from Vianna and all other living beings.

Eduardo no longer has anything. He never did. He thought he did, poor fool, but he was wrong. He no longer has anyone either. Never did. He feels so alone, so lonely that everything around him, all that is solid in his environment melts into thin air. He's just a stone flying through the air, an airplane, a meteorite. An acrobat freed from the pull of gravity. Nothing pulls him back to Earth anymore. He's just a body that doesn't attract anything, that isn't attracted by anything. Cut off from everything.

Eduardo thinks this must be the deepest feeling of loneliness. A body without any force of attraction, just drifting through the emptiness, the void, the hole in the universe. He has no other fate than to drift, wander through the rarefied atmosphere of the heavens, unaffected by the force of the winds, not even jostled from side to side like a leaf. Autumn. It's autumn out there. In his loneliness man has no weight. He's less dense than the air, that's why he just wafts. He's less dense than water, that's why he just floats on the waves. He floats and drifts aimlessly, without any ties. He now realizes he no longer has any ties.

To pretend having nothing is different from really having nothing. It's different, to forget once having had something from not being able to remember because you never had anything. Eduardo can't even want to remember anymore because he never forgot anything; nothing existed for him to forget. Nothing exists period. Nothingness exists. How does one touch it? And for what? How do you feel it? And for what? How do you coexist with it? How? How do you make your way down a road? And where to? Nothingness is out there and I'm here. I'm here inside of it and it's here inside of me. Siamese twins for eternity. Nothingness here and there. Me here and there. The two are inseparable.

We're both a stone, a rolling stone, with no direction home. I'm on my own, like a complete unknown. What a sweet joy it is to exist in nothingness. The sweet pleasure of letting nothingness exist. A feather in the wind doesn't want to know about the four cardinal points. And even if it did, it wouldn't gain anything by it.

Eduardo loses all sense of direction; he knows no shortcuts. He remembers always wanting to take the shortest route through life and save his steps. Now he realizes any and every attempt to save energy is hopeless and useless. If there is any principal, he may as well spend it, and fast, so his economy of steps matches the length of the road taken. Nothing is gained by keeping a few nickels in life's pocket if there's nothing to buy. Nothing exists and the coins only weigh down one's pocket. Might as well cast them to the wind and verify that they're denser than air; that's why they don't float (like he does), they just fall to the ground attracted by the pull of gravity.

Eduardo envies the coins with their weight and would like to imitate them. He lets go of his body and it falls to the bedroom floor like a coin. He's looking for a density greater than that of air. He wants to exist. He rolls on the floor, running into the furniture, feeling in his skin the marks of the hits and misses.

Eduardo wants all things to be reborn out of nothing right where they are and he invents magic tricks with the movements of his body rolling on the ground. Now the bed's legs are human legs and he rolls over to them so he can kiss them submissively. He wraps himself around one of them, in a semicircle, like a worm. He bends his legs and completes the circle as his hands touch his knees. His body is now a circumference around one of the bed's legs. Around a human leg. Eduardo rests and then starts turning the circumference of his body, slapping the bed's frame with his protruding parts. The rotating circumference frees his head from the pain caused by hitting against the frame. But now his knees hurt. Eduardo creates the movement of day and night like he does his own, the movement of fear and freedom like he does his own, the movement of pleasure and pain like he does his own. Life and death, they feel the same. How does one distinguish one's knee from one's head?

Eduardo recreates from nothing the possibility of the existence of the world, and within it, the possibility of the existence of the movement of life.

His body's circumference rotates with more difficulty. Eduardo is getting tired.

Now he rediscovers the possibility of force, and within it, the possibility of exhaustion.

Eduardo opens the circumference and stretches out his body on the ground. He turns over on his stomach and opens his arms to form a cross. He plays at not knowing where to put his nose. "Nose," he says and sniffs along the floor like a whiny dog. He plays at Pinocchio. He's in fairy-tale land. He makes believe he gets up and he makes believe he hits his head again against the frame. He would like to remember the pain caused by a bump on his forehead. He makes believe.

Eduardo rediscovers the possibility of remembering, and within it, the possibility of the present.

He guides his body outward from beneath the bed and stands up, fearing he might hurt himself.

He decides to phone Marcelo. But first he thinks it's necessary to know why he wants to call Marcelo. He grabs a pen and a piece of paper from the coffee table and makes a list:

1. Speak about last night; find out what happened at the Anvil.

2. Ask if he saw Ricky leave with the Bostonian.

3. Ask how he got back home. Was it with Marcelo's help or did he come back on his own like a sleepwalker.

Those are yesterday's matters. Now today's.

4. Send Marcelo to find out why the FBI got into the picture. It's important for him to tip off the group.

5. Complain bitterly about Vianna, but careful not to let the ace up his sleeve drop.

6. Ask Marcelo if he wouldn't like to change his name to Mário Correia Dias.

You'd do me a favor, Marcelo, it would save my hide.

Eduardo goes over to the phone. He has the paper in his hand. He dials Marcelo's number. He's about to change his mind when someone answers in English. Eduardo tries to identify the voice; it sounds familiar. He asks for Marcelo in English. The voice says Marcelo's not at home. Would he like to leave a message. Please say Eduardo called.

"Is it you, Eddie?"

Eduardo recognizes the voice.

"Ricky!"

Neither says anything. Ricky breaks the silence to say Marcelo went to a meeting and he answered the phone because he thought it might be him, Marcelo, with an urgent message.

"What are you doing in Marcelo's apartment?"

"I slept here."

"You slept there?"

"After leaving you in your own apartment last night. You really got wrecked, huh? You probably don't even remember."

"Did he invite you?"

"Yes."

Eduardo puts the receiver down gently as if in a trance. He doesn't want to hear another word. The call doesn't interest him anymore. He cut it off like one turns off the gas . . .

Eduardo goes out without closing his apartment door.

10

. . . .

Marcelo gets back to his apartment late.

Beset by disturbing news reports—transmitted to them from Brazil via Falcão—the meeting was intense and lasted too long. The repressive military machine was stockpiling more and newer weapons, readying itself for escalating its actions. The junta, composed of the three heads of the armed forces, had positioned the vice president, Pedro Aleixo, to take power. The air force had refined its perversities in matters of torture. It was a return to the gestapo. The scramble among the three branches to have their candidates named successor to the presidency manifested itself in all kinds of sabre rattling. To the victor the spoils. Victory was in the hands of the toughest.

The news from abroad was giving some of the companheiros cold feet. They could hang you upside down, apply electric shocks to your balls, your cunt, your ass, your nipples. They could put you in tubs of freezing water or in chambers that fluctuated wildly from hot to cold. The interrogations would be endless. All they could foresee was violence and more violence. Thirst, hunger, loneliness. Punches, kicks in the balls, deafening slaps over your ears. Then the corpses would be thrown from planes into the ocean, adding new names every day to the list of the disappeared. And to make matters worse, spies had infiltrated almost every organization. How would you go about detecting them?

The future government would be decided by the military. Liberal officers openly denounced the shameless tactics of the army in support of its hardline candidate, Medici. The entire country was a barracks in which the armed forces alone held elections. There were no rules for fair play and each branch had its own electoral college representing its interests. The army, the most brazen of the three, took the lead. They were the first to spurn the civilians who tried to cut a deal with them in 1964 and they carefully laid the trap that led to dissolving the national congress. Alone at the top. That's what they wanted, that's what they still want.

The euphoria felt after the American ambassador's kidnapping now gave way to concealed doubts and, in some cases, openly expressed fears. It reminded Marcelo of a poem by Drummond, which he quoted: "The spy sits at the dinner table with us." Another companheiro quoted the following line: "It's a time when the five senses condense into one."

Next came Marcelo's turn to report.

He said he couldn't see how to go about giving Professor Aníbal a good scare. Aníbal had taken every imaginable precaution as regards security and maybe even other measures which he hadn't been able to observe. The guy was a sly fox, no doubt about that. He had chosen a building with an intercom and a doorman who wouldn't let in a fly if it wasn't cleared with the tenant. Marcelo watched for a bit when he left Professor Aníbal's and noticed the doorman was absolutely strict about clearing all visitors. This wasn't a doorman but a security guard. Worse still, the apartment door had at least four locks and was made of steel. And on top of all this, Professor Aníbal was paralyzed from the waist down and could only move around in a wheelchair.

Eduardo (alias Rosebud) said he wouldn't have any problem pulling a Richard Widmark, running the wheelchair down a stairwell. He would even add that notorious villainous laugh. The more he found out about the man, he went on, the more certain he was that Aníbal was a real sonofabitch. Had the others read the article he wrote in William Buckley's *National Review* defending the military junta? Aníbal has established a close relationship with Republican right-wingers.

None of the others had read or heard of the article, so Rosebud promised to bring Xerox copies to the next meeting. He had done his homework, for which he was praised by Falcão.

Marcelo agreed with Rosebud, intellectually the guy was a real fuck-up. It was so difficult to put up with some of Aníbal's outlandish remarks that during the conversation Marcelo had lost his cool two or three times. He didn't regret it because that way his visit seemed more natural.

You'd better watch out, said another companheiro, he could turn you in right away. He's notorious among Brazilian academics for being quick on the draw with that accusing finger of his. It's probably itching right now.

His weak point, the only one he detected, Marcelo continued, is his wife, Leila. She gave the impression of being a little touched, maybe even crazy.

Rosebud asked him if she was a bleached blond. She might be modeling herself after that American look, the Jean Harlow look.

Marcelo said she's a pretty brunette, really built. She'd be right up Vasco's alley: she plays according to her man's rules and he controls her completely. He's too much, though. Vain, narcissistic, egocentric, so much so, in Marcelo's opinion, that if the companheiros did her in he'd be no sadder than if his neighbor's poodle were run over by a car. It's silly to worry about her, a waste of time, he thought. Aníbal was even capable of thanking them if they kidnapped her.

Vasco didn't agree with Marcelo. Very often it's not the blow itself that hurts people like Aníbal but its aftereffects. That's what they're afraid of, you know; they've got all kinds of important people around them to whom they've got to answer, they're easily controlled by the opinions of those people. Just look at Valdevinos, right now the fucker's shitting bricks. His wife will come home tomorrow and find his credit cards in the mail; the ambassador will receive his ID papers with a note informing him of the colonel's activities; the cops will receive his secret service papers . . . In the end, it's his comrades in arms here and back home who will put the screws on him. That's what they're afraid of.

One of the companheiros asked how he could be so sure of the attaché's ordeals.

Vasco told him he was fucking Valdevinos's maid and she gave him the lowdown on everything. He continued his reasoning: Valdevinos could easily get rid of the writing on the wall, all he had to do was have the wall painted over and all our work would be in vain. But now we've got him by the balls; everyone is going to know who's the most flaming queen of all. All it takes is for someone to spread the rumor and his reputation's down the drain, he'll never get another diplomatic post abroad as long as he lives. Vasco then asked Marcelo if he spoke to Eduardo as they had agreed and if everything went as planned.

No, things didn't exactly go as planned. Eduardo got stinking drunk. Marcelo was at least able to keep him from totally falling apart. But it's possible he'll go to Valdevinos.

The possibility made Vasco uneasy.

Marcelo said he exaggerated a bit; what he meant is that Eduardo wasn't easy to win over. He owed the attaché a big favor. He's the one who got him his job at the consulate. That was the only reason he let Valdevinos change his clothes in his apartment. He was reciprocating. Eduardo has principles.

Carlinhos asked Marcelo what he meant by principles.

Marcelo told him to cut the shit, man.

When Marcelo returns to his apartment he finds Ricky acting nervous. He has to go and he can't wait any longer. Marcelo insists he stay, at least until the end of the afternoon. They could go out for a bite. Marcelo invites him to lunch.

As Ricky goes out the door, he says, "Marcelo, Eddie called. He wanted to speak with you. I answered the phone because it kept ringing and I thought you might be trying to reach me. I was wrong, I'm sorry. Eddie was quite distressed ('depressed' is the word he used). You'd better call him."

Marcelo is upset Eduardo discovered his sneakiness; he's probably plotting his revenge right now. *I don't think I can come straight out and tell him; I'll have to have a few drinks, it's the only way.* It's the only way he can muster enough courage to tell him what happened Saturday night. Yes, he's going to call him; he says good-bye to Ricky.

The telephone is on the coffee table next to the sofa in the one-room apartment. He dials and waits. Nothing. He waits some more and then hangs up. He dials again. Nothing. He went out, it's not even worth going over there. He must have gone out to walk off his hangover and his depression. Then to Julio's to make a quick pickup. It's always crowded late Sunday afternoons. A quickie, as Eduardo is used to saying. It strikes Marcelo he might speak with the Cuban (yuck!) next door, they're good friends. When she's down, Stella probably goes to La Cuca's to listen to boleros—*help me make it through the night*—and to exchange tragic love stories. She must be going out of her head. Marcelo doesn't want to think he cheated on his friend behind her back. He tries to keep it out of his mind but he can't help thinking what Stella will do when they meet.

Out of her head, she'll greet me with her hand on her hip—shaking her head in an "okay, buster" gesture—and create the loudest ruckus ever heard in the neighborhood. Screaming like Flip Wilson's Geraldine, her voice will echo throughout the tenement: "You fucking bitch, you stole my man!" A sight to see. She'll grab her broom in the kitchen and she'll sweep me away, shoo, you bitch, you're no longer my friend. Get the fuck out! When Stella loses her head all hell breaks loose. *It won't do me any good to say I just wanted to see what it was like. You spoke so much about him I wanted to get a little piece of the action, but now you can have him all to yourself. He's all yours, girl, don't worry!* He imagines himself picking Ricky up in his arms and tossing him to Stella, who catches him and raises her face arrogantly, lowering her eyelids and shooting him a glance of infinite disdain: You scum! And what if Eduardo doesn't want Ricky back? He imagines a game of badminton in which they're tossing Ricky back and forth: you take him, no, you take him, he's yours. No way. Marcelo laughs to himself imagining Ricky as a shuttlecock. He's got the clap, you keep him. No, you take him. He could tell Stella Ricky's just a jerk; only Stella, lacking in taste as she is, could possibly think he's worth anything. You can find millions like him in the street, my dear. Millions, Stella. You must be blind. Just show up at any Halloween Day parade. Marcelo feels like a hypocrite. He's giving up on Ricky only on account of Stella. He imagines another scene: the three of them meet, Stella takes off her shoe and hits him with it. But he knows how to defuse Eduardo's anger: disparage the whore! He stinks like all gringos, that's some stench that comes from below. How can you stand it! For Marcelo it was pure torture. You'd never believe they were the ones who invented deodorants. And when he takes off his shoes, whew! his socks walk off on their own like cartoon characters, and you've got to hold your poor nostrils that beg for mercy. He doesn't bathe; Ricky is just like all the others, he doesn't wash. He's so dirty, if you don't tell him to wash first, it makes you nauseous. Who could stand him? Only your friend, the Black Widow. She gets off if a little shit's thrown in when the going gets hot. Marcelo's got to convince Eduardo. He'll fall for it. Like all Brazilian mulattos, he doesn't think about the quality of the meat; but just take away his shower and his deodorant and he'll go beserk. He'll fall for it. He'll say, hey, he's not with me. Here, take Ricky, he's yours. And me, I won't say no. Afterward he'll even be grateful for getting rid of the burden. He almost got stuck with that nincompoop in his apartment but he'll be thankful he was saved from making a big mistake. It hadn't struck Marcelo before that the gringo doesn't even have a place to sleep. Can you imagine? The gringo settles into your apartment like it's a hotel and the next thing you know he'll want home-cooked meals and his laundry done. You'll turn into Gloria Swanson in *Sunset Boulevard* giving him money by day and pussy by night. You'll be slaving away at the consulate and he'll just laze around, having a good time. The guy's a good-for-nothing. Don't say you weren't warned. The night he stayed over all Marcelo did was give him a little wink and he wanted to settle right in. He said he had no place to sleep, that it was late and looked like it was going to rain. Marcelo told him it was okay for the night but in the morning he'd have to leave. Well, as you know, there's only one bed in the apartment and in the middle of the night, before you could say lickety split, Marcelo was on top of him. Saint Marcelo he ain't. Nor would Eduardo want him to be, or would he?

Feeling obligated, Marcelo goes over to Eduardo's apartment. He rings the bell but no one answers. He decides to ring his neighbor's bell.

Paco, distrustful, opens the door; he had already had more than his share of cops that day.

Marcelo identifies himself.

Paco feels relieved and tells him Eduardo always speaks about him. He asks him in and closes the door after first looking up and down the hallway. It's only a humble apartment but Marcelo should make himself at home just the same. A friend of Eduardo's is a friend of his.

Marcelo notices the Cuban looks less nervous now, but he doesn't want to or know how to get too comfy with him. He's only there to find out if Paco knows Eduardo's whereabouts. He'll be caught dead before he lets this reactionary get familiar. He resists. He knows the Cuban is sincere in what he says, but he's got to put up resistance. He either says nothing or answers in monosyllables.

"I came by to find out if you knew Eduardo's whereabouts."

"Oh, you can't stand there in the middle of the living room. Go on, chico, siéntate, sit down."

Marcelo refuses. He resists the Cuban's invitation. He knows his friendliness is sincere but he resists just the same.

"Listen, forget the formalities, please. We have so much to speak about. I'm really confused and I need to talk to someone."

Marcelo yields to his curiosity. He takes the seat on the sofa that Paco offers him. He says he can't imagine why Paco's confused. He figures something unusual must have happened to him or to Eduardo. If that's the case he should confide in him. That's why he's there.

"You don't know the half of it, chico. There's so much going on I don't know what to think or what to do."

Marcelo notices Paco is sad, anxious, and disheartened. It makes him even more curious, but he conceals his interest. He looks around the apartment, registering the decor. He doesn't bring up the subject, he doesn't want the conversation to go off track. Paco, silent and absorbed in thought, doesn't take notice of Marcelo's eyes. Finally he opens up:

"I don't know what I can do to save Eduardo."

"Save him?"

"Yes, save him."

"Is someone trying to kill him?"

"I know who it is. I'm the only one who knows. His life is in danger. He knows it and I know he knows it. But he won't tell me anything nor will he go to the police. It can only be blackmail, a serious case of blackmail," Paco whispers the final words as if the walls had ears.

"Don't you think he's imagining those things; after all, he was drunk when you saw him."

"He didn't tell me anything; I discovered it on my own. I saw it with my own eyes."

"What did you discover?"

"That the guy in black leather wants to kill him. He's afraid of that guy."

"Why don't you explain it to me from the start, Paco. What man in black are you talking about? Did he have a gun? How do you know he wanted to kill Eduardo?"

"She's an S & M queen. Ever since she came by yesterday after-noon Eduardo hasn't been the same. The bitch has complete control over him. I no longer know him."

"Everyone knows he helped out a friend who was in a bind. That's all it was, Paco. I don't understand how you can jump from that to such conclusions: death, murder, blackmail. And the stuff about Eduardo no longer being the same, I don't understand it. Listen, Paco, are you sure you're not seeing things?"

Marcelo thinks Paco is off his rocker. Has he always been this way? He heard the rooster crow this morning and now he thinks Armageddon is upon us.

"I don't even understand myself anymore. I tried to help him but he no longer wanted my help. He wouldn't let me inside his apartment after the two cops came by. All I wanted was to help . . ."

"Two cops, Paco? Don't you think you're exaggerating a little too much, making a mountain out of a mole hill?"

"Two cops, I swear it!" He makes a cross out of his right thumb and forefinger, brings it to his lips and kisses it. "I swear on my mother's grave, I'm telling you the truth. Why would I want to lie? They came to question him and they stayed in his apartment for more than an hour."

Suddenly Marcelo begins to worry. He changes his tactics.

2

As Marcelo leaves Paco's apartment, he notices a cop stationed outside Eduardo's door and another one in a patrol car. He feels he's lucky to have avoided running into them. Had he arrived at Eduardo's door a few moments later than he did, he'd be answering to these cops now.

He calls Falcão from a phone booth on the corner.

3

Late on Sunday afternoon, just as he's reading the article "Brazil in Turmoil" in the *New York Times,* Professor Aníbal gets a call from Washington.

It's from FBI headquarters. After identifying itself, the voice on the phone apologizes for bothering him so late on a Sunday afternoon, but the urgency of the matter justifies the inconvenience. He explains that the SNI in Brasília gave the professor's name as a trustworthy contact. They thought he could help the Bureau solve a mystery that threatened to become a problem for the two friendly nations.

Professor Aníbal can't imagine how he can help but they can count on him. He'll do his best. He adds he'll be on call for the Bureau if they wish.

The voice asks if he's willing to meet with two agents in a short while. They're the best in the New York office. They'll fill him in on all pertinent details and together the three will hopefully come up with some helpful suggestions. The Bureau has hit a dead end, Professor Aníbal will understand when he meets the agents.

Professor Aníbal says very well, he'll be expecting them.

Aníbal calls Leila, he wants her to come into his study. He needs to talk to her.

Leila appears in the doorway.

Aníbal asks if she wouldn't mind going out for a walk, maybe take in a movie. If she hurries she can make the six o'clock screening. Or she can go out and do whatever she likes but please not return before eight.

She says she can't take it anymore, she can't even spend one whole afternoon at home. Yesterday it was that young man, Marcelo. Today he won't even tell her who it is. She can't understand why all the secrecy. But don't get all worked up, she adds, she won't give away her treasure. If she hasn't given it up yet, she's not about to do so now.

Aníbal cuts her short and tells her to stop breaking his balls. Cut the shit!

She interrupts him saying, look here, what kind of language is that? Who'd ever think Professor Aníbal of Columbia University speaks like that!

The comment rolls off his back. He goes on: he's asking her to be understanding, she did it yesterday, didn't she? He went along with all of her whims and all for the insignificant price of going out for a walk so he could receive Marcelo.

"My whims? Or yours?" she insists ironically.

"Listen, there's no time to discuss your flights of fancy, my visitors will be here any moment. What do you want? For people to see us quarrelling?"

Leila goes to the dressing room but readies herself so slowly she'll still be there when the visitors arrive.

Aníbal wheels himself to the kitchen, to the intercom, and bellows hysterically that she's taking too long, that she's doing it on purpose, he knows her well. She's stalling.

Leila thinks, *he really knows me,* but she denies it saying she couldn't find the right outfit for the weather. The temperature was fine at this hour but later on when she returned it was she and not he who would have to put up with the windy streets.

The intercom buzzes. Aníbal, already stationed next to it, answers. The doorman tells him he's got two visitors, Messers. Marshall and Robbins.

The professor says okay and wheels himself to the bedroom where Leila has just finished getting ready and is looking at herself in the mirror. It's too late now, he'll have to introduce her, but please tell them you're sorry and that you're on your way out. He wheels himself back to the vestibule, followed by his wife.

The doorbell rings.

Aníbal signals for her to wait and then tells Leila to open the door. She opens the locks under her husband's hawklike gaze. She asks the two gentlemen to come in. She excuses herself, she's on her way out. She kisses her husband honey good-bye. She goes out and locks the door behind her.

The chief and his assistant can't hide their surprise on seeing the professor in a wheelchair. The chief tries to figure out whether it was a recent accident or if he was born with a physical defect. Not being able to say for sure and not wanting to prolong their host's obvious embarrassment, the chief extends his hand: "Professor Paes Leme, I presume." He says his name is Mr. Marshall, of the FBI, and in his left hand holds up his badge. "This is Mr. Robbins, my assistant."

The professor shakes his hand; he'll be very pleased if he can be of some help.

"We've gone through some difficult times in our recent history," says Aníbal to initiate the conversation. "Rebellion in the barracks, student unrest in the universities, bank robberies, urban guerrillas murdering innocent people in cold blood, and now the kidnapping of the ambassador of a friendly neighbor. Just when my country— the sleeping giant (he smiles)—is about to wake up and leap into the future."

The agents understand little of what the professor says but they keep their professional smiles in place, silently expressing their agreement.

"But they won't prevail, no matter how hard they try. We're on to them and they'll be weeded from Brazilian society, even if we have to use violence. The revolutionary military government is not inherently violent nor does it want to resort to violence. It's those criminals who are responsible, they're forcing it to be violent, reluctantly, I can assure you. The military wants peace, harmony, and prosperity."

The chief takes advantage of Aníbal's brief pause to tell him he can see why Brasília gave his name as that of a trustworthy contact.

"You gentlemen cannot imagine how happy it makes me that our two intelligence services are working together, even after what happened in September."

Aníbal just now realizes the two agents are still standing in the vestibule. He apologizes:

"How could I be so absentminded! Here I am talking away and you're still standing there; where's my hospitality? But please, come in." He maneuvers his wheelchair as close to the wall as possible so the two men can get by him.

He wheels himself right behind them. He points to a sofa and invites them to sit down and then positions his wheelchair in its usual place in the living room.

The chief says he doesn't want to take too much of Professor Paes Leme's precious time; he knows it's Sunday, a day of rest, and so it would be better to get right down to business. He takes out of the inside pocket of his suit jacket a notebook with a list of all the facts of the case.

Agent Marshall had his doubts ever since he received orders from Washington to interview Professor Paes Leme of Columbia University. The voice on the phone said he was one of the greatest minds in Brazil; he should treat him as if he were requesting the cooperation of an authority of the stature of Arthur Schlesinger. Marshall was against the idea—the FBI doesn't like getting involved with intellectuals ("eggheads" is the word he used). His experience told him they always end up criticizing what you do. But orders are orders.

Glancing from time to time at his notebook, Marshall gives a summary of the case, emphasizing those points that seemed most enigmatic to him. He finishes the summary by noting that the investigation was moving along fine until Mr. Silva disappeared mysteriously a few hours ago. He disappeared from his apartment without even closing his door.

The assistant adds that, perhaps, in retaliation, the group of terrorists had kidnapped the young man. Maybe he was the one they were after and not the other man.

The chief continues, informing the professor that since Mr. Silva is an official of the Brazilian consulate—even at the low rank of clerk—Washington does not want any misunderstandings with the Brazilian authorities. They might think the whole affair was planned by the CIA—on a minor scale, of course, compared with the kidnapping of the U.S. ambassador—in order to work out some kind of exchange of hostages.

The professor listened attentively, adding here and there a "strange, very strange," which punctuated the agents' account.

At the end of the account the two agents looked at the professor to see if he had the key to unlock the mystery.

The professor nods his head, his face glowing with a victorious grin: "Gentlemen, I think I can be helpful, very helpful." He pauses and then continues: "It's incredible how subversives only think about disturbing the peace. In Brazil it's the same. The citizen is no longer safe in his own apartment, car, or place of work. When you least expect it, they show up wearing masks and wielding machine guns; they tell you to put your hands up, this is a robbery or this is a kidnapping. As if the solution to the real problems of Brazil were this cheap imitation of a cops-and-robbers movie. It's obvious the disruptions are nothing more than the work of disaffected youths."

The chief wants to lead the conversation in such a way that the professor won't digress from the business at hand. He figures intellectuals are like that, they talk about everything except the topic at hand. But he draws on his experience, foreseeing that he has to be patient with the professor.

"What I don't understand is the American press. There's no way of making sense of it. Today I read an article in the *Times*—perhaps you also read it?—in which the Brazilian revolution is characterized as a coup. It criticizes the repression, the censorship, but praises what is referred to as the Aesopic language of the arts. If you read between the lines you can readily see that article defends the terrorists who kidnapped your ambassador. You can't tell what side the reporters are on. But, in effect, only fools don't know. Basically, they're against you." He gives the agents a penetrating glance, which surprises them, making them think they're being criticized.

The chief can't hide a Yankee Doodle Dandy show of displeasure when he realizes the professor's reasoning is actually an attack:

"Thank God we have a free press here in the United States. And we're very proud of keeping it that way."

"So you think it's freedom, eh? Tell me now, in all sincerity, doesn't the press publish reports that one day are unfavorable and the next day favorable to the Black Panthers? I can tell you what freedom of the press in the United States and in France really is."

The chief changes his opinion of the professor, he's one of us, a different kind of intellectual. He begins to pay more attention to what he says.

"Listen, when it's a matter of foreign policy, journalists here and abroad are all incendiary critics. But when it's national matters that are at stake—national security and the welfare of the citizenry—they're conservative through and through."

The chief tells the professor he's sorry for his outburst before but since he doesn't understand foreign policy matters too well—he explains that he trained for the FBI and not the CIA—he's not in a position to judge the irresponsibility of American journalists. What he was really referring to were national problems, about which he and the *Times* had little to disagree on.

"Ah, you can't know what the commie press in Brazil does with the pro-terrorist articles that appear here. They republish them on the first page and raise as much enthusiasm as a holiday parade for which workers get the day off."

The chief listens and learns, all the while casting glances of approval at his assistant.

"And that's what subversives call the negative image of the regime in the foreign press. Since everything today goes through the media, they speak of the tarnished image of our country abroad. They speak of all kinds of images but eventually hit the nail on the head when they point to the military regime's image as an authoritarian dictatorship. You've got to see it. Any of those articles will do to rally people to the subversives' cause."

"And how can the government rule with the pressure put on it by the press?" the assistant asks, curiosity having gotten the better of him.

"It can't, no regime in the world can rule under such conditions. That's why we had to create laws to protect the rule of government. And what does the press have to say about that? You'll never guess. They cry censorship! Censorship, can you believe that?"

"I understand what you're saying," said the chief.

"But is there or isn't there censorship," the assistant middle-classedly asks.

"Do you think there's censorship in your country just because no newspaper will publish the incendiary writings of Malcolm X or Jerry Rubin?"

"Newspapers can't waste their precious space on that rubbish; if they did, we'd have a real loony bin on our hands here."

"It's the same in Brazil. The only difference is that there we've institutionalized the self-protection of the regime under the form of law. It's necessary in a young country like ours, in which many politicians are irresponsible and a large percentage of the population is illiterate. Here you can leave the whole thing on automatic pilot; the owners of the press themselves are the first to impose self-censorship."

"Self-censorship . . ." the chief repeats, as if repeating it he'll understand it better.

The assistant tells the professor he'll read the *Times* article and then send a letter of protest to the editor. He's also going to start a publicity campaign in favor of the military regime. It's those commie journalists that are our enemies. To get the ball rolling, he's going to reproduce the professor's words for the next meeting of the American Legion. He's their secretary.

The assistant's ability to express himself surprises the chief, who hastens to take the lead in the conversation.

"What you say is very important and we understand your frustrations, Professor Paes Leme. I assure you you have our support. But the best way of helping your country, and ours as well, is by helping us bring our investigation to a successful conclusion. Let's get to work, shall we?"

Professor Aníbal realizes he's taken a long detour from the matter at hand and apologizes.

The chief says there's no need to apologize, his words were very instructive and looks at the assistant for support.

The assistant nods his assent.

"To work then!" says Aníbal, agreeing and taking the lead. He begins by remembering that while the chief gave his account several ideas occurred to him that might be of help in solving the mystery of the apartment broken into on Amsterdam Avenue. He tells them he's always been very suspicious of an organization founded by Brazilian students and artists in a Protestant church on 46th Street. He did a little investigating and discovered it was a group of subversives.

The chief asks him for the name of the church.

Aníbal has it on the tip of his tongue: Saint Clement's Episcopal Church.

The chief recognizes the name; it has appeared in several investigations into political matters. He tells the assistant to make a note of it.

Aníbal gets back on course again and gives them the name of the organization: "Brazil-U.S. People's Fraternity." He adds that once he knew the name he said to himself the word *people* wasn't fooling anyone; it smacked of China.

"China?" the assistant, surprised, asks.

"In a manner of speaking," the professor explains. "They can't even camouflage the purpose of the group. The name itself points in the direction of the ideologies that animate the group."

"And the Chinese are involved?"

"I doubt it. In my humble opinion, they smoke cigars, drink rum, and dance the rumba."

The two agents look at each other perplexed.

The professor now knows he's controlling the conversation and gives them a mini-lesson on Cuba's infiltration into Latin America.

"And now the Cuban commies want to infiltrate the United States? Is that what you're saying, professor? You mean we don't have enough with the ones who get a free ride to Miami?"

"It's a hypothesis!" says Aníbal triumphantly. And he goes on giving them information on the People's Fraternity. The organization didn't work out too well so it was disbanded. But the members are still roaming about the city.

The chief would like to have some names. Would it be too much of an inconvenience for the professor to . . . ?

They're Brazilian.

That's why we came to you in the first place.

Aníbal says he doesn't know the majority of them personally. He knows some of them by name because they're protégés of the commie press. He gives the names of Saul Ferreira, a painter, Eduardo Lima, a filmmaker, and Flávio Leitão, a writer.

The chief asks the professor if he wouldn't write the names down for him in the assistant's notebook; the assistant gets up and hands it to the professor along with his pen. The professor writes the names down and adds two others, whom he thinks are the founders of the organization. They're probably the ones who make the political contacts. The other three are useful to them but innocent. They help camouflage the real purpose of the organization.

The professor adds he has some additional information, maybe not too relevant to the case at hand, but you never know. He'll give it to them on the condition that they do not include it in any of their reports.

"Off the record," the chief agrees.

The professor is referring to the military attaché at the consulate, Eduardo's protector.

Agent Marshall is taken aback and keeps silent.

The professor drums his fingers on the wheelchair's armrest waiting for their reaction. Nothing. He starts all over, asking them again not to let it out of these four walls; it's a delicate and intimate matter. If it ever became public it could affect the ambassador and imagine the consequences. As for the attaché and Eduardo it seems there's more than just friendship there. How should we say it, a kind of male bonding.

The chief doesn't dare ask the attaché's name. He can still hear the Dominican bodeguero's words, which he committed to memory. He described a middle-aged queen who often used the apartment. But he doesn't remember the graffiti sprayed on the wall making any references to homosexual relations. Their tone was definitely political. He's about to background the information in his memory when the professor takes up the matter again, remarking that no one at the consulate can understand why the military attaché has lunch every week with a mere clerk, preferring him over all other colleagues of his own rank.

"But this is another kettle of fish," the assistant dares to say. "I think we've got enough information for our case."

The professor is not about to quit so early in the game. He tells them he's known colleagues from Rio to come to New York who've had a suspicious past back home. Now, how could a consulate hire someone like that? Wouldn't they check his background? The professor doesn't want to implicate this young man in anything—far from it, let him earn his living as he can—but what bothers him—and, please, don't get him wrong—is the image of Brazilians that Americans are likely to have. Soon everyone's going to think Brazil is an enormous fruit orchard; a new stereotype to replace the one you all had of us running around the Amazon in loin cloths.

The chief tells the professor not to worry, Americans are very tolerant nowadays. They're not going to throw stones at their neighbor's house if their own is made of glass. Has the professor ever been to San Francisco?

"Tolerance, my foot. Let's not get things confused here. When you see a kid like that you don't think twice about it, he sells sexual favors. You know more than I do about all the scandals in Washington."

The chief is convinced. He says he'll go to the consulate the following day and by hook or by crook he'll find the young man. He'll also make an appointment with the ambassador. He asks the professor if he thinks he should say anything to the ambassador about the young man. Off the cuff, you know, as if for no special reason.

The professor doesn't say anything.

The chief asks him again, this time with his eyes. He'd like an answer to his question.

"It can't do any harm. Especially if he's involved up to his eyebrows in terrorism. Yes, I think you may ask about him. You may . . . actually, you ought to. The ambassador should be able to trust his military attaché."

"And what if the young man is not guilty of anything? If he's only the victim of some mix-up?" the assistant interjects. "It could be, you know, we don't have anything concrete on him. And who knows? Maybe he's infiltrated the terrorist group. Maybe he's a spy in the service of the military attaché?"

"That's unlikely; if you knew what these Brazilian terrorists are like . . . ? They're all queer, excuse the expression, but it's about time we crossed our t's and dotted our i's. The young man and the terrorists are not enemies; on the contrary, they understand each other. They're all cut from the same cloth and they're all into the same dirty business."

11

· · · ·

On that same Sunday around four in the afternoon, agents Marshall and Robbins returned to Mr. Silva's apartment on orders from Washington. As is evident from the preceding page, the informant did not tell the truth when first questioned. Columbia University rosters do not include anyone named Mário Correia Dias, or any Brazilian student with a name even remotely like it. The agents inspected this year's rosters as well as those of the preceding five years. Furthermore, the declarations made by the two local businessmen indicate that the real tenant of the apartment in question is a well-groomed foreigner in his fifties (possibly of Brazilian origin), evidently a man of means and of questionable moral conduct.

It was the agents' intention to question Mr. Silva again. They wanted to find out the tenant's true identity. Mrs. Simon was not very helpful in this regard because she had dealt with him only on a few brief occasions. The agents believed that without the tenant's identity, it would be difficult to: (a) continue their investigation, (b) come to any hypotheses about the defacement of the apartment (except that the graffiti were of a political nature), and (c) devise a plan for the capture of the possible "terrorists" involved in this crime.

The agents were convinced that Eduardo was crucial for the successful outcome of the investigation. The declarations of an informant recommended by the Washington office, a Professor X (he asked to remain anonymous in any official reports), contradicted that assumption. He provided the agents with valuable, clear, and exact information. It was not difficult, as will be explained below, to break up the newly formed New York chapter of a group of terrorists based in Brazil or Cuba. As for Mr. Silva, his disappearance has remained a mystery and it seems as if it will stay that way.

After the meeting with Professor X, the agents realized that the case needed further attention; it might possibly lead them to even more dramatic subversive activity. With this in mind, they sought help from the New York Police Department, which provided (a) a guard stationed at Mr. Silva's door (the agents decided to transfer him inside the premises so as not to arouse too much curiosity among the other tenants) and (b) a patrol car in case of an emergency. The Police Department's assistance was subsequently increased; the agents also sought help from the Missing Persons Department, since it was not unlikely that Mr. Silva had been kidnapped.

Mr. Silva's neighbor, Mr. Ayala, a Cuban refugee, was peremptory in his declaration on Monday morning. There is no reason to doubt his statement, although agent Robbins classified the witness as having a "fantasmatonic imagination" (for a definition of the term see the chapter on "Witnesses" in the pamphlet *Interrogation Procedures*). He testified that Mr. Silva left his apartment alone and ran like a beast down the stairs (it should be remembered that said apartment is on the fifth floor) for a meeting he couldn't miss. This piece of testimony eliminates the kidnapping hypothesis. The motive for the sudden departure in such a rampaging manner remained unclear and Mr. Ayala was not much help in clearing it up. Careful analysis of passenger lists of flights bound for Brazil led the investigators to conclude that he did not leave the city or the country. The suspect's family, which was contacted in the city of Rio de Janeiro (Brazil), declared they did not know his whereabouts in recent days.

The following account was drafted by the Department of Missing Persons of the New York Police Department.

On the first of December, almost two days after the warrant for the suspect's arrest was issued, a patrol car on duty in the Bowery detected—among a group of winos causing a commotion in the entrance to a liquor store—a young man who fit Mr. Silva's description. He was carrying a bottle of Four Roses in his hand. Officer Williams separated him from the group and questioned him.

In his log, filed in the archives of the Bowery Precinct, it is stated that the suspect had no identification papers of any kind. He was wearing clothing of high quality, which was dirty and ragged (the FBI explains in a footnote that this detail is of little consequence since the affluent residents of the area buy expensive clothing which, after a season or two, they donate to the Salvation Army). He had a very bushy Afro, a hairstyle popular among blacks; he was unshaven and his face was grimy. It was evident, however, that his skin was darker than indicated on the papers provided by the Brazilian consulate. The suspect was in a state of extreme destitution and drunkenness. He was probably starving, according to Officer Williams's interpretation of the suspect's total apathy and lack of aggressiveness.

He also did not have the appearance or accent of a stranger (Brazilian in this case). He looked more like a Hispanic, born and raised in this country, taking into consideration that he spoke English natively and had no detectable accent. He did not answer the questions put to him by the officers, either because he was inebriated or because he refused on personal grounds. When he did speak, he did so in a haphazard manner. Neither of the officers was able to make any sense of his words. He did not react when the officers asked him if he was Mr. Silva.

Despite the possibility that the man was not the suspect under investigation, he was taken to the precinct to make a deposition.

Since it was impossible to get a deposition from him that made sense, the sergeant in charge that night decided to book him and incarcerate him for loitering. The man was led to a cell despite the commotion he caused, begging hysterically for his bottle of Four Roses as if he were a spoiled child. At a certain moment, before he was led away, he had what looked like an epileptic fit, squirming on the floor like an animal, his whole body shaking uncontrollably. After a brief examination, the precinct medical officer determined that the detainee was faking the attack with the express purpose of obtaining the alcohol that his body demanded. The medic gave him a sedative. Both the medic and the sergeant in charge believed that once the crisis was over and the detainee was sober, he would be able to answer their questions. The above is the night sergeant's report to the sergeant in charge during the day.

Once he quieted down, the detainee was taken to the "cage" where others were waiting to be arraigned. The night went by without any outbursts or commotions, even though it was Saturday night, when detainees are particularly rowdy and rebellious. Nevertheless, the next morning the sergeant in charge was called to the detainee's cell to examine his, Mr. Silva's, corpse, which had its head smashed and blood all over it. The drunk had apparently committed suicide during the night. The other detainees' statements did not help to determine what, exactly, had happened. They had nothing to report; they had seen nothing and heard nothing.

The autopsy revealed that before the alleged suicide, the other detainees had violently abused the victim. There were indications of a sadistic sexual attack although the victim was still dressed; his underclothes were stained with blood and semen. The autopsy confirmed the suicide hypothesis. It is believed—despite the lack of cooperation from the eye witnesses and possible perpetrators—that the victim had banged his head against the wall like a madman. Against the hypothesis of this spontaneous and crazed act, the prison guard testified that he heard no screams throughout the entire night.

Subsequent action was postponed until an inquest was held. The New York Police Department's report ends here.

On the recommendation of agents Marshall and Robbins, which was accepted by the head of the New York office, the Bureau decided that the man detained at the Bowery precinct could *not* be identified as Mr. Silva until there was evidence to the contrary. Consequently, the Bureau decided not to inform the Brazilian authorities and other parties involved with the suspect about said incident. According to the investigating agents, any violence within an American precinct involving, even remotely, antiterrorist actions by the Brazilian military, aided and abetted by the CIA, would certainly provoke a campaign by the U.S. and international press to defame the two countries and their respective intelligence services.

Nor was it ruled out that the Brazilian military itself, involved as it is in antiterrorist acts of repression, including physical and mental torture, might not resort to criticizing the American police in order to demonstrate to the rest of the world that they are not alone in permitting such violations of human rights to take place in their prisons.

Terezinha: He really put one over on us.

Da Gloria: Who would have thought Eduardo could do that. I would have put my hand in the fire for him. May God and the Most Holy Virgin protect me.

Maria da Graça: I made believe I didn't suspect anything, but I was no dummy. I never told you two anything before because I just knew you were going to say I had the dirtiest mind on this Earth. He certainly was no saint and anyone could have seen that if they wanted to.

Terezinha: It was no great surprise for me either. Only you, da Gloria, fell for it. All those little mannerisms didn't fool me. You remember when he let his hair grow? He looked like a little girl all full of vanities.

Maria da Graça: If he had put on lipstick and high heels, who could have seen the difference? No one. That he was effiminate, there's no doubt about that.

Terezinha: If he had put on earrings he could have appeared in one of those night clubs in the Village. He would have been a hit.

Maria da Graça: He was losing time and money working here. He could have been a millionaire by now. Do you remember the story of that guy or gal, who knows anymore, who went to France and a count or some noble fell madly in love with her? I read about it in *People* and you know *People* never lies.

Terezinha: What I never imagined, though, is that he'd get involved with terrorists. Can you believe it? With criminals on the FBI's most wanted list?. Ugh! It makes me sick to think about it.

Da Gloria: God help us, Ave Maria!

Maria da Graça: They say he was kidnapped right in his own apartment. Kidnapped by his own cronies, that's what they say.

Terezinha: And you believe everything you read in the papers? Only you! You're so naive!

Maria da Graça: Me? Naive? When you're just getting started I've already been there and back. Who does she think she's kidding? She thinks she has a monopoly on the truth just because she got promoted.

Da Gloria: And there's no one who can do anything for him?

Maria da Graça: Not even Colonel Vianna. And he's a colonel!

What could we possibly do? Didn't you hear what he said? That even the FBI was called in but they couldn't crack the case. Two expert agents, police officers, patrol cars . . . they did all they could.

Terezinha (whispering to Maria da Graça): He thinks he's clever, that he can fool everyone! Well, we know those two were always having lunch together . . . together at the dinner table and in bed, for sure. Anyone could have seen it if they wanted to. He doesn't fool me!

Maria da Graça (whispering): Have you gone crazy, menina?

Da Gloria: What are you two whispering about?

Maria da Graça: Oh, nothing. Nothing at all, menina. Terezinha was telling me that the colonel must be really suffering. They were such good friends.

Da Gloria: He is. He told me Eduardo was like a son to him. The son he never had. Neither he nor his wife dona Sílvia ever imagined he had such personal problems. He asked me to tell that to Titio, to my uncle.

Terezinha: And you told him?

Da Gloria: Well, didn't he ask me to?

Maria da Graça: Have you thought about what they must be saying about us in Brazil? That we're running some kind of whorehouse here! They're mean spirited and jealous.

Da Gloria: I don't even want to think about it. Titio already asked me if I would like to be transferred to another consulate.

Terezinha: And?

Da Gloria: I told him no, that it's really nice working here, there's a good mood here. Those things can happen to anyone, even to the best of families.

Terezinha: And?

Da Gloria: And he agreed.

Maria da Graça: You two have got your heads in Brazil; I've got mine here. What worries me, especially after yesterday's front page story in the *Daily News* is what people must be saying here. They're going to think all us Brazilians are like that.

Da Gloria: Titio calls me every night and tells me not to worry about what journalists say. They're just a bunch of gossipmongers. They're after anyone's scalp.

Maria da Graça: Terezinha, tell the truth; do you really think he was kidnapped?

Terezinha: If you want to know the truth, I really don't know for sure. If you want my opinion, though, which is a different matter, I think he's hiding in some fleabag hotel. Someone's covering for him, of course. I won't say who, I won't give the name of the person covering up for him. I'm no fool, and I'm not about to be treated as a gossip by my two best friends. He's no fool, he wouldn't be showing his face here at the office after such a scandal. But you'll see, and I want to be sure to be here when it happens. You'll see, he'll show up here one of these days all bright-eyed and bushy-tailed. He's only waiting for the dust to settle.

Da Gloria: God help us! You too, Terezinha? Don't you have pity on anyone? Poor guy! He's probably in dire straits right now and here you are maligning him.

Terezinha: Maligning him? You've got to be kidding? He gets into all kinds of scrapes and I'm the one who bears the brunt. And that's why I'm not going to say anything. I don't want any of you coming to me afterward and saying you already knew everything. I'll just say you both are lying, that you're liars, you hear me? Right to your faces: liars!

3

Carlinhos (at the airport): You couldn't trust the sonofabitch. You're all witnesses; when the going got rough, he didn't think twice about it, he just took off. Puto faggot sonofabitch. A neighbor of his told me he's the one who put the finger on us. I can see you don't believe me. You think he's innocent, that I'm the one who's nuts. Okay. So tell me, how could the other side have known so much about us. Only the guy who turned us in. He gave the FBI a full profile. You're all witnesses that the FBI knew absolutely everything about our group. Even the brief period we set up that organization in the church. Nothing escaped those fuckers. He blabbed and now the FBI is hiding him somewhere. They say he just disappeared into thin air (he snaps his fingers) just like that! He disappeared, my ass! What he wanted most of all was to fuck us, right up the ass. And he did. By now the puto's probably already had plastic surgery, changed his identity and who the fuck is going to recognize him, lying on the beach on some tropical island in the Pacific. That's where American intelligence sends their stoolies. Don't you remember that spy who defected from Russia and turned in the entire spy network that had infiltrated the United Nations? One of those magazines, I don't remember if it was *Time* or *Newsweek,* said they ran into him in Hawaii sunning himself and drinking a daiquiri by the edge of the pool in a deluxe hotel. The CIA suggested it was only a look-alike, but it was obvious it was him, you could see it in his face. Where is the American people's money going? the magazine asked. Where? It's going to pay for plastic surgery, five-star hotels, pools, daiquiris, and some pin money for Eduardo. Poor Eduardo! How it must have hurt when they cut off half of that big flat nose. And you know who's to blame for all this, who doesn't have the balls to admit it and assume the responsibility? Marcelo. We're here because he fucked up. He came to us with all that shit about trusting his old college mate, that he was a good person, trustworthy, partial to our cause . . . A lot of bullshit. And now? Here we are, SCREWED! A friend of the military attaché, that's what he was, that's what he is. Anyone could see it if he wanted to. That's the truth no one wanted to listen to when I warned you all. The two of them whispering to each other in the corner of the restaurant week in week out, and me serving those two motherfuckers like a fucking fool. Tell me! What the fuck for? So he can rat on us and turn us in as if we were just a pack of ghetto thugs. You all preferred not to listen to me, to take Marcelo at his word. Now look what's happened. They roped us, bound us, and branded us like a pack of ponies; fucked us up the ass. And those two . . . Shit, it makes me so fucking angry . . .

4

Dear Sergio,
You can't imagine how sad and depressed Silvia and I feel about our dear Eduardo's disappearance. We know you and Teresa are very distressed, so in this sad hour we join our prayers to yours that Almighty God may illuminate Eduardo's mind and guide his steps onto the straight and narrow path from which he never should have strayed.
Only yesterday, Silvia had a mass said for him in our parish. Although she had only met him once or twice, she told me the image she had of him was of an angel who lost his way here on

Earth. She remembered the gentleness of his eyes and the refinement of his words and manners, his kind and generous soul always ready to give.

Eduardo was, of course, a problematic young man, for the many reasons you know and told me, just like so many other youth of today, influenced by the most pernicious things in this permissive society which we are reluctantly bequeathing to subsequent generations. But it's better to forget all that in this hour of suffering. I prefer to remember, as does Silvia, the better side of his lively personality; that will bring him back to those who love him.

I should inform you that Eduardo's disappearance provoked a great commotion among his fellow workers in the foreign service and even among the diplomatic corps. By this time you should have received a letter from the ambassador. I can assure you I had nothing to do with it; it was his own idea. He wanted to tell you about all the efforts he made to aid the New York Police in bringing their investigations to a successful conclusion. Unfortunately, it was all in vain. I should add that, in my presence, the ambassador praised Eduardo's work at the consulate.

In the end, that's what counts. I can see Eduardo all over again arriving at Kennedy airport. I was holding a photo of him in my hand, he was apprehensive and uncertain of his new life in a foreign country. But he was also enthusiastic about the possibility of proving to himself and his own that he could meet and triumph over any challenge. I think he triumphed, even if life got the better of him in the end, but isn't that the fate that awaits us all? He triumphed because he proved he was capable of grappling with the responsibilities of a job and a home. I never before had the occasion to speak of his apartment. It was very comfortable and inviting. He used to entertain his friends there, both Brazilian and American. He had many friends.

It's too bad he never confided in me about the difficulties and problems that perplexed and preoccupied him. They had a harmful effect on this inexperienced young man. I don't know if I could have helped him as I would have liked to. Unfortunately, we are often impotent before the plans of Our Lord, but maybe the friendship of an older and more experienced couple might have helped him bear his inner conflicts and combat the self-destructive forces taking hold of him. Silvia and I will never forgive ourselves for not having invited him over more often. We erred in thinking a young man full of life like Eduardo would not have enjoyed our company. And we live so far away, in Queens. Well, we were wrong. He could have learned a lot with us, as he learned with you. We failed and we must now accept our sorrow. We ask you to forgive us. God, in His infinite bounty, must have already forgiven the both of us. We wait expectantly for your charitable words.

I probably shouldn't bring up this delicate matter in this sad and painful moment, but I feel obliged, as a friend and, even more importantly, as an official of the armed forces, to clarify certain things. The press declared that Eduardo's disappearance was the result of his involvement with a terrorist organization in this city. It even suggested the possibility of a kidnapping, as if the madness that has gotten hold of our country had contaminated these northern latitudes.

Don't believe a word of it, Sérgio. You should not be made to suffer the agony of thinking your son betrayed his country, this country that we love so dearly, or worse, that he betrayed the civic responsibilities you both instilled in him. It's all a lie propagated by the communist press that dominates us and imposes upon us as truth the most outlandish lies. It's a calumny of the worst sort. They are using our Eduardo to make life more difficult for our citizens and they are trying to turn a loving family against the military. I can guarantee (and here it's not so much a friend, but the military attaché who speaks) that our Eduardo was never involved with those criminals detained by the FBI and expelled from this country that had so generously opened its doors to them. We should at least preserve the dignified memory of "our" son—you will forgive, I hope, the egoism of a couple who needs to share in the intimacy of your sorrow.

5

"Damn it! " Ricky exclaims when Marcelo tells him about Eduardo's disappearance. "Poor fellow!" You should have told me about it before."

"How could I? I'm not a fortune teller, you know! I only found out yesterday, in the newspapers."

"He disappeared the morning we took him home after a night

of hard drinking . . . I must have been one of the last people he spoke to."

"I don't doubt it."

"And it's only now his best friend finds out about his death, and in the newspapers!? What a friend!"

"Now hold on here! Don't exaggerate, I didn't say anything about his dying; the newspapers didn't either. They said he disap-peared, Ricky. Dis-ap-peared!"

"What got into him? Did he go nuts or something?"

"Who knows? The guy just took off, that's all. Either a person says something, leaves a note, explains what he's up to, or he leaves an open field for everyone to imagine what happened, to form what-ever hypotheses occur to them."

"And what's yours?"

"I don't have one, thank God. I'm just waiting for the return of the myth. Billy the Kid rides again."

"Nothing occurs to you?"

"Nothing, absolutely nothing, unless it was a cool breeze sweep-ing the forlorn from this Earth."

"Was he like that?"

"Like what?"

"You sonofabitch."

"You mean Eduardo? Don't make me laugh. He was happy-go-lucky, nothing forlorn about him. A happy man if ever I saw one, who'll live as long as they'll let him live the way he likes."

"And who wasn't going to 'let' him live anymore?"

"What? You trying to get something out of me? Trying to spy on me, eh? You sonofabitch. I won't say another word. I'll just keep my mouth shut from now on. You speak."

"Egoist."

"Keep me out of it."

"How? If you and he are identical. If you, he, and I are cut from the same piece of cloth. There's the three stooges, isn't there? The three musketeers too, no? And now, ladies and gentlemen, distin-guished public, I have the great honor and pleasure of introduc-ing . . . the three silent ones."

"Or the three egoists."

"I prefer the silent ones."

"But the three stooges were really four. One is missing."

"The three musketeers were also four. You're right. Hmmm. We're missing one. The fourth of the silent trinity. Who can it be?"

"The kidnapper."

"Bite your tongue! Eduardo wasn't kidnapped, he just skipped town."

"If it's not the kidnapper then it's the taxi driver, the bus driver or the truck driver. Or the machinist, better still the airplane pilot."

"Less imagination, my dear, we need less imagination. Eduardo is somewhere in New York, in Manhattan, which both he and I love so much, especially to walk around in. And his name is not Ricky. Think about it: Eduardo's name is not Ricky."

"You sure you don't know where he is? You trying to hide something from me?"

"I don't know anything for sure. But I'm sure you were suggesting your room is the fourth element of the trinity."

"I'm lost."

"It's elementary, my dear. You noted that you and he invented the same fate. The very same."

"No, I didn't note anything. Why don't you tell me about it, Sherlock."

"Who left his city in Arizona one fine day without telling anyone, huh? Who is it that took a train to I-don't-know-where and then a bus to San Francisco? And who is it that subsequently took a plane to New York? Tell me!"

"Okay, you win. Now what?"

"Now what? That no one in your family, no relative of yours knows where you are right now. You're missing."

"That's different."

"The only difference is he's 'Wanted' and you're 'Missing.' That's all."

"That's different."

"Forget different, my man. You enlisted in the army, you're a soldier, you're in Vietnam, on the battlefield. You fuck up, you're interrogated, you turn in your friends, you get a jail sentence, you're expelled from the country. Where do you go? Everyone is afraid of his own Vietnam. His was the police, or the FBI. Yours is the Pentagon and a little man dressed in khaki."

"Do you really think he was involved?"

"I don't think. I know for sure."

"If you know for sure, then you were also involved. You're in the same boat. How is it you alone got off? You just told me the others were expelled from the country."

"They left me off the list of names. So I could become Billy the Kid's evangelist. They had the decency of saying nothing about me. Whoever ratted to the SNI or the FBI left me out of it. I can't imagine why. Your guess is as good as mine."

"If Eduardo reappears, do you think . . ."

"I don't think. I know for sure."

"You betrayed him. He's got to be mad as hell with you."

"On the contrary."

"Eduardo wanted me for himself."

"Just like he wanted thousands of others back home and here."

"We'll fly down to Brazil."

"Don't think he prized you above the others, Mr. Masked Man."

"Don't change the subject. You're afraid of him. Of Billy the Kid's return."

"Have you gone nuts?"

6

(Flyer distributed throughout New York by Paco, who wrote it and had it printed. The letters E. C. S. are written with blood. The four points above the name of the Grand Wizard of the Order refer to the power he has to decree death sentences.

Two skulls are drawn in each of the upper corners of this sheet. Beneath them are two words: on the left, "Sadness," and on the right, "Death." The letters are written above two crossbones. The skulls are attached by a ribbon that goes straight down to the lower corners of this sheet, where another two skulls are found. Two other words are written below them: on the left, "Terror," and on the right, "Mourning." The ribbon is tied in a bow in the lower center of the sheet.)

I, F. A., promise and swear on this sword, avenging instrument of false oaths, to keep E. C. S.'s secret and not to write, draw, or paint anything that might refer to Him without obtaining His permission. If I break my oath, I hereby express my consent and desire that my body be quartered, burned and my ashes be deposited in the Chalice so that it and my name may be publicly and universally cursed.

He said to me:

> *The voice is to be heard by the ear*
> *Hear the voice of the master*
> *Start out on the road*
> *The road to salvation*
> *I am in all places*

I shall never again wait for anyone to help me. I shall never again ask anyone's help. I turn my eyes toward the Messenger of Moses. Deliver me, O My Lord Jesus Christ, from evil men. Preserve me, O Supreme Divinity, One of the Seven, from violent men.

> *For the Pure of Heart*
> *Everything is pure*
> *Be like the child.*

Thus spoke He to me, as I have written it.
Thus also did He order me to record His persecution and martyrdom, and to write this Proclamation.

Proclamation

I must now speak to you about a state of affairs that has shocked and grieved the faithful, a state of affairs that only man's faithlessness makes possible: International Communism. Incontestably the greatest evil that has ever afflicted humanity, whose star once shone brightly.

Now, however, there is no longer any security because the Cuban government has invented the means to exterminate religion from the world more efficiently than ever before. I cannot but admire the effective methods of those who have opted for the realization of Communism, that barbarous oppressor of the Church and its Faithful. They have even taken the inconceivable step of prohibiting the priesthood.

Who is not shocked by such a degrading procedure? Who would have ever thought men could have such ideas?

Communism is the triumph of tyranny against the Faithful. It is impossible to adequately describe the methods of those who plotted to see the horrendous effects of Communism. They are men who look through a prism, when they should impugn Communism every chance they get, thus confirming the brilliant power of religion.

It is hereby proven that Communism intends to erradicate Christianity, God's masterpiece, which has existed for twenty centuries and will last until the end of the World. Because God protects the fruit of His labor, it has survived persecutions and always triumphed over impiety. No matter how ignorant, man knows that human power is incapable of destroying God's creation.

The supreme head of the communists, well known by everyone, moved to action by his incredulity, which has attracted to him so many people's illusions, believes that he can govern the World as if he were a monarch legitimately installed by God. Catholics bitterly look upon such a great injustice.

Oh, incredulous men, how awful is your faithlessness to God!

All legitimate power emanates from the eternal Omnipotence of God and is subject to His divine rule. This holds for the temporal as well as the spiritual orders, such that by obeying the Pope, the King, or one's Father, who are God's ministers of goodness, one is really obeying God.

Christianity sanctifies everything and destroys nothing, except Sin.

Thus did He bid me record His words so that all the peoples of the Future would know them. Thus did He bid me record this dialogue between Him and the Inquisitor.

Inquisitor: Why don't you and your fellow exiles renounce the Cause of Christianity?

He: We are fighting for Fellowship.

Inquisitor: What do you mean by Fellowship?

He: The Holy Faith in our Christian religion.

Inquisitor: But you know quite well that our religion is opposed to those who decree the Death Sentence. Only the State can decree it. It is superior to everything and everyone.

He: We are fighting for Christian Fellowship among all peoples of good will. We have been blessed by the Pope. If I had not lost the document sent from Rome you would no doubt believe me, wouldn't you?

Inquisitor: What kind of document was it?

He: It was a letter from Rome, signed by the Pope.

Inquisitor: What did that letter say?

He: It said that the exiled persons who fight for the Holy Cause of the Pope and Christian Fellowship will not be guilty of any crime or sin.

Inquisitor: Do you remember anything else in that document?

He: It said that the real murderers, those who commit all kinds of cruelties and impious and barbarous acts, are Fidel's soldiers, who have taken possession of the Kingdom of the Guajiros. It said that they were excommunicated and that we have received the Pope's blessing.

Inquisitor: What color were the ribbon and the seal on the letter? What was inscribed on the seal?

He: The ribbon was white, it seemed to be made of linen. The seal was also white and it bore the figure of Philip II; it was inscribed with words referring to Rome and Catholic Spain.

Inquisitor: How is it possible to admit or suppose that the Pope could bless such iniquities or that Philip II could permit the degradation of his dignity as King?

He: Just as I know that I shall be sentenced to death by the Communists, thus also do I tell you that I had possession of that document and that everything written on it is exactly as I have told you. And if any of my followers is also captured, like me, you will be convinced by their words that everything I have said is the Truth, nothing but the Truth.

When He was told that the hour of the execution had come, He said:

Because Christian Fellowship among the peoples of Good Will must continue to exist, anyone failing to uphold the meaning of Fellowship shall be punished.

7

Woman across the way: I always told you he was a dangerous man, a very dangerous man. You didn't believe me. Now you can see for yourself, there's all those cops in front of the building.

Paralytic husband lying in bed: What are you talking about?

Woman: The newspaper says he's a communist.

Husband: Who's a communist?

Woman: Are you deaf and dumb? I'm not going to speak to you anymore.

Husband: Who's a communist, tell me?

Woman: I won't, I won't. You never pay any attention to what I say. You're always muttering that I go on like a nut—you thought I didn't know that, huh?

Husband: You're lying, I never said such a thing about you. You're not crazy.

Woman: I know I'm not nuts, you dope.

Husband: Go on, tell me.

Woman: First you've got to say "please."

Husband: Please, tell me who's a communist?

Woman: The Puerto Rican, you dope.

Husband: I'll bet he is. They all are. That's why they come to this country, to bring it down.

Woman: You don't have to worry, this time they're really going to kill him.